**Here's what critics are saying about
the Marty Hudson Mysteries:**

"This is a terrific new series featuring modern updated
Sherlock Holmes characters. I've been looking forward to
reading this book as a fan of Sherlock Holmes and I was
not disappointed. This is a fun and entertaining book with
great characters. The story had many twists that kept me
guessing until the end. I look forward to reading more
books in this series."
—*A Cozy Booknook*

"One of the most anticipated of the fall releases happens to
be one of THE BEST of the fall releases! Halliday and Rey
have joined forces to create a SUPERLATIVE new cozy
mystery series that will leave readers clamoring for more."
—*Blogcritics, Diane Morasco*

"This well-written book is loaded with fantastic, lovable
characters. Marty's story is full of humor, mystery and
suspense."
—*BookLikes*

# BOOKS BY KELLY REY

*Jamie Winters Mysteries*:
Motion for Murder
Mistletoe & Misdemeanors (holiday short story)
Death of a Diva
The Sassy Suspect
Verdicts & Vixens
A Playboy in Peril

*Marty Hudson Mysteries*
Sherlock Holmes and the Case of the Brash Blonde
Sherlock Holmes and the Case of the Disappearing Diva

# BOOKS BY GEMMA HALLIDAY

### *High Heels Mysteries*
Spying in High Heels
Killer in High Heels
Undercover in High Heels
Christmas in High Heels
(short story)
Alibi in High Heels
Mayhem in High Heels
Honeymoon in High Heels
(short story)
Sweetheart in High Heels
(short story)
Fearless in High Heels
Danger in High Heels
Homicide in High Heels
Deadly in High Heels
Suspect in High Heels
Peril in High Heels
Jeopardy in High Heels

### *Wine & Dine Mysteries*
A Sip Before Dying
Chocolate Covered Death
Victim in the Vineyard
Marriage, Merlot & Murder
Death in Wine Country
Fashion, Rosé & Foul Play
Witness at the Winery

### *Hollywood Headlines Mysteries*
Hollywood Scandals
Hollywood Secrets
Hollywood Confessions
Hollywood Holiday
(short story)
Hollywood Deception

### *Marty Hudson Mysteries*
Sherlock Holmes and the Case
of the Brash Blonde
Sherlock Holmes and the Case
of the Disappearing Diva
Sherlock Holmes and the Case
of the Wealthy Widow

### *Tahoe Tessie Mysteries*
Luck Be A Lady
Hey Big Spender
Baby It's Cold Outside
(holiday short story)

### *Jamie Bond Mysteries*
Unbreakable Bond
Secret Bond
Bond Bombshell
(short story)
Lethal Bond
Dangerous Bond
Bond Ambition
(short story)
Fatal Bond
Deadly Bond

### *Hartley Grace Featherstone Mysteries*
Deadly Cool
Social Suicide
Wicked Games

### *Other Works*
Play Dead
Viva Las Vegas
A High Heels Haunting
Watching You (short story)
Confessions of a Bombshell
Bandit (short story)

# SHERLOCK HOLMES AND THE CASE OF THE DISAPPEARING DIVA

a Marty Hudson mystery

GEMMA HALLIDAY

AND

KELLY REY

# SHERLOCK HOLMES AND THE CASE OF THE DISAPPEARING DIVA

# CHAPTER ONE

"I want to hire Sherlock Holmes to find my sister. Everyone says he's the very best."

I stared at our prospective, if seriously deluded, client Barbara Lowery Bristol as we stood in the foyer of my newly inherited Victorian money pit at 221 Baker Street in San Francisco. It was unclear exactly who she meant by "everyone," since Sherlock Holmes had solved exactly one case. And the "client" in that case had been me. Sure, Mr. Sherlock Holmes, private investigator, had gotten a mention in the *San Francisco Chronicle*, and the story *could* have had legs thanks to a few social media shares. But he was hardly a celebrity. Especially considering he didn't actually exist.

Not that that little technicality had stopped my best friend, Irene Adler, from creating an entire business around him. After all, Irene was the queen when it came to business, being one of the Silicon Valley's youngest venture capitalists herself. And she'd sure capitalized on our small and semi-successful run at using the made-up name in the past, quickly creating fake credentials, a website, some business cards with a PO box address, and—voila!—Sherlock Holmes Investigations. I was 50/50 on whether it had been a great idea or a harebrained scheme. Holmes had been born out of necessity, a little desperation, and a lot of boldness. I still wasn't convinced we shouldn't have buried him shortly afterward.

However, my Victorian money pit demanded to be filled, so I smiled at Barbara Lowery Bristol anyway.

"You heard right," Irene told her. "Mr. Holmes is the best. Unfortunately, he isn't available right now, but we'll be happy to present your case to him. I'm Irene Adler, and this is Martha Hudson. We work with Mr. Holmes."

I still marveled at how she could say that without her head bursting into flames. Of course, even if it did, it would probably just add more glimmer to her auburn hair. Irene was the sort of girl they'd modeled Barbie dolls after—only her version had a degree from MIT and too many millions in the bank to need a Ken to support her. We'd met during a lecture about social media's impact on political and economic culture. I'd been crashing it. She'd been giving it. Irene was a computer prodigy turned VC, providing her funds to various start-ups that she deemed promising. So far, like with everything else in her life, she'd had the Midas touch. Irene could make money in her sleep, and probably did. So, while I was in this ruse for the cash, I think she was in it for the kicks.

I gave Barbara my most reassuring smile. "Please call me Marty."

Barbara gathered her lapels with a shiver. "Mr. Holmes certainly keeps it chilly in here, doesn't he?"

"That's just the hole in the roof," Irene said. "It'll warm up when the fog burns off."

"Hole in the…" Barbara's gaze traveled upward.

"It's an old house," I explained. Actually, the truth was, it was an old house, and I was a homeowner without old money to fix it. Or new money. Or any money, really. The last storm had taken what was left of my rotting shingles, leaving me with an unintended skylight over the master bedroom. And since my *actual* job as a barista at the Stanford University Bookstore Café paid barely enough to keep me in Top Ramen, I'd have to wait until I won the lottery to repair it.

"Why don't we go into the living room and make ourselves comfortable?" I suggested.

Barbara followed us under the foyer's multifaceted (and dusty) crystal chandelier into the living room, where she settled onto the overstuffed sofa, and I shoved the remaining few boxes of inherited junk out of sight with my foot before facing her from the love seat. She didn't look very comfortable. In fact, she hadn't loosened her grip on her lapels, and I knew why. It might have been warmer in a meat locker.

Irene adjusted her off-the-shoulder Stella McCartney dress just a little more on her shoulders, and I got up again to close the ancient insulated drapes. As she readied her laptop on the coffee table, I moved through the room switching on the Tiffany table lamps, pleased to notice I hadn't missed any dust on the end tables while straightening up for Barbara Bristol's appointment.

Irene waited until I'd taken a seat beside her before turning to Barbara. "You mentioned on the phone that your sister is missing?"

Barbara nodded. "Yes."

"Why don't we start with your sister's name."

"Rebecca," she said. "Rebecca Lowery. She was a coloratura."

I blinked at her. A *what?*

Irene had typed *Rebecca Lowery* before her fingers hesitated over the keyboard. "I beg your pardon?"

"A coloratura," she repeated. "It's a kind of soprano. Rebecca was an opera singer. She was in rehearsal for the traveling company of *Ethereal Love.* I'm sure you've heard of it."

"Of course." Irene typed *Not a word*, then passed me a wry sideways glance from beneath her lashes.

I hadn't heard of it either. In fact, the only thing I knew about opera was that there were sopranos, tenors, and basses. And when the fat lady sang, it was all over.

"The things she could do with her instrument," Barbara said on a sigh. "Have you ever heard a truly gifted coloratura perform? It can bring tears to your eyes."

*Is it that bad?* Irene typed.

I bit the inside of my cheek to stem a smile. "I'm sure she was wonderful," I said. I was sure of no such thing, being more of a pop-rock girl myself. While I'd crashed a couple of college lectures in the past on the history of classical music, I only had a passing knowledge of Italian, and my German was *nicht gut.* The nuances of opera were lost on me.

Barbara's hands shook as she worried the handle of her knock-off designer handbag. She wore a gray linen blazer over black cotton slacks and a burgundy blouse with an artificial sheen, which spoke to polyester rather than silk. Low-heeled pumps. A practical outfit for a woman of modest means who'd traveled from Des Moines to look for her missing sister.

"Would you like a glass of water?" I asked her, noticing her discomfort.

Her smile was grateful. "That's very kind. I'm sorry. I'm really not sure what to think right now. I never thought I'd find myself in this situation."

They waited while I retrieved her water from the kitchen, wishing I'd thought to stash some instant coffee or tea bags in a cupboard. It was a little embarrassing to hand over a plain glass of water, sans ice cubes, but Barbara didn't seem to mind. She took an immediate sip and clutched the glass in both hands.

"I'm sure we can find your sister." I kept my voice gentle. "When did you last see her?"

"Alive? Almost five years ago. Not since our mother passed."

Irene looked up sharply. "I'm sorry—did you say 'alive'?"

Her hand faltered as she lowered the glass to the coffee table. "Maybe I wasn't clear," she said. "My sister is dead."

*Then she should be easy to find*, Irene typed.

I frowned at her. She shrugged and hit the backspace key, deleting the comment.

"Maybe you'd better start from the beginning," I told Ms. Bristol.

She took a deep breath and let it out on a shaky sigh. "On Monday I got a call from the medical examiner's office informing me of Rebecca's death. He was a very kind man. Dr. Watson, I think his name was."

I felt myself flush at the name.

She must have noticed, as she paused and asked, "Do you know him?"

Broad shoulders, thick blond hair, deep blue eyes, pouty lower lip. *That* Dr. Watson?

"We're familiar with him," I told her, ignoring the tiny smirk Irene shot my way. Barbara Lowery Bristol didn't need to know that Dr. Watson had cost me a few sleepless nights and a couple of distracted days as well. Bad enough that Irene knew it and was not about to let me live it down anytime soon.

Barbara seemed satisfied with that answer. "Well, after speaking with him, I made arrangements with a local mortuary and caught a flight out here to view the...to see her."

"And did you see her?" I asked carefully.

Barbara shook her head. "No. I retained Gordon's Mortuary to start the arrangements. Except..." She hesitated again.

Irene and I traded glances.

"Except?" Irene prodded.

Barbara picked up the glass of water and sipped from it. "When I went to the mortuary," she said, "Rebecca was gone."

I blinked at her, vision of a zombie Rebecca fleeing the scene running through my mind.

"What do you mean 'gone'?" Irene repeated. She typed the word *zombie?*

I swear it was almost like she was in my head sometimes. I stifled a snicker.

"Well, just gone." Barbara paused. "I don't really know where she is. The ME assured me she was positively identified at the morgue. But the bod—er, *person* at the funeral home? That wasn't Rebecca. It was some other woman."

"Do you know who the other woman was?" Irene asked.

Barbara shook her head. "Obviously they thought it was my sister."

"So...did the mortuary tell you how they lost her?" I asked.

A small frown formed between her eyebrows. "They didn't, really. Mr. Gordon was very apologetic—"

"I would hope so," Irene muttered.

"—but they can't seem to find Rebecca. No one seems to know what happened. Or at least, they're not telling *me*."

"Did you call the police?" I asked, thinking that would have been my first move.

She nodded. "I did. I tried to file a missing persons report but...well, I guess that wasn't quite the right division."

*Missing Corpses Division?* Irene typed.

I ignored her with no small effort. "What did the police say?"

Barbara shook her head. "Not much. I don't think they were taking it very seriously. They said they'd look into it, but I had the feeling they weren't going to look very hard." She paused. "They told me she was already deceased and had already been seen by the ME. She wasn't a priority. That's when I called you."

"And the mortuary has no idea what happened to her?"

Barbara Lowery Bristol shook her head.

"Well," Irene said, "we know one thing that *didn't* happen. Your sister didn't get up and walk away. No offense intended," she added.

"None taken," Barbara said, though she didn't sound confident about it.

"We don't mean to be insensitive," I said, shooting Irene a look. *Ix-nay on the ombies-zay.* "But you just said it's been a few years since you've seen your sister. You're sure the woman at the mortuary was not her?"

The ensuing silence swelled into awkwardness before Barbara finally said, "Alright, it's true, my sister and I had been estranged, and I hadn't seen her in years. But she was my *sister.* I'd recognize her under any circumstances. How could I not?"

I could think of a few circumstances, suddenly wondering how Rebecca had died and what state her body might be in.

"Here." Barbara slid a photograph from her wallet and passed it to me. "This is the most current picture I have."

Rebecca Lowery had been a beauty, her blonde hair swept into an intricate updo over deep brown eyes, sculpted cheekbones, and a generous mouth.

"She was beautiful," Irene said.

"Yes." There was a subtle tension running beneath that single word as Barbara returned the photograph to its sleeve, running a finger over it before closing her wallet. "And she knew how to use her beauty to get what she wanted, even if what she wanted was to get out of trouble. Especially then." Her cheeks reddened, as if she hadn't meant to say that aloud. "It's not entirely her fault she could be difficult. She'd always been spoiled and a drama queen. Especially once her singing started to draw acclaim. In fact, you could call her a bit of a diva."

"I'm sure it goes with the territory," Irene said.

Barbara shrugged. "Look, I don't know if Mr. Holmes handles this type of case."

"He handles *any* type of case," Irene assured her.

I shot her a look. Mr. Holmes didn't handle any type of case—he'd only handled one before. Or, more accurately, Irene and I had *stumbled* through one before. And it had been one thing to investigate my own great-aunt's death using Private Investigator Sherlock Holmes to open those doors that had slammed squarely in the face of two curious female civilians. But it was something else entirely to track down a missing corpse. Something morbid. Something I wasn't all that interested in doing, even if it did lead me back to Dr. Watson again. I was content to admire him from afar, despite what the stalker laws said.

Then again…

My glance lingered on the ancient drapes billowing in the draft from the upstairs where a gaping hole sat in my ancient roof. While the retainer check Barbara had sent wasn't lottery-winnings large, it might be enough to patch a small hole. Maybe even put a down payment on a whole new roof. Heck, if I stretched it, I might even be able to spring for a couple of ice cube trays for the freezer.

"At its heart, this is a simple missing persons matter," Irene said, shooting Barbra a winning smile. "We can get started right away."

"But I thought Sherlock Holmes…" She looked at us uncertainly. "That is, I had hoped to meet Mr. Holmes before…" The thought trailed off again, while the implication hung in the air between us. For whatever reason, she doubted our capability. Smart woman.

"Mr. Holmes travels extensively," Irene said. "But you have nothing to worry about. Marty and I do most of the legwork anyway."

"I see." She hesitated. "I've never hired a private investigator before."

"We'll take care of everything," Irene told her. "We have your contact information, and we'll be in touch very soon."

Barbara took a last bracing sip of water before standing. "I'll wait to hear from you, then. Please call me anytime—day or night—when you find her."

"We will," I promised. "Let us show you out."

Irene and I stood at the door, watching her drive off in her rental sedan.

"What do you think of her?" Irene asked when we'd returned to the living room.

I drew my legs up beneath me on the sofa. "She seemed genuinely upset. And I thought she was credible."

"I agree. She did throw a little shade at Rebecca though."

"That sounded like something that goes way back," I said. "Maybe even as far as childhood. If Rebecca was the pretty one or the golden child in the family, it's only natural that Barbara would resent that a little, with sibling rivalry and all."

"Yeah, I guess so." Irene scrolled through her notes. "A missing corpse. That's a first, huh?"

A first I could have happily done without. "Can we please just call her 'Rebecca'?" I asked with a shudder.

"We can call her anything you want," Irene said. "As long as we find her."

"Where do we start?"

She smiled. "I think you already know the answer to that. Go put on some makeup and skinny jeans. We're going to pay Watson a visit."

*　*　*

The first time I'd met Dr. Watson, I wasn't sure what kind of impression I'd made. At 5'5" and 120 pounds (give or take, depending on how much pizza I'd consumed that day), I wasn't exactly what you'd consider a bombshell. I *was* a natural blonde, though in the San Francisco fog I tended more toward frizz than shampoo-commercial curls. And at the time of our first encounter, I'd been practically begging him to release my great-aunt's autopsy report—which I'm sure was a pickup line lots of girls used on cute doctors, right? Unluckily for me, Watson was and is a stickler for rules and regulations and had refused to budge from his official position. *Luckily* for me, Irene has the imagination of a wizard and dreamed up our employer, Sherlock Holmes. Watson had seemed skeptical at the time. Skepticism that only grew as our boss was perennially absent. I was never quite sure if Watson believed us or just didn't want to deal with the paperwork that catching us in a lie would create.

As I sat across from him in his utilitarian office with its cinderblock walls painted institutional green, his face held much the same expression of semi-belief now.

"Sherlock Holmes is tracking down a missing corpse?" he repeated, giving me a poker-faced stare.

I nodded, feeling a little claustrophobic in the basement office. It offered no personal touches, no plants, no framed diplomas, no family photos of any kind. Overhead fluorescent lighting was a harsh substitute for sunlight, and stark metal file cabinets lined two walls, adding to the cold feel. A desktop computer with an enormous monitor sat on his desk, along with piles of manila file folders and lab reports. For Dr. Watson, business was always good.

"It sounds morbid, I know," I agreed.

"That's one word for it," he replied.

"Her name's Rebecca Lowery," Irene piped up beside me. "She's a blonde. Well, a dead blonde."

I would have rolled my eyes, but I was too busy using them to stare at Watson. Not for the first time, it occurred to me that the man had picked the wrong profession. He was doing a total disservice to female humanity by hiding those looks in a basement every day. His thick blond hair gleamed even under the crappy fluorescents, his pouty lower lip looked practically nibbleable, his startlingly blue eyes, with their feathery little laugh lines, were complemented by a crisp blue chambray shirt that enhanced the muscular lines of his chest and shoulders. His black slacks, while not tight, suggested strong legs. I'd seen those legs in action, chasing an intruder through the backyard of the Victorian. I'd pay to see that again. If I had any money.

I struggled to bring my concentration back to the case. "She's an opera singer."

"Was," Irene added.

"A coloratura soprano," I said.

He nodded. "I'm familiar. She came through here on Monday, and we released the body to the mortuary the next day. Gordon's, I believe it was." He slipped a folder from one of the piles in front of him and flipped it open.

"That's right," Irene said. "Only it wasn't Rebecca at Gordon's when her sister arrived to pay her respects."

Watson frowned. "I'm not sure how that could be."

"Who identified the body here at the morgue?" I asked.

"Her director. She had missed a rehearsal, and when he went to check on her at her home, he found her deceased. He's the one who positively IDed her here." Watson checked the file of papers in front of him. "Phillip Sterling Rossi."

"And you're sure the right body was released the next day?" Irene asked.

He looked up, a shadow darkening his face.

"Never mind," she said quickly. "No offense. We're all professionals here, right?"

His expression suggested he had his doubts about *some* of us.

"What about the other...decedent," I asked. "The woman at the mortuary who wasn't Rebecca Lowery."

"What about her?" he asked.

"Do you know who she was?"

"No, she didn't come through my offices. Though, unless there had been something odd about her death in the first place, she wouldn't have. You'd have to ask Gordon's who she is."

"What was the cause of death?"

"For Rebecca?" He referred to his notes. "Occipital blunt force trauma. According to the police report, she slipped and struck her head on the corner of a granite countertop."

Granite countertops were the holy grail in my own fantasy kitchen, along with cherry cabinets, stainless steel appliances, and a gorgeous natural stone floor. But death by granite countertop was a new and tragic possibility I'd never considered. One small vote for keeping the chipped Formica.

"So it was accidental," Irene murmured.

He gave a single nod. "I explained to the sister"—he referred to his notes again—"Barbara Bristol, that Ms. Lowery hadn't been the victim of foul play. I'd assumed that was understood when she left."

"It was," I assured him. "She hired us to locate her sister's remains, nothing more."

"Did you do an autopsy?" Irene pressed.

I shot her a look.

Watson paused. "Partial. We did an external examination, drew bodily fluids, and ran a tox screen. But based on the obvious injuries and my discussion with the detective involved about how the deceased was found, we determined a full autopsy wasn't warranted."

"How was she found?" Irene asked.

"In a position consistent with a fall. If you want more details, you'll have to ask Detective Lestrade," he offered.

I shuddered at the idea. Lestrade was an SFPD detective with a long case list and a short temper. While his office rivaled a tornado in terms of organization, I knew he wasn't as dumb as he looked. The farther we kept "Sherlock Holmes" from Lestrade, the better chance Irene and I had of not ending up in a jail cell.

"Do you know how long she'd been dead?" I asked, trying to construct a timeline.

"Hard to pinpoint exactly, but based on liver temp, I'd say she'd died sometime late Saturday night or early Sunday morning."

"And you're positive the same body that came into your morgue left to go to Gordon's?" Irene pressed.

Watson closed his notes with a little more force than was strictly necessary. "Yes, as I've told everyone, Rebecca Lowery's body was properly tagged when it left this office."

I jumped on that first part of the sentence. "*Everyone*? Has someone else contacted you about Rebecca Lowery?"

He paused, shooting me a look that said he'd be watching his wording around me in the future. "Yes," he admitted. "A reporter."

I felt my eyebrows rise. Had Barbara Bristol been contacting the press as well as engaging a private investigator? "What did he want?"

Watson pinched the bridge of his nose with a sigh. "A story, I guess. He showed up here yesterday with a lot of questions about how we could lose a body."

"What did you tell him?" Irene asked.

"Nothing at all," he said. "Just that Rebecca's body left here, and what happened to it after that is out of my hands. But he made threats of a coming FOIA request."

"FOIA?" Irene repeated.

"Freedom of Information Act," I supplied. "But your records wouldn't fall under FOIA, would they?"

"Doubtful," Dr. Watson said. "HIPAA privacy rules extend fifty years past date of death, but there have been rulings that records requests supersede HIPAA. I would consider it an invasion of personal privacy, but of course, I'm bound by the law." He stood. "Was there anything else?"

"One thing," Irene said. "What kind of window are we talking about between the time Rebecca's was positively IDed here and when her sister saw Not-Her at Gordon's Mortuary?"

He steepled his hands. "The decedent was received at this office on Monday, positively identified by Mr. Rossi that evening, released to Gordon's Mortuary on Tuesday morning. That's all I know."

"Which means," Irene said, "Gordon's lost her." She paused. "Unless the hearse was carjacked after they picked her up and Rebecca's now doing a *Weekend at Bernie's* thing on Venice Beach."

Watson stared at her. "That ghoulishness must be such a comfort to your clients. But I highly doubt that's what happened."

"Agreed," Irene said. "Who'd carjack a hearse? Not a big market for parts there."

I resisted the urge to kick her in the shin.

"You know," I said, more to myself than anyone else. "A body is a pretty big thing to just lose. I mean, it's not like car keys."

Irene turned to me, one eyebrow raised. "What are you saying?"

"I'm saying, I can see maybe accidentally mixing two bodies up and thinking the other woman was Rebecca...but in that case Rebecca would be where the other woman is supposed to be now. And presumably she's not. How do you accidentally *lose* a body altogether?"

"You think someone *took* Rebecca Lowery?" Watson said slowly.

I shrugged.

"But why would someone steal a dead body?" Irene asked.

"I can't imagine." His gaze remained steady. "That's where Mr. Holmes comes in, right?"

Right. If only he would.

# CHAPTER TWO

———

"Promise me that if I die, you won't bring me here," Irene said an hour later as we stood in the lobby of Gordon's Mortuary. "Freeze me cryogenically, or just prop me in the corner like a broom. Anything but this. What was Barbara Bristol thinking?"

"Give her a break. She doesn't know the area," I said. "She probably picked it out online."

"You're being too kind," she said. "There isn't enough photoshopping in the world to make this place look appealing."

The dim lighting in the lobby was a blessing, given the dingy wallpaper and mismatched furniture. A grandfather clock stood silent to our right, having long ago stopped keeping time. A rickety side table practically creaked under the weight of a stack of generic *Scenes Across America* calendars, bearing the funeral home's imprint, and a few pamphlets, exhorting well-organized people with disposable income to preplan their "life celebration." A cheap-looking accordion style folding door stood latched closed to our right, probably concealing a viewing room. Across the lobby to our left was a closed door with a tarnished gold nameplate reading *Private*. No soothing background music, no hushed voices, and no evidence of good taste.

"Décor by flea market," I muttered.

"No kidding." Irene glanced around. "Where is everybody? This place is quiet, even for a funeral home. You'd think they'd at least be playing Muzak or something."

"Guess they didn't hear us come in," I said.

"They who?" she asked. "There doesn't even seem to be a staff. You could walk right in and steal the furniture, no problem."

We looked at the two ancient wing chairs pushed against the wall. Dust powdered the arms and lined the butt-shaped concavities on the seat cushions.

"Who'd want to?" I asked.

She smirked. "Okay, then you could walk in and steal a body."

"Touché." I paused. "Although, again, I still can't imagine why anyone would."

"Black market organs?"

"Those have to be harvested soon after death to remain viable," I said.

Irene shot me a look.

"What? I sat in on a class about transplant hepatology last month." One of the perks of my job as a barista on the Stanford campus was easy access to some of the world's brightest minds. Which I took full advantage of on a regular basis, even if crashing classes meant I didn't pay full tuition.

She wrinkled her nose. "Why would you do that?"

"One can never be too careful about one's liver," I told her. Especially when one, like me, enjoyed her occasional cocktail.

Irene shrugged. "Okay, well, maybe someone wanted Rebecca's liver."

But I shook my head in the negative. "Watson said he received Rebecca's body on Monday and it—*she*—had likely been dead at least 24 hours by then. Too much time had passed."

"Oh, right. So forget that angle. By then her organs would have spoiled like day-old fish."

I stared at her. "Maybe we could *try* to be respectful?"

She shrugged. "Just trying to lighten the mood. You think I don't know this is spooky stuff?"

It was hard to tell sometimes. I looked across the lobby. "Do you think we should knock on that door?"

"I think we should leave and never come back," Irene said. "Rebecca Lowery probably jumped out of her casket and ran off by herself when she got a look at this place."

"Can I help you ladies?" boomed a voice behind us.

Irene and I spun around as one.

Then I froze. I was pretty sure my mouth was hanging open like a cartoon character as I stared at the man in front of me. He could have been an extra in a vampire movie. Black hair accentuated a pale, gaunt face with sharp cheekbones under intense black eyes. A chilly smile emanated from his lipless mouth. His black suit, draped on a skeletal frame, was standard issue mortician wear, as were the shiny black wingtips. I was fairly sure I'd seen an animatronic version of him holding a butler's tray in the local Home Depot Halloween display.

He extended a heavily veined hand. "Dominic Gordon. And you are?"

*Terrified.* "Martha Hudson," I said. His hand was dry and cold, as you would expect from a cadaver. I tried not to meet his eyes. Their blackness was unnerving, almost soulless.

"Charmed," Gordon said, completely without charm. He turned to Irene with a raised eyebrow.

"Uh, this is my partner, Irene Adler. We're private detectives investigating Rebecca Lowery's disappearance."

A little vertical crease appeared between his eyebrows. "Private detectives? I don't understand."

"Then you have something in common with our client," Irene said, having taken a moment to find her voice. I was pretty sure she was imagining him turning into a little bat and flying away, just like I was. "Ms. Lowry's sister doesn't understand either. She doesn't understand how her sister's body vanished from your funeral home."

His eyebrows shot up in alarm, and he did a *not so loud* gesture, patting the air with both palms. I couldn't imagine who he might fear would overhear us. His clients weren't the listening type.

"Maybe we should step into my office." He gestured toward the *Private* sign.

"I'm comfortable right here," Irene said.

Which was more than *I* could say, though standing out here was preferable to holing up in a small office with the Vampire Lestat.

"What can you tell us about Rebecca Lowery?" she asked.

He stroked his chin, thinking. "Redhead, rather corpulent, died in a car accident?"

"Blonde, thin, died from head trauma," I said. And I couldn't imagine what he considered corpulent, given that he probably topped the scales at 150, even with his pockets full of embalming fluid.

"Yes, of course." He smiled fleetingly. "Lovely woman."

Nothing creepy about *that*. My skin prickled like it was getting ready to crawl off.

"Are you sure about that?" Irene asked. "You might be thinking of the Jane Doe you tried to pass off as our client's sister."

His eyes narrowed. "I'm not sure insults are called for, under the circumstances."

"Mr. Gordon," I cut in, "Rebecca Lowery's body was positively identified at the medical examiner's office on Monday evening. We understand the body was released to you the following day."

He nodded. "We picked up the deceased at Mrs. Lowery Bristol's request and scheduled the cremation."

Irene gave a start. "Cremation?"

Another nod. "That's right. Her sister specifically requested that cremation be carried out as soon as possible."

I couldn't help but wonder why Barbara had neglected to mention that. Not that it was any of our business. It was entirely possible the sisters had no living relatives and therefore no need for a formal visitation. Or it might have been Rebecca's wish simply to be cremated. It might have even been an attempt at frugality on Barbara's part. There was nothing wrong with frugality. It was my life's guiding principle.

"But it wasn't done," Irene was saying.

Gordon shook his head. "The deceased's lawyer informed me that Miss Lowery's will specifically stipulated a visitation with an open casket and full cosmetics. We immediately rescheduled her for embalming." He drew himself up straighter. "We honor the final wishes of our clients here."

Clearly Barbara wasn't up on her sister's wishes. Then again, if they'd been estranged, I'd hardly expect her to know what her sister's will said.

"Regrettably," Gordon went on, "in the exchange of the necessary paperwork, the deceased…well…"

"Disappeared," Irene said.

"Quite." He ran a finger inside his collar to loosen it around his neck. "Regrettably," he repeated.

"Yeah," Irene said. "We got that part."

"I want to understand the timeline," I said. "You picked up the deceased on Tuesday morning. And you met with her sister when?"

He ran a hand down the back of his head. "She engaged our services by phone on Monday afternoon. Tuesday we received the body from the morgue. The sister came in on Wednesday to complete the paperwork for the change from a simple cremation to a viewing. And to make the necessary payment arrangements."

I could practically read Irene's mind. *How much do you charge to lose a body?* But she managed to stay silent.

"And did she see her sister at that point?" I asked.

"Regret—" He glanced at Irene. "*Unfortunately*, no. I mean, she asked to. We didn't have the body ready, of course, so we discouraged it. Such a shock to see one's loved ones in that sort of state, you know."

"Almost as much shock as finding out they'd been lost."

Dominic's eyebrows pinched together. "But she was quite insistent on seeing her sister."

"And that's when she realized you had the wrong body."

"Er…quite."

"Who was the other woman?" Irene cut in.

"I'm sorry?" he asked, blinking at her.

"The body in Rebecca's place. Who was she?"

"Oh, uh, er…we're not entirely sure."

I felt my eyebrows rise. "You're telling me that a random dead body showed up in Rebecca Lowery's place?"

"Uh, yes. I mean, no. She…well, she was tagged as Rebecca Lowery, so we're still trying to find her proper identification."

"So no other bodies are missing? This wasn't a simple mix-up?" I shot a look toward Irene. Unfortunately, our theory was carrying more and more weight—this wasn't a case of poor filing. Someone had deliberately taken Rebecca Lowery and left a Jane Doe in her place.

"No one else is missing!" Dominic said, looking over both shoulders as if hordes of prospective clients might be listening. "Look, we'll figure out who the other woman is. I'm sure it's a simple misunderstanding."

"Age? Coloring?" Irene jumped in.

"Excuse me?"

"Of the Jane Doe."

He paused. "If you're asking if she could be mistaken for Rebecca Lowery, the answer is yes. They looked very similar."

Funny, Dominic suddenly had an excellent memory when it came to what Rebecca Lowery looked like. I wondered how much of his act was trying to cover up the fact that his mortuary had lost a body.

"So Rebecca Lowery actually disappeared from this location," Irene said. "Not in transport. Who has access to this building?"

"No one who doesn't need access." His Adam's apple boomeranged in his throat when he swallowed. "If you're assuming we pass out keys like dinner mints, Miss Adler, you're mistaken."

"I'm not assuming anything," she said evenly. "Where do you put the bodies when you bring them in? You know, before the embalming and cosmetics?"

"Downstairs, of course." He plugged a finger into his collar again and yanked it around. "But I couldn't possibly take you there. It would be improper."

"As opposed to losing a body," Irene muttered.

If it was possible, Dominic Gordon paled even further.

She raised her voice. "What sort of security measures do you employ?"

He stiffened. "I'll have you know, we have a state-of-the-art security system."

She pointed to the keypad mounted beside the front door. "Is that it?"

He nodded.

"No security cameras?"

"Why would we need them?" he asked.

Good point. His clients didn't usually get frisky.

Irene walked over to the keypad and punched in some numbers while studying the readout. "That's what I thought." She turned to me. "I think we're about finished here." She glanced at Dominic Gordon. "We'll be in touch if we think of anything else."

"Fine." His tone suggested it was anything but. "You might find it more convenient to call. My card." He handed me a flimsy gray business card. "Let me see you out." He rushed past us to open the door, practically shoving us onto the sagging porch.

When the door closed behind us, Irene said, "He just made number one on the suspect list."

We had a suspect list? We'd only talked to two people. "Why?" I asked.

"You have to ask?" She shuddered. "You look up the word *creepy*, and that guy's picture is right there. I can just see him pulling a Norman Bates and keeping a dead body at his house for company."

"Thanks for that disturbing image," I said. "But it's not a crime to be creepy."

We got into the car.

"True enough," Irene admitted. "If it was, some of the guys I've dated would be in jail."

"What was that with the keypad?" I asked.

"Just seeing how easy it would be to bypass."

"And?"

"Child's play."

What was child's play for Irene and what was child's play for the rest of the world were two different things. Irene had started her computing career at age twelve by hacking into a government mainframe. She'd graduated MIT at fourteen, and she'd sold her first company on her twenty-first birthday, making her a multimillionaire before she'd ever bought her first beer. However, I tended to believe her when she said Gordon was skimping on security. He hadn't struck me as the overly vigilant type. Case in point—the missing body.

"So, anyone could have broken in?" I asked.

Irene nodded. "The real question is why. I mean, I get why someone would want to steal cash or jewelry. But why steal a body?"

"Medical research?" I offered.

"Totally great reason." She paused and shot me a look. "*If* this were the eighteenth century and you wanted to know how to cure the vapors."

I gave her a playful punch in the arm. "You have a better idea?"

She paused a moment, pursing her lips as she walked. "Okay, I can think of one reason," she said. "Necrophilia."

"That is not a *better* reason," I told her.

"I can easily picture Dominic Gordon propping Rebecca in a chair and going home to play Old Maid with her every night."

"Really disturbing," I told her.

"Tell me you can't see it happening."

Thing was, I kind of could.

"Okay, as ick as that is…but then why would he substitute another cadaver in her place? I mean, one body is as good as another, right?"

"Hmm." Irene mulled that one over. "You're right. I mean, the only reason to sub bodies is so the missing Rebecca wouldn't be noticed."

"Like at a viewing."

Irene raised an eyebrow my way. "Now you're onto something, Sherlock."

I flinched. "I wish you wouldn't call me that."

But she ignored me, her mental hamster having jumped on his wheel. "Rebecca was originally schedule for cremation. It wasn't until *after* the last minute change to an open casket viewing that she went missing. Someone didn't want Rebecca viewed. Instead, they broke in, took Rebecca's body, and substituted a similar-looking corpse, hoping to pass it off as Rebecca for the viewing."

I hated to admit it, but that was the best theory we'd come up with so far. "They might have gotten away with it too. I mean, it had been five years since her sister had seen Rebecca.

And with the mortuary makeup and a little grief clouding Barbara's vision, it wasn't a half bad plan."

"If Barbara hadn't insisted on seeing her sister before she was made up, it's possible no one would have noticed," Irene added.

"So what about Rebecca did someone not want seen?"

Irene turned to me, her eyes shining. Uh-oh. I knew that look. It was the same one she'd gotten when she'd made Forbes 30 Under 30 list—glee mixed with just enough determination to be scary.

"Evidence of her murder."

"Murder?" I choked out. "Wait—we're only looking for a missing person here. Dr. Watson said her death was accidental."

"But what if it wasn't? What if she was *pushed* into that granite counter instead of falling?"

I paused. "That would be hard to prove. The wound would look identical whether it was from a fall or push."

"But it's possible."

I nodded. "Watson is thorough. I don't think he'd miss evidence of a crime."

"If he were looking for it," Irene cut in. "This was a simple slip and fall when it came to him. I mean, what if the evidence wasn't glaring? What if it was just enough that an open casket and visitation made the killer too nervous?"

"I supposed it's possible," I said slowly. "But we're being paid to find Rebecca…not find out how she died."

Irene grinned at me. "If we find out *who* killed Rebecca and took the body, it'll lead us to *where* the body was taken."

While I could point out a couple of flaws in her logic and I had my doubts that Watson would miss a murder, it was becoming more and more clear that Rebecca's body hadn't just been misplaced—it had been taken. Someone had intentionally left Jane Doe in her place. Not something innocent people did.

I nodded. "Fine. We can do it your way."

"You won't regret it," Irene said.

I already kind of did.

# CHAPTER THREE

———

Irene had a charity dinner to go to, so she gave me a ride home and said we'd resume our efforts in the morning. I wasn't sure if it was more of a threat or a promise. Until my Victorian became habitable with an actual roof over my head, I lived in a second-floor shoebox in a building that time had forgotten. While it was a slight step up from the Victorian, the plumbing still groaned, linoleum still had more chips than Frito-Lays, and the walls were no thicker than cheap bath towels. And being that it was in Palo Alto, in the heart of the Silicon Valley, rent was exorbitantly high. I probably paid more for my just-above-the-poverty-level dwelling than most Americans paid for their McMansions. Fortunately, my landlord didn't live on the premises and didn't seem to want to step foot in the building any more than most of the tenants did, so I'd only had to escape down the back stairwell to avoid him once or twice when my day job as a barista hadn't quite paid off in "exorbitant" levels.

When I opened the door, my basset hound, Toby, hurled himself at my legs, panting and licking furiously, aiming for my chin, my hands, or my kneecaps. Toby was another inheritance from my great-aunt Kate, and what he lacked in coordination he more than made up for in affection. Maybe because he'd come from living in the Victorian, Toby didn't seem to mind my apartment. It was a small step up.

I took him out for a quick walk before returning home to change his water and put some food in his bowl. While he gobbled his dinner, I spent a few minutes going through the mail and surveying the food in the fridge for my own dinner possibilities. I settled on two slices of cold pizza, washed down with a glass of Pepsi. Toby and I were sharing an oatmeal cookie for dessert when the phone rang.

"Is that old goat Isaac in there with you?"

It was Mrs. Frist, who lived down the hall from me and spent most of her day glued to the peephole so she could catalog the comings and goings of everyone on the second floor. Especially my next-door neighbor, Isaac Bitterman, an 83-year-old myopic widower with an appalling lack of culinary talent, which didn't deter him one bit from sharing his creations. I'd already had to replace my microwave oven, a saucepan, and a few utensils thanks to his alleged cooking and its perpetually lingering smells and near cement-like textures. I couldn't afford to share too many more meals with Mr. Bitterman.

Fortunately, the senior female population in the building helped distract his attention. The ladies considered him quite a catch, since he still had some hair, an ill-conceived sense of adventure, and a healthy railroad pension.

Mrs. Frist had staked her claim early on and protected it jealously. She was a wiry octogenarian package of silver hair and gold jewelry in a velour track suit, and she had it bad for Mr. Bitterman. For some reason, she viewed me as competition for his affections. I wasn't quite sure how to take that.

"If he's in there with you…" Mrs. Frist trailed off, leaving the threat hanging.

"If you mean Mr. Bitterman," I said, "I haven't seen him."

"I thought we had a dinner date. He'd best not stand me up, if he knows what's good for him."

If she knew what was good for *her*, she'd order takeout.

I glanced at the clock. "Well, it's still early. I'm sure he'll show up."

"He got a grocery delivery earlier," she said, managing to sound accusatory about it. "And I saw french bread. You don't eat alone when you have french bread."

"I'm sure he's not sharing his French bread," I assured her.

"He'd best not be cooking dinner for Mrs. Streelman in 4E," she huffed. "I caught him giving her the eye last week in the lobby. Isaac does like a nice turn of ankle, I can tell you that."

Too much information right there.

"Maybe he's just downstairs playing poker with Mr. Orgeron, and he's lost track of time."

"We'll see about that," she huffed, and then she hung up on me.

Toby looked at me from his doggy bed, his head cocked quizzically.

"If she comes knocking," I told him, "don't answer the door."

\* \* \*

"I don't understand. The medical examiner said she fell and hit her head." Barbara Lowery Bristol emptied a fourth packet of sugar into her coffee the next morning. Her plastic spoon made little scraping sounds against the cup when she stirred, as if she were digging her way through the bottom of the cup. We'd managed to find a window table at the coffee shop down the street from Irene's place, just outside The City. It was out of the flow of customer traffic, if not away from the morning white noise. As an added bonus, it was warm and smelled much better than the Victorian. Less musty, more spicy and sugary.

My stomach rumbled softly. "That may well be true," I told her. "We just need to learn a little more about your sister so we can be sure it was nothing more than an awful accident."

"Don't you believe the doctor?" She tasted the coffee, grimaced, and added a fifth sugar packet.

*Trust, believe, lust after.* I took a bite of my banana walnut muffin to staunch the warmth rising in my belly.

"Of course we believe him," Irene said. "But sometimes there are extenuating circumstances he might not be aware of. That's what makes us private detectives."

Well, that, and a PO box and some imagination.

"Was Rebecca having problems with anyone?" I asked. "Maybe a boyfriend? Someone in the opera company?"

"I don't really know." *Scrape, scrape.* "As I told you before, we hadn't spoken in several years. I only knew she'd joined the company because I saw an article about the show in the Sunday paper." She hesitated. "That sounds pathetic, doesn't it, that I had to learn about my sister's career from a newspaper."

"Families can be complicated," Irene said.

"Complicated." She considered that before shaking her head with a soft snort. "I never would have expected it to come to that, but I had no choice. I couldn't watch Rebecca destroy herself anymore."

Irene took a sip of her chai tea, her gaze sliding briefly to me above the rim of the cup. "What do you mean, destroy herself?"

Barbara looked pained. "Is this relevant?"

"Anything could be relevant at this point," Irene said.

She set the spoon carefully on her napkin, where a milky beige stain immediately blossomed, and took a moment to gather her thoughts. "It's embarrassing to admit this," she said finally, "but my sister had a history of drug use. At first I wasn't sure, but after a while...well, you couldn't miss the signs, the way she acted, the way she spoke, even the way she *looked*. Sort of...cloudy, if you know what I mean. Like she wasn't quite there." She paused.

"Go on," I said softly.

Her mouth twisted with remembered pain. "Rebecca tried to hide it on the few occasions that she visited, of course, and when she couldn't do that, she let my parents ignore it. Which they were all too happy to do, and when they couldn't do *that*, everyone tried to justify it. It must have been the pain meds from her car accident that triggered the descent, or her latest boyfriend was a bad influence, or one of her friends introduced her to that life. It couldn't have been *Rebecca's* fault. She hadn't intended for it to happen. She was *better* than that. The talented golden child just *couldn't* be an addict."

"I'm sorry," I said quietly, struck by the pain in her voice.

She steeled her shoulders, gathering herself. "Anyway, by the time my parents died, I'd had enough. I needed to be away from her. Away from her drama. She reached out to me a few times, but I never returned her calls."

"So you never spoke to her after your parents died?" Irene asked.

Barbara shook her head. "In her last call, she claimed she'd cleaned herself up, but I know enough about addiction to know how fleeting those moments can be. Given Rebecca's lack of impulse control, it probably wouldn't have lasted. It didn't surprise me at all that she fell in her own home and killed herself." She paused to take a sip of coffee. "And I do believe that's what happened," she added. "I'd seen her stumbling around my parents' house in a drug-induced haze all too many times."

Irene and I traded glances, and I could tell we shared a thought: *ask Watson about the tox screen*. While being high might have contributed to Rebecca's death, it could also have given someone a good reason to ditch the body. Designer drugs were like fingerprints—depending on the mix, they pointed directly at a certain dealer.

"Do you know of anyone who was close with Rebecca?" I asked. "Someone who might know whom she'd been seeing, what she'd been doing for the past few years?"

Barbara shook her head. "I'm sorry. I really don't know anything about her private life. But I do know she'd always been most comfortable at the theater. Even from high school, I think it was the place where she felt she could most be herself. Isn't that ironic? Rebecca was most herself when she was playing someone else." She glanced at us in turn. "Maybe a member of that opera company can give you more information."

"We'll give it a try," I said. "And we'll let you know what we find."

"Don't." She pushed her coffee aside, grim-faced. "Just let me know when you find her body so I can put this ugly business behind me."

\* \* \*

"She's not exactly wracked with grief, is she?" Irene said fifteen minutes later when we were in her Porsche headed for the Bayside Theater, where, according to the theater's website, rehearsals were underway for *Ethereal Love* under the guidance of one Patrick Sterling Rossi. I'd done a quick internet search, finding little of note about Mr. Rossi. He didn't seem to be one of the leading lights in the opera world.

"I think she's been grieving her sister for years." I slipped my phone into my pocket. "Besides, people grieve in different ways."

Irene braked to allow some pedestrians through the crosswalk. "Did it strike you that she really didn't seem to care if her sister was the victim of foul play?"

"That's not fair. We don't know her well enough to make that judgment."

"Right. Maybe she's just the stoic type."

I ignored that. "You're the one who said families are complicated. Besides, she flew out here, didn't she?"

Irene shrugged. "Maybe she was hoping for a fat payday."

"You're getting cynical," I told her.

"That can happen to a detective," she said.

"So what's *your* excuse?"

She wrinkled her nose at me. We drove the rest of the way lost in thought. At least I was lost in thought. Irene was probably writing computer code in her head for the next must-have app.

Once we parked a few blocks down the street from the theater, we got out of the car and headed for the frosted glass entrance doors. I'd never attended a live performance at the Bayside, but I knew the theater was fairly large, seating roughly 1500 people, and had been refurbished a few times throughout the forty years of its existence. Performances ranged from ballet and dance troupes to Broadway productions and live musical acts. Its only drawback was its location bordering an industrial area, which reduced both foot and vehicular traffic, although it did make for easier parking in a city where that was notoriously difficult.

We entered the cool, dimly lit lobby. Multiple crystal chandeliers sparkled overhead. The glass-enclosed box office stretched along the wall to our right. A broad open staircase to our left led to balcony seating. The theater proper lay directly ahead, behind two sets of closed double doors.

Beyond the doors, someone sang in a high, clear soprano.

"I can't understand a word she's saying," Irene complained. "What is that, German?"

"Italian, I think." I hesitated. "We probably shouldn't go in there."

"What do you want us to do, shout questions through the door?" Irene grabbed the handle. "Let's be bold."

She did bold better than I did, but I followed her anyway. Pausing at the top of the aisle, we took in the plush red seats, the sparkling chandeliers, the expansive stage bracketed by red velvet curtains. A redheaded woman glowed in the single spotlight while minions orbited around a tall dark-haired man in jeans standing behind the orchestra pit, watching her.

"That's probably the director, Patrick Sterling Rossi," I whispered. "We should start with him."

Irene started down the aisle, but I grabbed her arm. "After she's done."

"Fine." She dropped into a seat, arms crossed. "I can take it if you can."

I sat behind her. "It's kind of pretty, actually."

We listened for a few moments.

"Wonder what she's saying," Irene said again.

"Whatever it is, she seems upset."

"Got any gum?"

I blinked at her.

"What? I've got coffee breath."

"You can't chew gum in an opera house," I hissed.

"Why not?"

"Because this isn't the county fair. It's—"

"Hey!" The dark-haired man glared up at us. He made a *cut* gesture, and the music and singing instantly stopped while every head turned our way.

"Uh-oh," I whispered.

"This is a closed rehearsal!" he snapped.

"Then you should have locked the doors," Irene murmured. She stood. "Are you Patrick Sterling Rossi?"

He frowned. "That's right. Who are you?"

"We're detectives," she called back. "We have some questions for you about Rebecca Lowery. You can answer them here and now or later in our office."

I noticed a hush seemed to fall over the theater at the mention of Rebecca's name.

"He'll think you're a cop," I whispered.

"That's the point," she whispered back.

Rossi made a gesture with his hands toward the stage that must have meant *take five*, as the rest of the crew scattered, and he made his way up the aisle to us. "I'm sorry we'll have to make this quick. It's been tumultuous around here since Rebecca passed, and we're on a tight timeline." If he was cut up about Rebecca's passing, he didn't show it. I was starting to wonder if anyone was grieving for her.

"Irene Adler," Irene offered as he approached. She stuck her hand out to shake. "And this is my associate, Martha Hudson."

"PS Rossi. I'm the director of the show."

We shook his hand. Up close, he was a handsome man, with a few silvery strands woven into jet black hair, light laugh lines at the corners of gray eyes, the suggestion of a five o'clock shadow, and a tantalizing faint scent Chanel Égoïste cologne.

"You, uh, said you're police detectives?"

"Consulting investigators," Irene explained without really explaining anything.

Rossi frowned but nodded. "Why don't we step into the lobby?" he suggested. "We'll have more privacy there."

We followed him back to the lobby, waiting while he fished a pack of cigarettes from his pocket, extracted one with his lips, and lit it with a gold lighter, completely ignoring the smoking-ban laws. "What is it you wanted to know?" he asked impatiently, the cigarette bobbing up and down in his mouth.

"What can you tell us about Rebecca Lowery?" I asked, trying not to inhale the secondhand smoke too deeply.

He shrugged. "What would you like to know? She was a very talented singer. Her death came as a real shock." While the words were sympathetic, the tone didn't match. He could have just as easily been talking about a hangnail.

"What role was she playing?" I asked.

"The Spirit of Love." He looked from Irene to me. "Are you familiar with the story?"

I'd never even *heard* of the story. But, then again, I didn't follow opera.

"Of course," Irene lied. "I love that opera. I've seen it half a dozen times."

I suppressed a sigh. One day Irene's fibs were going to catch up to her. And I had a bad feeling I'd be standing right beside her when they did.

"Rebecca was perfect for the part and excited to have it. We were set to open in two weeks for a limited engagement before the national tour."

"How were her relationships with the rest of the company?" Irene asked. "Did she get along with everyone? Any arguments that you know of?"

He shrugged. "I don't pry into my talents' lives. All I can tell you is, Rebecca was very talented and gone too soon."

"Did she have a drug problem?" Irene asked bluntly.

He looked startled. "A reporter asked me the same question."

I perked up. That was the second mention of a reporter. Someone was definitely following Rebecca's disappearance for a story. And they seemed to be following our same line of thought. "Did the reporter give a name?" I asked.

Rossi shook his head. "I don't know. I don't remember. Look, I don't know where the idea of our star being an addict came from, but it's the last thing our backer needs to hear at this point. He's invested a lot of money into this production, and he's rightly concerned about potential bad press from her death."

Interesting non-answer.

"Is that a no?" I asked him.

He leveled those gray eyes on mine. "It's a firm no. I never personally saw any signs of drug use."

I studied him. While he was looking me straight in the eyes, he was making way too much of an effort to do it. He was hiding something. "You never personally saw it…but you suspected." I paused. "Heard rumors maybe?"

He seemed reluctant to answer. "No rumors," he said finally. "Just observation. I thought she might have had some history of substance abuse."

"Why?" I asked. "What did you observe?"

He blew out a final stream of smoke and dropped the cigarette into a paper cup on the floor filled with similar butts. This wasn't the first time he'd illegally indulged in the lobby. "When the company got together socially, Rebecca always stuck to club soda—no alcohol of any sort. Not even a glass of wine. And I never even saw her take so much as an aspirin for a headache. At the time I just assumed…well, you'd be surprised what some singers do to protect their instrument." He paused. "Of course, this is all speculation."

"I understand you were the one to find her?" I asked.

His eyebrows drew together, as if the memory was playing out in front of him. "Yes. She, uh, missed rehearsal that morning. Truth be told, she'd missed a few lately. When she just didn't show up on Monday, I was worried she might be really ill. I went to her apartment, and when she didn't answer the door, I got the super to let me in. That's when we found…" He trailed off, as if mentally trying to wipe away the image.

"You said she'd missed a few rehearsals lately?" I asked. "Any particular reason why?"

He shrugged. "Said she wasn't feeling well. That flu's been going around."

This was the first I'd heard of any flu. It sounded like a convenient cover. Suddenly I wondered just what Rebecca had been doing in her last few days when she'd been calling in sick.

"Were there any other problems in her life that you knew about? Issues with other cast members?"

He shook his head again. "I told you, I didn't pay attention to her social life. No one came to me with any problems. As far as I can tell you, she was a model prima donna. If I had an entire company of Rebeccas, my life would be much easier."

"So she was beautiful and talented and easy as pie," Irene said. "Yet she's dead."

Rossi's mouth twisted in a grimace. "I don't understand. I was told she'd hit her head in a fall, but if the police are involved—"

I shook my head. "Oh, we're not—"

"Strictly routine," Irene cut in. "Dotting *i*'s, crossing *t*'s, that sort of thing. Would you mind if we talk to some other members of the company?"

He paused, looking as if he very much did mind. "Please, be discreet. Everyone is upset as it is."

"Don't worry," Irene said. "You won't even know we're here."

\* \* \*

"Sorry again about knocking over that music stand," Irene said. "I didn't realize they could make so much noise."

"Don't sweat it, honey." Diana Rossi was a plump fortysomething brunette with ruddy cheeks and a perpetually wet brow—the sort of woman who looked overworked even while sitting still. Her eyes were fixed on the redhead in front of her as she adjusted the puce colored velvet costume in place on her tiny derriere. "The rehearsal needed to end anyway. My husband tends to let them drag on and on until the lights start to melt the stage. It's just the way he works."

"We're sorry to bother you, but as my colleague here said"—I gestured to Irene—"we're working for Rebecca's sister. We're…tying up some loose ends for her estate." Which was almost the truth and sounded a lot better than looking for her missing corpse.

"Right. Hold still, Tara. I haven't pinned you yet," Diana told the girl in front of her.

I didn't think it was possible for Tara to stand still. Everything on her seemed to be moving at once, starting with her shimmering Disney-princess red hair, to her incredibly large bosom, to the long legs fidgeting impatiently beneath the gown that Diana was currently trying to pin. We'd learned that Tara Tarnowski, the woman we'd seen on stage when we'd entered, had been Rebecca's understudy for the Spirit of Love role in *Ethereal Love*, which meant she was the new female lead. Not that the promotion stoked my suspicion that Tara could have had something to do with Rebecca's death.

Until she began speaking.

"Rebecca was a total B-word." She twisted to glare down at us from the wooden box she was standing on, surrounded by racks of costumes and shoes and accessories. "Thought she was better than everyone around here just because she'd studied in Europe under Giovanni Maximiliano. At least she *claimed* she had."

"Hold still," Diana said around a mouthful of pins.

"Claimed? You mean you didn't believe her?" Irene asked.

Tara shrugged. "Rebecca had a knack for telling people what they wanted to hear. Especially if it meant getting ahead. I mean, if I thought it would get me the lead, I could have made up some credentials too. But some of us have morals."

"So, you think Rebecca lied to get the lead role?"

But Diana answered instead. "You know that's ridiculous. My husband wouldn't have given her the lead if she didn't deserve it."

Tara made a harrumphing sound, as if she didn't believe that for a second. "Well, all I'm saying is that Rebecca put the *D* in diva. I mean, we're two weeks out, and she hasn't even shown up for rehearsals in like, a week."

"PS said she was sick," I said.

"*Called* in sick. Big difference," Tara said, twisting to look at us to make her point.

"Hold still!" Diana admonished.

"Well, hurry it up," Tara said. "I haven't got all day to stand here and—*ow!*"

"I told you to stand still," Diana said. She winked at us.

I couldn't help but like her a little.

"Do you know if Rebecca had any issue with anyone in the cast?" I asked carefully, not adding *other than you*, in Tara's direction.

Diana shook her head. "Not that I knew of. Sorry."

"Was she seeing anyone?" Irene asked. "A boyfriend?"

"I remember one guy coming around a few times," Diana responded. "Big guy. Looked like a bodybuilder or something."

Irene's eyebrows went north. "Really?"

I gave her a *down girl* look. "Did you get his name?" I asked.

She shook her head. "Sorry, she didn't introduce me. Give me a quarter turn, please."

Tara pivoted obediently to her right. "As if she would! Queen Rebecca thought she was so far above us."

"Tara," Diana chided.

"Well, it's true," she mumbled under her breath.

"You know, now that you mention it," Diana said, her wet brow furrowing. "I seem to recall an argument between Rebecca and the bodybuilder. A couple weeks ago. You remember that, don't you, Tara?"

"An argument?" Irene looked practically giddy. "Do tell."

"There's not a lot to tell. The guy showed up after rehearsal a couple of weeks ago, and they got into it backstage."

"What did he say?" I asked.

"Sorry, I didn't really hear what they were arguing over," Diana admitted.

Irene looked to Tara. "Did you?"

Tara shrugged. "I wasn't interested in her drama. But I can bet whatever it was, it was Rebecca's fault."

Drama seemed to be a common theme when it came to Rebecca. Barbara had even referred to her sister as a drama queen. Hard to know if the drama derived from the real or the imagined, and maybe it didn't matter. Rebecca's life had been short, but it hadn't been boring.

"Did Rebecca ever mention other fights with the boyfriend?" I prodded. "Anything that might have gotten heated…or violent?"

Tara shrugged. "I don't remember."

I looked to Diana, but she shook her head. "Sorry. I don't remember her saying much about him. She didn't really talk about her private life."

Tara snorted. "At least not with the likes of *us*."

"Did she ever come to rehearsal with any bruises…or maybe a black eye?" Irene pressed, clearly thinking along the same lines I was. A *hotheaded* boyfriend sounded promising.

And slightly preferable to tracking down drug dealers or necrophilics.

Diana looked concerned. "Are you asking me if he ever hit her?"

"That's what we're asking," Irene said.

Diana shook her head. "No. I never saw anything like that."

But that didn't mean the boyfriend hadn't gotten violent. It just meant if he had, Rebecca had covered it up.

"I guess we should congratulate you," Irene said, switching gears and addressing Tara. "You're the female lead now, right?"

Diana's hands stilled briefly, but she kept her expression neutral as she resumed her work.

Tara, on the other hand, gave us a self-satisfied smile. "The Spirit of Love role was meant for me."

"But it didn't become yours until Rebecca died," Irene pointed out. She paused while Tara's face darkened. "Had you been her understudy in any other productions?"

Tara's lips tightened. "Never. And I shouldn't have been this time."

"Oh? Why's that?"

"Clearly you know nothing about opera," she said with a sniff.

"I think I know enough," Irene said levelly.

"Let me tell you—"

Diana touched Tara's arm. "We're done here. Go on and change out so I can get to work."

Tara speared us with an icy glare before stepping off the box and stomping off without a backward glance.

Diana busied herself sliding her unused pins into the pin cushion on her wrist. "Don't mind her. Being an understudy is a sensitive topic for her. She's actually very talented in her own right."

"I'm sure she is," I said. "We didn't mean to imply otherwise."

"I know you didn't." She smiled. "We were very lucky to have two talented coloraturas in the company. It's just that Tara saw the understudy role as second best, when it's not that at all. She'll be wonderful playing the lead."

"Had Tara and Rebecca known each other before *Ethereal Love* was cast?" Irene asked. "Did they travel in the same circles?"

"I really couldn't say. I think they both considered me more of a den mother than a confidant." Her smile was rueful. "If you'll excuse me, I really should get started on her costume. Can I help you find your way out?"

We declined the offer, said our thanks, and threaded a path through the wardrobe room and the backstage labyrinth of halls and doorways back to the stairs at stage left. A few straggling members of the orchestra were still putting their instruments away as we made our way up the aisle.

"Well," Irene said, "that was enlightening."

"In more ways than one," I mumbled, thinking about the way Tara had insinuated at least three untoward different things about Rebecca in the course of a few minutes.

"What do we think of the understudy?" she asked, as if reading my mind.

I shrugged. "I think she's catty and jealous, but I'm not sure about killer."

Irene blinked at me. "Come on! Really? Professional rivalry is a fabulous reason to kill."

"But what about the boyfriend. You'd really put your money on the waif-thin redhead over the bodybuilder?"

Irene shrugged. "Hey, if the opera world is anything like the business world, rivals will do just about anything to get ahead. And, let's not forget, so far Tara is the only person who seems to have benefited from Rebecca's death. That makes her number one on my suspect list."

She had a point. "Okay," I conceded. "But I still like the boyfriend. He'd have access to her home and much more opportunity. Plus he'd be strong enough to give her a good hard shove into the granite countertop, *and* don't forget, he was a hothead."

"We don't know that for sure," Irene said. "We know they had at least one fight. Lots of couples fight, and it doesn't necessarily end in murder."

"Still," I said. "It's worth looking into."

"What's worth looking into?" a voice resonated behind us.

I turned to see PS Rossi reentering the theater from the lobby, presumably after another cigarette break.

"Is there anything else we can help you with?" he asked again, looking like helping us was the last thing he wanted to do.

I glanced at Irene. "As a matter of fact, there is," I said. "Did you know Rebecca Lowery's boyfriend?"

"Her boyfriend?" He frowned, thinking. "Why?"

"We just wanted to make sure someone had informed him of her death," Irene quickly lied.

He frowned and shook his head. "I'm sure he already knows. He is a police officer, after all."

"A *police officer*?" Irene repeated. "Are you sure about that?"

He nodded. "I mean, I never met him, but I heard Rebecca mention him once or twice."

"Did she mention a name?" I asked. Funny that Tara hadn't thought the boyfriend's occupation important to note. A police officer would know exactly what kind of evidence could condemn a killer…and be in a better position than anyone to make a body disappear to hide that evidence.

"I think his name was Bruce…or no, Bryan. Bryan Steele."

Irene looked at me. "A police officer."

I had the feeling Tara had just become the understudy again. This time on our suspect list.

# CHAPTER FOUR

"He'll be retired by the time we find a parking spot," Irene complained.

"Don't give up now," I urged her. "We've only been around the block three times."

According to Irene's online searches, Bryan Steele's precinct was a one-story historic brick building three blocks south of Golden Gate Park. A chilly wind scented with saltwater and fast food swept in through our open windows, hurling wispy filaments of fog at the patrol cars parked up and down the narrow street, hogging every inch of curb.

"I love the idea of a police officer stealing a corpse," Irene said.

*Love* wasn't exactly the word I would use. In fact, the idea of one sworn to protect-and-serve actually shove-and-running and taking the body with him made me shiver. I pointed. "Someone's pulling out up there."

A few minutes later, we were looking through a window of bulletproof glass at the desk sergeant—a barrel-chested man with flat eyes and one hair wound around his scalp seventeen times. Telephones rang faintly in the background, and the garlicky scent of takeout laced the air.

"Officer Steele's out on leave," he told us.

"When is he due back?" I asked.

His shoulders lifted and fell.

"When did he go on leave?" I asked.

His shoulders lifted and fell again.

"How long has he been gone?" I asked.

His shoulders stayed still while he glared at me.

"Excuse me." Irene flashed her phone screen at me out of Sergeant Coif's view, beneath the window. The note *keep him talking* was scrolled across it. Easier said than done. First I had to *get* him talking.

I slid her a sideways glance. "What…?"

She shook her head very slightly. "I'm waiting for an important email," she said in a loud, clear voice. "I'll just step aside to check it."

I resisted the urge to follow her. Great. Now what?

Two uniformed officers entered the lobby, chatting about the upcoming football season. They did a double take when they noticed Irene—obviously auburn-haired bombshells carrying Birkin bags weren't par for the course at the station. They glanced briefly at me—blondes in not-so-chic shabby jeans clearly didn't seem so out of place. Then they nodded to Sergeant Coif, who wordlessly buzzed them into the inner sanctum.

So all I needed was a uniform, a badge, and a gun to get his attention.

"Is Officer Steele picking up his messages?" I asked him.

"Sure. His secretary comes in for them every morning," he said, without a trace of humor.

Hilarious. I glanced over my shoulder to see Irene sitting with her back to us, typing furiously on her phone. Whatever she was doing, she wasn't done yet. And I had a feeling email had nothing to do with it

I turned back to the window. "Did I mention that we're friends of Rebecca Lowery?"

Nothing.

"Officer Steele's girlfriend?" I prompted.

Less than nothing. He actually looked bored.

I suppressed a sigh. "How are the Niners looking this year?"

His eyes lit up. "Garoppalo's the best move they've made in a long time. Long as the injury bug doesn't bite, they should be able to go twelve and—"

"Time to go," Irene cut in from behind me.

Naturally, just when I'd solved the Rubik's Cube.

She smiled at the sergeant. "Thanks for all your help."

He actually had the nerve to say "You're welcome" before she dragged me by the arm out of the station.

"What's wrong with you?" I asked when we'd reached the sidewalk.

"While you were busy charming the desk sergeant—nice job, by the way—I was taking a tiny peek at Bryan Steele's file."

I gasped. "You hacked into a police file?"

"I just peeked."

"What were you thinking?"

"The same thing you were," she said, grinning proudly. "That it would be easier to turn water into wine than to get anything out of Sergeant Tight Lips back there."

I shook my head. "Great. So when is Steele coming back from leave?"

The grin grew. "That's the thing. The file I hacked—I mean, *peeked* at? It was an IA file."

I resisted the urge to shake her. "You hacked into an *Internal Affairs* file?" I glanced over both shoulders as if expecting a swarm of officers to follow after us shouting Miranda rights. "Do you know how illegal that is?" I hissed.

She nodded. "Very." If anything, she looked even more proud of herself as she practically propelled me down the block. "Listen, Bryan Steele's not out on leave. He's been *suspended* for use of excessive force against an arrestee."

I stared at her. "Are you sure?"

"Marty." Her tone was withering. "If I know one thing in this life, it's computer hacking. And finding a killer shoe sale. But mostly computer hacking."

I noticed she'd dropped the peeking ruse altogether.

"Also," she added, "I know how to read. Bryan Steele's not only a hothead. He's a *violent* hothead. He's also totally our number one suspect."

"Has it occurred to you," I said, "that the last person you talk to always seems to become your number one suspect?"

"That's because I'm flexible," she said. "I'm telling you, Mar, this Steele guy has what it takes."

Great. A violent hothead who just happened to also be a police officer. What could go wrong there? Suddenly, I was rethinking our theory on nice, safe Tara.

"So what are we going to do about it?" I asked her. "You saw the kind of cooperation we got from that desk sergeant. Cops look out for one another. I highly doubt any of them would be interested in helping us."

Irene checked her Piaget watch. "I can't do anything about it right now. I'm due at a meeting."

"New baby entrepreneurs?" I asked.

She nodded. "Yep. I've got a couple of Cal kids who have an AI property they're trying to sell."

"Artificial intelligence?"

She nodded. "Yeah, this one's really cool. It's a hairless, poopless cat robot."

The wonders of technology.

"I'll track down Steele's home address after," she promised, "and we can pay him a visit tomorrow."

"Looking forward to it."

If Irene detected my sarcasm, she didn't mention it. "Can I drop you off at 221?" she asked as we got into her car.

I thought about my options. Rent was due this week at my apartment. Then again, at the Victorian I had a hole in the roof, broken hot water heater, peeling and possibly lead-contaminated paint…

"Actually, mind swinging by my apartment instead?"

Irene gave me a small nod of pity before pulling away from the curb. "Not quite livable yet, huh?"

"Depends on how much you enjoy fresh air."

"Cheer up. A few more cases and you'll be able to get enough of the repairs done at the house to move in. There's some good news for you, right?"

A few more cases? I didn't know if that was good news or bad.

* * *

My neighbor across the hall, 2B, was sitting in the hallway, back against his door, legs outstretched, when I climbed the stairs with the day's assortment of circulars and bills in my hand. Legally speaking, 2B was named Ed Something-with-twenty-letters-and-no-vowels, and he was a throwback to the

Woodstock era that he was about twenty years too young to have actually experienced, with torn jeans and an endless wardrobe of rock band and old album cover art T-shirts. His long, thin face was accented with devilish arched eyebrows and scrubby whiskers. He'd lived across the hall from me for about a year, and for eleven months and three weeks, he'd been trying to get me to go out with him. I had nothing against 2B, but I'd rather have dinner with Mr. Bitterman.

"Hey, Marty." He scrambled to his feet and stood with his hands stuffed into his pockets, shifting back and forth. "Have you got a spare key to my place?"

I shook my head. "You've never gave me a spare key, Ed." Thank God for small favors.

"I didn't?" He pulled one hand from his pocket to scratch his head. "I'm gonna get one made for you. Soon as I get back inside. See, I kind of locked myself out."

I stuck my key in the lock and heard the frantic scrabble of paws followed by a thud on the other side of the door.

"I'd rather you didn't." I unlocked the door. "I don't want that kind of responsibility."

Suddenly 2B was right over my shoulder, following me inside. I left the door cracked so he could find his way back out. Quickly.

Toby danced around me with a happy smile, his tail wagging furiously. When I knelt to pet his wriggling little body, he paused to sniff my hands, punctuating his inspection with a sloppy kiss to my palm. Having fulfilled his canine obligations, he trotted back to his doggy bed, where he lay muzzle on paws, watching us intently so he didn't miss anything.

2B followed me into the kitchen. "If you don't have a key, who'll feed the bird when I'm on vacation?"

"You don't have a bird," I said wearily.

"Not yet," he said. "But I'm working on it. I leave the window open all the time in case one flies in. Thing is, it's supposed to rain, and I got my Bose on the floor right below the window. Speakers don't like water. Can I borrow a lock pick so I can get inside?"

I dropped the mail on the table. It was nothing that couldn't wait—for months if necessary. "I don't have a lockpick either, Ed."

"You don't?" His mouth twisted. "Wow, Marty, I thought you were some kind of PI or something."

"Or something," I mumbled.

Someone knocked on the door. I knew from the smell that roiled into the apartment that my day had just gone from *meh* to *ugh*.

Sure enough, Isaac Bitterman shuffled into the room wearing green plaid pants under a yellow striped polo shirt with pristine white Adidas. Gray hair poked from his collar. And his sleeves. And his ears. His black-framed glasses magnified his eyes into golf balls.

He carried a plate loaded with what looked like crisp, skinny asparagus stalks slathered with some noxious-smelling green sauce. "I've been waiting for you to get home, Martha Hudson. I developed a new dip." He thrust the plate under my nose.

Immediately the carbon monoxide detector on the ceiling beeped once in protest at the rising fumes. Toby let out a sharp bark and fled to the safety of my bedroom.

"Whoa!" 2B took a step back, pinching his nostrils shut. "What *is* that, dude?"

"It's a secret recipe," Mr. Bitterman said with obvious, if misplaced, pride.

"It should've stayed a secret," 2B told him.

"Mrs. Frist was looking for you yesterday," I told him. "She said you had a dinner date."

He snorted. "In her dreams. She's too old for me. I'm a cougar."

"Pretty sure you can't be a cougar, dude," 2B said. "You've got the wrong equipment."

"What equipment?" Mr. Bitterman asked. "I've got equipment for any project, thanks to my friends Black & Decker."

2B laughed. "Can I have some of what you're smoking?"

Mr. Bitterman scowled at him. "Is that how you dress for dinner, young man?"

"He's not here for dinner," I said immediately. "He's locked himself out of his apartment and thought I had a spare key." I eyed the plate of asparagus spears, hoping *I* wasn't here for dinner either.

"What's wrong with how I dress?" 2B asked. "Lynyrd Skynyrd rocks."

Mr. Bitterman took his time looking 2B up and down before shoving the plate at him. "People should eat more vegetables. Try one."

2B backed up with an expression of horror, and if there had been a window behind him, he might have dived through it to escape. "I don't eat vegetables, dude. I'm a carnivore."

"Come on, they're good for you," I said, egging Mr. Bitterman to take a step closer to 2B. Which caused 2B to take a step closer to my door.

"N-n-no thank you!" 2B said, backing up just a bit further. "I'm on a strictly cheeseburger diet."

"Those things will clog your arteries, son. Trust me. I've had three bypass surgeries." Bitterman shoved the plate toward him again.

2B stumbled over the threshold of my front door.

"Good luck with the birds," I told him as I swiftly closed it shut.

Bitterman shook his head at me. "You could do better than him."

God, I hoped so.

Mr. Bitterman set the plate on the table. "Now that I've got you to myself, Martha Hudson, what say we order a pizza?"

I crossed my arms, amused and relieved, since I'd been afraid he'd expect me to sample that green sauce, which on closer inspection, appeared to be bubbling, although it was cold. "What about 'people should eat more vegetables'?"

He shrugged his thin shoulders. "Win some, lose some."

Story of my life.

# CHAPTER FIVE

———

I'd checked my phone a total of fifteen times by mid-shift the next morning, anxious for word from Irene about Bryan Steele. The silence on her end was making me jumpy. That and the four cups of coffee I'd downed trying to pump some life into my veins as I took the early shift—which started at 5 a.m. to prep pastries and lattes for the students who'd pulled midterm all-nighters. As early as it sometimes started, I actually kinda liked my job. The coffee bar sat on the mezzanine floor of the Stanford Bookstore, filling my days with the heavenly scents of dark roast and freshly printed paperbacks. The tips paid the bills (mostly), free caffeine was an employee perk (no pun intended), and being on the university campus gave me unfettered access to dozens of classes, of which I'd audited (or crashed) enough to qualify as a PhD candidate. Unfortunately, since college tuition had never been in the budget for the single mother who'd raised me, and auditing classes didn't earn actual credits, a degree eluded me. Which was fine. It saved me the trouble of picking just one subject to focus all my time on. My brain was a virtual Jill-of-all-trades, full of the random facts I'd picked up over time. All very useful in my career of filling paper cups for cramming college students.

My fellow barista, Pam Lockwood, slipped behind the counter with an armful of empty cups, which she dumped in the recycling bin. Pam was one of those rare always-happy people, pink-cheeked with a general air of softness about her, in appearance and in personality. She'd only worked at the coffee bar for a few quarters, but she was convinced she'd find her Mr. Right someday behind a macchiato or a cappuccino, if only she kept flossing. Pam was a big believer in good oral hygiene and the appeal of a winning smile.

"Do you see that blond guy sitting by the stairs?" She blew a wisp of brown hair from her eyes. "Maybe I should ask him out. What do you think?"

Blond guy? My mind went instantly to Watson. I glanced over, relieved and irritated to see it wasn't him. Of course it wasn't. Watson was buried in his cinderblock Batcave solving the eternal mysteries of unexplained death. "You mean the guy in head-to-toe leather? With the motorcycle helmet on the chair beside him?"

"I don't think he's a student," she said. "He doesn't have any books or a laptop or anything. Just his helmet. And his…leather."

The way she breathed that last word, whispered of hidden fetishes. One I wanted to know nothing about.

"Motorcycles are so sexy," Pam said with a little shiver. "I mean, sure, there's the chance you could get flattened into ribbon by a tractor trailer on the freeway, but it's the fear of death that makes you *live*, right?"

Except Pam's idea of living was hitting up Bed Bath & Beyond on payday to browse for the latest kitchen gadget and stock up on fluffy bath towels.

"You can just tell he's born to be wild," she added in a rapturous whisper.

"I think he might be just passing through," I told her. "You might want to wait for someone more…rooted."

"That's good advice, Marty." She bent to retrieve a spray bottle of cleanser from the storage cabinet. "Do you know where I can rent a motorcycle helmet?"

So much for good advice.

"Why don't you start with buying him another coffee?" I suggested.

Pam considered it. "You're probably right. I can work a coffee into my budget. I'm trying to be frugal, since I've got my eye on a new juicer." She found the folded newspaper. "Thanks, Marty. Let me know if I can give you advice sometime."

I hoped she didn't mean that.

After checking my phone for time number sixteen, I decided to take advantage of the lull in the customers by wiping down the tables. Ten minutes later, I gathered two abandoned cups from the last one, turned, and nearly bumped into a tall blond man. And not one dressed in leather and carrying a motorcycle helmet this time.

Watson. Apparently he'd escaped from the Batcave after all.

I blinked up at him, trying to cover my surprise. "I'm so sorry," I said on a gasp. "Did I spill anything on you?"

"I don't think so." Smiling, he patted down his chest and stomach just to be sure, while I thought, *I could do that for you.* A thought followed immediately by an intense flush of heat in my face.

"Not a drop," he said. "Have you got a minute?"

*For that smile, I have a lifetime.*

Good Lord. I really needed to get a grip. I glanced at the emptiness around us. "Sure."

I suddenly felt nervous. Watson and I weren't exactly on drop-by-your-work-to-hang terms. Granted, what terms we were on was still a bit ambiguous. Sure, we'd had dinner together before, but that had been purely work related. Sure, he'd been to the Victorian, even in the bedroom—which hadn't been as exciting as it might sound since he'd been chasing after an intruder at the time—and he'd even been to my apartment. But in all that time he'd been a perfect gentleman.

That just had to end.

"Do you want something to drink?" I asked him.

He shook his head. "No, thanks. I just came to talk to you."

The nerves kicked up a notch. We certainly weren't on drove-all-the-way-to-Palo-Alto-just-to-talk-to-you terms.

"Is there a problem?" I asked, gesturing to a table we could sit at.

"There might be." He held a chair for me. "I wanted to chat about Mr. Holmes."

I froze. This was it then. The end of the Sherlock Holmes ruse. I'd known it would come someday, but I hadn't expected it so soon. Well, that wasn't entirely true. I'd kind of expected it as soon as Irene had first showed Watson that fake PI license. It seemed strange that he'd question its validity now, but the gears of bureaucracy ground slowly.

I stifled a sigh, thinking the least I could do was offer an explanation. I owed him that much.

"Listen," I said, "let me—"

"Detective Lestrade paid me a visit this morning," he said.

The words stuck in my throat. It was worse than I thought. Lestrade had made the discovery and had issued a warrant for our arrest on fraud charges. Watson probably thought he'd warn me in case I wanted to turn myself in. I arranged my features into an expression of complete neutrality while I raised my eyebrows in question, pretending my heart wasn't trying to crash through my ribs.

He sat back, crossing his legs. He wore gray slacks and a black shirt with a burgundy tie and looked like a recent med school graduate. I wondered if he'd visit me in jail.

"Someone hacked into the police database yesterday," he said. "Specifically, the Internal Affairs database."

"Did they?" An image of Irene bent over her phone at the police station sprang to mind. "You read about things like this all the time," I said. "No one is safe from hacking these days, are they?"

"Apparently not. Funny thing, though. He said the files that were hacked had to do with an officer named Bryan Steele." He paused. "Ever heard of him?"

I thought about lying, but that shtick seemed done to death in this situation. "Of course," I said. "I'm a detective." Oops. There went another lie. "I know that Steele dated Rebecca Lowery."

"Whose body just happens to be missing."

"Talk about coincidence," I said. I gave him my toothiest grin.

"Yes, let's talk about coincidence." He crossed his arms.

Crossed legs and crossed arms were a bad sign. It meant he was closed off to a perfectly innocent explanation. If only I had one.

"Does Mr. Holmes happen to know anything about this?" he asked.

"Mr. Holmes?" I scrubbed at a nonexistent stain on the table. "No. In fact, I'm sure he doesn't." Mostly because he didn't exist.

"How about you?"

"Me?" I squeaked out on a laugh that sounded totally forced even to my own ears. "I wouldn't know how to hack into anything. I can barely figure out most of the apps on my phone." I gave him a sheepish grin meant to impart my embarrassing lack of technical know-how, when the cell phone in my pocket chimed with an incoming text.

I didn't move. Not even my frozen grin.

He frowned. "Aren't you going to check that?"

"Oh, was that mine?" I pulled the phone from my pocket.

*Steele lives at 479 7th Ave.*

I put the phone facedown on the table, resolved to talk to Irene about her timing. "It's nothing important."

"You seem upset."

"Do I?" Dang, the grin had thawed.

"Do you need to call someone back?"

I shook my head. "It was a wrong number."

Another text chimed.

Watson's eyes dropped to my phone before rising to meet mine. "Maybe you want to let them know that."

"Good idea," I said. Except if I did that, he might catch a glimpse of the screen. "I'll do it later. This happens all the time. Now, what were we talking about?"

"Hacking."

"Oh. Yeah. Right." Rats. So much for my seamless change of topic. "So, uh, do the police have any leads as to who might have been the hacker?"

"Not yet," he said, watching me closely. "But they're working on it. I thought you might want to talk to your boss about it."

"My boss?"

A frown flirted with his perfect features. "Yes."

I glanced behind myself, checking to see if Alberta, the day manager, was at the coffee bar. "I don't know what she'd have to do with—"

"Sherlock Holmes," he said flatly.

Oh, right. That boss. I swallowed hard. "I'll be sure to let him know," I said. "Or see if he knows. Or anyone else. I mean, I'm not the only detective."

He stared at me.

"Sure I can't get you some coffee?" I asked brightly.

"Thanks, no." He made a move to stand, then hesitated. "One more thing."

Customers were starting to trickle in again, much to my relief, lining up at the counter for service.

I grabbed my phone and leaped to my feet. "I'm sorry. Pam's on break, and I'm working alone right now. I have to go take care of them."

"Marty, wait."

The urgency in his voice compelled me to turn back to him.

"Are you available for dinner tomorrow night?" he asked.

Pure adrenaline surged through me. *Dinner? I'm available for dinner, dessert, a midnight snack, and breakfast. In bed.* But probably I should play it a little cooler than that.

"I'm not sure," I said. "I'll have to check. Why?"

He sighed. "The thing is, I'd really like a chance to discuss what you've learned about Rebecca Lowery. To be honest, the circumstances of this…" He ran a hand through his hair, his expression pained. "Let's just say it's concerning to me. Professionally."

My excitement was swept away in a flood of disappointment. And sympathy. "But you had nothing to do with it. *You* didn't lose the body. You followed protocol."

"I know, and I wish I could put it out of my mind," he said. "But I can't. What do you say? Dinner?"

How could I refuse? He was genuinely disturbed by the case, and I couldn't blame him. In fact, I felt the same way. Still, did I want to sit through another dinner with him while posing as a detective, afraid that I might say the wrong thing at any moment and reveal my flagrant deception?

I glanced at his wide shoulders and pouty lips.

On second thought, maybe I'd take the chance.

My cell phone chimed with another incoming text. I shoved it into my pocket without looking at it.

"Alright," I said. "Dinner tomorrow night."

He smiled. "I'm looking forward to it."

I wished I could say the same.

\* \* \*

I felt like I'd worked a double shift by the time I slid into the passenger seat of Irene's car idling in the Tresidder parking lot.

"Hey," I said wearily.

"Hey, yourself." She paused, giving me a quick once-over. "What happened?"

"Huh?"

She rolled her eyes. "Your cheeks are flushed, you've been biting your nails, and your forehead is so wrinkled it's screaming for Botox."

I sighed. She knew me so well. "Watson came to see me today," I confessed.

"Nice." She pulled out onto Mayfield, toward Campus Drive. "How'd he look?"

*Hot.* "That's not important."

"It's *always* important. So what'd he want?"

"We're going out to dinner tomorrow night," I said as casually as I could.

She hit the brakes at a stop sign, lurching me forward. "He asked you out on a date? This is huge, Mar!"

"It's not a date. We're just…having dinner."

Irene grinned. "Uh-huh. Dinner. Together?"

"Yes."

"Alone?"

"I guess."

"Someplace nice?"

"He hasn't specified yet…" I trailed off.

"Dude. That's a date. That man's hot for you."

I felt my cheeks grow warm. "He's hot—that much is true. Hot for me? That's debatable."

"You've got to wear that cute little drop-waist Moschino dress and—"

"That's not all," I cut in.

"Of course it's not! You need shoes too. I've got just the pair." At the insistence of the cars behind her, she finally pulled forward again.

"No, I mean, that's not all Watson said. He told me the police know someone hacked into their database," I told her.

She shrugged. "So what?"

"So Watson asked me if I knew anything about it," I said. "I said no, of course, but I don't know if he believed me. Which is *why* he asked me out to dinner. Purely to interrogate."

"He can't prove anything," Irene said. "And neither can the police." She narrowed her eyes. "You didn't confess, did you?"

"Of course not," I snapped. "I played dumb." I paused. "Then we're fine."

"You seem pretty sure of yourself," I hedged.

"There's a reason I make the big bucks," she said lightly.

Which was true. She *did* make the big bucks, but she was the most low-key billionaire I'd ever met. Granted, she was probably the *only* billionaire I'd ever met.

"Don't think I'm going to let you off the hook about that dress," she said. "

"It's just a business meeting," I insisted. "With a side of interrogation."

"Just don't let him tie you up." She paused. "Or maybe you should." She waggled her eyebrows at me suggestively.

I shook my head. "Pay attention to the road, will you?"

Nearly an hour later, we found Bryan Steele's house sitting in the middle of the block in the Inner Richmond District. The place was a monument to *boring*, a square, two-story building with four square windows above a square garage door and gated front entry. The outside was 1970s baby-poo-brown stucco, the windows all barred, and the garage door was a utilitarian rust color. No flowerpots, no kitschy architecture The

City was known for, and no personality. Even the windows were boring, covered in simple white horizontal blinds beyond their prison cages. Clearly there'd been no feminine touch at play here.

Irene turned to me. "Ready to talk to Officer Steele or what?"

My choice was "or what," but she was already out of the car, so I hurried after her, trying to ignore the anxious flutters in my stomach. It was one thing to play PI with Barbara Lowery Bristol. It was another to do it with a police officer, especially a police officer with a temper. I wasn't at all sure we could pull this off.

When he answered Irene's knock on the door, Bryan Steele's appearance immediately betrayed his profession. He stood a little over six feet tall, with a broad chest, close-cropped brown hair, and suspicious brown eyes. He was not smiling, and I wasn't sure if he ever had. "Yeah?"

Irene stepped forward, unflinching. "Bryan Steele? We'd like to ask you some questions about Rebecca Lowery."

"I don't talk to reporters," he said flatly.

"Good thing we're not reporters then." She smiled at him, to no discernible effect. "My name is Irene," she said. "This is my partner, Marty."

"Partner," he repeated. "You on the job?"

"Private," she said. "We've been hired to find Rebecca Lowery. Her body, that is."

"Hired," he repeated. If he felt any grief at the mention of his deceased girlfriend, he hid it well.

She nodded. "We're private investigators. We work for Sherlock Holmes. Have you heard of him?"

"No."

This was like trying to interview Mt. Rushmore.

To Irene's credit, she forged ahead. "You do know Rebecca Lowery's body is missing, right?"

He crossed his arms, making his biceps bulge, probably as a means of intimidation. "Who hired you, exactly?"

So he *could* form actual sentences.

I stepped forward so that Irene didn't have to do *all* the heavy lifting. "Barbara Lowery Bristol," I said. "Her sister."

He let out a derisive snort. "That's rich. Barb couldn't have cared less about Rebecca."

Irene's glance silently entreated me to continue.

"Why would you say that?" I asked. "She cared enough to hire us to find her."

"Probably wanted to make sure she's really dead," he said. "She tell you they hadn't spoken in years?"

I nodded. "Yes, she did."

"She feels bad about that," Irene added.

"Suckers," he muttered under his breath.

I bristled. "What's that supposed to mean?"

Steele leaned a shoulder against the doorframe, arms still crossed, perfectly at ease in his derision. "She also tell you Rebecca was going to sue her?"

I tried to hide my surprise. "Maybe she didn't know."

"Oh, she knew. Just like she knew what she was doing when she moved into their dead parents' house instead of selling it and splitting the proceeds like she was supposed to. Barb is all about the money."

My shock must have registered on my face, as his expression held a hint of a smile for the first time. "Bet she didn't mention that, did she?" he pressed.

"You said *going* to sue her," I said instead of answering. "Does that mean Rebecca never went through with it?"

He focused on a point somewhere over our heads, out in the trees. "Rebecca gave her sister a break and waited, hoping she'd come to her senses. I told her that wasn't going to happen, but she wouldn't listen. Finally, when she realized the truth, Rebecca decided to sue for her rightful half of the inheritance."

That couldn't be farther from the story Barbara had given us. True, she hadn't been wracked with grief when it came to her sister, but she *had* flown halfway across the country and hired private investigators—or at least us—to find her. That had to count for something.

"When, exactly, did she finally decide to sue?" Irene asked.

Bryan pinned us with a stony look. "A couple weeks ago. Rebecca called her sister and warned her about it."

If Bryan Steele was telling the truth, it was hard to deny the timeliness of Rebecca's death as far as Barbara was concerned. If she was as money-hungry as he suggested, Barbara could have removed the threat to her inheritance by removing her own sister.

Which meant we could be working for a killer.

"When was the last time you saw Rebecca?" Irene asked him.

He reverted to his default scowl. "I dunno. Why?"

"You were seen at the theater arguing with her just days before her death."

"What do you care? Her death was an accident, right?"

"Officially," Irene said.

He narrowed his eyes. "What kind of crap is her sister trying to stir up, huh?"

"Is there anything to stir up here?" Irene pressed.

I bit my lip. The way Bryan's jaw was setting and his muscles tensing, I wasn't too keen on stirring anything else up.

"What, you thinking I killed her and dumped her in a vat of acid or something?"

Ugh. *Now* I was.

"Let me help you out. I didn't." He glanced at his watch. "You finished?"

"Not quite," Irene said. "What did you two fight about at the Bayside Theater?"

His expression turned to granite. "We're done here." He stepped back and slammed the door in our faces.

Irene stared at it. I could feel her eyes narrowing and her spine straightening. Irene was not used to doors slamming in her face.

"Let's go," I urged her. "Before he gets his gun."

She let me pull her away from the house. "What a charmer. How could any woman resist him?"

"It might be grief talking."

"It might be *guilt* talking."

We got into the car.

"Do you believe him?" I asked.

"You mean that not-so-subtle implication that Barbara had her own sister killed?"

I nodded.

"I don't know. I mean, he *is* being investigated by Internal Affairs. Doesn't exactly paint him as an upright citizen."

"But it seems an odd thing to make up," I reasoned. "It would be easy enough to check public records to find out about the inheritance from the parents."

Irene chewed her lower lip, thinking. "Okay," she said finally, "this is diabolical, but let's say Barbara did have Rebecca killed. Why go to the trouble of hiring us then?"

"As a red herring," I said slowly. "I mean, maybe she thought it made her look innocent."

"So, Barbara stole the body herself to cover up the crime, then hired us to look for it?"

"Assuming we'd never find her sister." Suddenly I felt a dip in my stomach. Had Barbara Bristol hired us not because we had a stellar reputation but because we had virtually no reputation? Had she hired us because she thought we'd fail?

I blew out a breath so hard it ruffled my hair. I didn't feel good about cashing a possible killer's check. And I certainly didn't want to help one cover up her crime.

"So, what do we do now?" I asked. "I mean, what do we tell Barbara Bristol? 'Thanks but no thanks for hiring us...'" I hesitated.

"Even though it was because you thought we'd never be skilled enough to find her?" Irene finished, following my same train of thought.

I nodded. "Yeah. That."

"It's pretty clever, really," Irene mused. "It also supports any future claim of innocence Barbara might need to make. Can't you just imagine it? 'But Judge, if I'd killed her, I'd never have hired a private investigator to find her.'"

"Believing she wouldn't be found." I paused.

"Like I said, diabolical."

I sighed. "Normal baristas don't need to worry about dealing with this kind of thing."

"They also can't afford to renovate pricey Victorians," she pointed out.

I knew that. I just didn't know if it was enough.

"Know what I think?" Irene started the car. "I think we need to find out more about our client. Maybe Steele's story wasn't even true."

I could only hope. The case was unsettling enough without working for a body-snatching murderer.

# CHAPTER SIX

———

"I don't understand." Dominic Gordon frowned at us over the top of a huge arrangement of pink carnations, baby's breath, and lush greens in a pink vase. The flowers would have been lovely, except he was holding them while standing in Viewing Room Two, beside a pearl gray casket that was presently occupied by a pink-cheeked, white-haired lady who, for reasons I couldn't understand, was still wearing her glasses. "Why do you need to contact Miss Lowery's attorney?" he asked. "I followed all his directives. Do you think I've done something wrong?"

I didn't *think* it.

"It's routine," Irene said. "We just have a few questions for him."

"Questions about me?" He settled the vase on the floor beside a smaller arrangement of daisies, which seemed incongruously cheerful for a wake. It turned out that Viewing Room Two was no improvement over the lobby. Faded flocked wallpaper, thin dirt-colored carpet, dusty faux crystal sconces. Viewing Room Two made my apartment look luxe. A visitor's book lay open to its first blank page on a podium near the doorway, along with a few pens and a stack of prayer cards. I wished the pink-cheeked lady well in the afterlife. It seemed to me she'd already paid her dues, being buried out of such a bargain basement mortuary.

"Listen." Gordon dropped a thin, cold hand on my shoulder to steer me away from the casket to the rows of folding chairs that faced it. When he sat beside me, I could have sworn I felt a rush of cold air envelop me. Instinctively, I leaned away.

Irene remained near the casket, her distrust evident in her expression.

His long, thin fingers intertwined, dancing like anemones in an aquarium. "I have an idea," he said. "You don't call the lawyer on me, and I'll give you both a 5 percent discount on a preplanned life celebration. How about that?"

I planned to celebrate my life while I was alive.

"To be honest," I began.

"Ten percent," he cut in, clearly not interested in *honest*. "Ten percent and I'll throw in my top-of-the-line casket, the Sleeping Beauty." He stood and glided toward Irene. "You'll look like a movie star," he assured her.

"I don't think so," she hedged, looking like a trapped gazelle between Mr. Creepy and the occupied casket.

"Okay. Alright." He pressed his hands to his mouth, considering. "How does this sound? Fifteen percent off and free embalming. That's some deal. Don't make the mistake of waiting. You can't plan your life celebration soon enough."

I was pretty sure you could.

"Or maybe you want to be cremated," he suggested. "We can handle that too. We'll treat your cremains with white glove service, even put you in a nice box. Gold, bronze, platinum— we've got urns to fit any budget." His gaze flicked to my outfit. "Even ceramic."

I tried not to be insulted.

"Oh, I know," he said, snapping his fingers as he took another step toward Irene. "Or you could have your ashes spread over San Francisco Bay. Spend eternity admiring the Golden Gate Bridge. How'd you like that?"

Irene shot me a helpless look.

"How about this," I said slowly, my eyes pinging around the room. "You give us the name of that lawyer…and we won't tell anyone you're planning a trip to the Cayman Islands to deposit your clients' hard earned preplanning money in your secret offshore bank account."

Gordon froze, his gaze turning my way. "What…I…how did you…" he sputtered, his train of thought clearly jumping from rail to rail.

"I think it's a fair trade," Irene said, grinning like a cat that ate a canary—or at least escaped embalming.

Gordon's mouth moved up and down without making any sounds. Finally he seemed to find his voice. "I'll get his card."

\* \* \*

"That was awesome back there," Irene said a little later, when we were in the elevator ascending to the fourteenth floor offices of Becker, Becker & Becker, Counselors at Law.

I did a mock bow. "All in a day's work, my dear Adler."

"So, let me guess." She put her finger to her chin in mock thought. "You noticed that on his suit he had the hair of some rat indigenous only on the Cayman Islands, he had stains on his fingers from counting dirty cash money, and his lack of a tan meant he was planning a trip to the Caymans?"

I laughed and shot her a look. "Get real. I peeked in the door of his office as we walked in. His laptop was open to his Travelocity account."

Irene slapped her palm against her forehead. "Genius."

"And a little lucky guessing. I mean, there are only so many reasons one visits the Cayman Islands."

"And he doesn't seem the surfing type," Irene agreed.

I nodded. "Stood to reason he was doing something shady." I only hoped it was the only shady thing he was doing.

The elevator doors slid open to reveal a swanky lobby filled with lots of dark wood, plush sound-deadening carpet, and an air of rampant self-importance. If Gordon's Mortuary had a polar opposite, the Law Offices of Becker, Becker & Becker would be it. A glass-walled conference room lay behind a horseshoe-shaped receptionist's desk, and door-lined corridors stretched toward the Bay on the right and the Pacific on the left.

A pretty blonde sat behind the desk, wearing a red wrap dress and a headset. She smiled at us. "Can I help you?"

Irene passed her a business card. "We're here to see Mr. Becker."

She glanced at the card before looking up, the smile steady. "Which one?"

Irene consulted the card Dominic Gordon had supplied. "Anthony Becker."

"Senior, Junior, or the Third?"

Irene consulted the card again. It didn't specify. "Senior?"

The blonde's smile morphed smoothly from expectant to regretful. "I'm afraid he's in trial all week."

"Junior," Irene said.

"Again," the blonde began.

"The Third." Impatience tinged Irene's voice.

"I'm sorry, but he's out of town."

Irene blinked. "Then why did you ask which—never mind. Just give me whoever you've got."

Confusion etched a tiny vertical line between the blonde's carefully groomed eyebrows. "I don't understand."

"Someone outside the Becker trinity," Irene said. "An associate. A law student. Anyone who has familiarity with Rebecca Lowery."

"Just a moment please." She turned away, tapped in an extension with long, gray-polished nails, and kept her voice low when she spoke to whomever was on the other end. When she turned back, the smooth smile was intact. "Mr. Becker will see you."

Irene scowled at her. "But you said—"

"No relation," the blonde said cheerfully. "Here he is."

We turned to see another of the firm's complement of Beckers emerging from the Pacific hallway with an aura of impatient busyness riding on his suspenders-clad shoulders. This Becker looked like a testimonial to the P90X workout right down to the aquiline nose and lantern jaw. His eyes widened slightly when he saw Irene. She had that effect on men. Irene was *Yowza!* by every criterion. "Can I help you ladies?"

I didn't seem to be included in that offer, which also happened a lot when I stood next to my best friend. Because of his focus on Irene, I let her take the lead.

"Don't you think it would be better to talk in your office?" she asked him. "This is a confidential matter."

"I've only got a moment," he said with insincere regret. "I'm afraid I'm already late for another obligation."

Irene shrugged. "Have it your way." She flashed another business card. "We work for a private investigator named Sherlock Holmes. We'd like to ask you a few questions about Rebecca Lowery. I understand she was represented by this firm and that you're handling the matter of her estate."

He didn't look at the card. "I'm sure you understand I'm limited by the attorney/client privilege."

"We won't impinge on the privilege," I assured him.

"We'll be general," Irene agreed. "Was Miss Lowery suing her sister, Barbara Bristol, over a house that became part of their parents' estate?"

A tiny grin chiseled itself into his humorless expression. "General," he repeated. "That question sounds rather specific."

"Don't be a lawyer about it," Irene told him with a flirtatious smile. "It's a simple question."

"As I said, the attorney/client privilege—"

"Nod once for yes, twice for no," she cut in.

He considered for a long moment before nodding once. "Miss Lowery had contacted us to initiate that paperwork. I'm afraid I can't go into details beyond that."

"We understand," I said. He didn't have to. Filed complaints would be accessible as public records anyway.

"Let me ask you a hypothetical question," Irene said. "If two siblings—let's call them Dick and Jane—inherit a house, and Jane dies, doesn't that mean the house passes entirely to Dick?"

"I don't deal in hypotheticals," he said.

She let out a short laugh. "Seriously? I thought lawyers took a whole semester in hypotheticals."

I was surprised, and relieved, when his tiny grin returned. He probably found her charming and insouciant. Something I couldn't pull off.

"Let me rephrase," he said. "I don't deal in hypotheticals for less than $500 an hour."

For a second, I expected her to call his bluff, since she probably walked around with four times that amount in her purse on any given day.

"Doesn't matter," she said instead. "We know that Dick would take the house whether he was entitled to it or not."

"But can he *stay* there." His grin graduated to a smile. "That's the question. Maybe we can address that on your next visit."

Irene smiled back. "I do love a cliffhanger," she said.

* * *

"I was not flirting with him." She angled the Porsche to the curb at 221 Baker Street. "It's just my experience that charm takes you further than frost."

I had to agree. Unfortunately, as Irene had found out as she'd accessed the public records after our visit with Mr. Charm, there was nothing for Rebecca. Whoever had killed her had done it before any of her initiated paperwork had been filed. And, flirt as she might, Irene had been unable to get anything out of Becker about Rebecca's will. Though, without any other next of kin, unless she'd specified who would get her half of the inheritance she'd yet to receive, it would revert to Barbara. Even if she had specified, it was a sticky situation in legal terms—one that I could easily see Barbara coming out victorious in, being that all other parties were deceased.

Irene killed the engine and glanced at the Victorian. "You sure you want me to drop you here? It looks like rain," she said, her gaze going to the gathering clouds above us.

I nodded. "The roofers are coming to put a tarp up."

"A tarp?"

"It's all I could afford." I paused. "Plus the lights keep flickering, so I wanted to get an electrician to check it out. He's coming to give me an estimate I probably can't afford. But at least I'll know how in debt I'm going to be."

"Electrical is nothing to mess with. You know I can cover it. Or I can lend it to you. Whatever you want."

I shook my head. "Thanks, but you know I'm not comfortable borrowing money from you all the time."

"Marty, you *never* borrow from me. You're the only person I know who doesn't borrow from me."

"And I want to keep it that way."

"Then we'll cash Barbara Bristol's check," she said firmly. "I can take a few dollars of it if it makes you feel better, but the rest is yours."

I knew *a few dollars* to Irene meant just that. And it was tempting, since that would more than cover any deposit I might need for repairs. Still...

"I'm not sure I want to do that yet," I said. "Not until we know she's innocent."

"You and those inconvenient principles of yours," Irene said with affection.

"Don't pretend you don't feel the same way," I said.

"Yeah. We'll have to work on that. Won't we?" She smiled. "Good luck."

My experience so far with the Victorian told me I was going to need it.

*   *   *

"I got good news, and I got bad news." My electrical contractor, Anthony Delvecchio, told me half an hour later. He was fiftysomething with a belly that overhung the waistband of his jeans and a beard that could house a small animal. He also had kind eyes, but those eyes didn't fool me. He was moving in for the kill on my bank account.

"Let me have it," I said wearily. It couldn't be worse than the ancient roof, the ancient windows, the ancient plumbing, and the ancient HVAC system.

"You've got knob-and-tube wiring," he said. "Knob and tube's not up to code. The whole place should be rewired."

I was wrong. It *could* be worse. "How much would that cost?"

He scratched his belly. "Place this size? Roughly ten grand."

I couldn't breathe. "Ten *thousand* dollars?" There weren't enough extra shifts at the coffee bar to cover that if I worked around the clock. "Can't I just live with what I've got?"

He shook his head. "You was my daughter, I wouldn't let you do that. It's not safe. You don't want the place to burn down."

Said who? I looked around, trying to see beyond the expensive repair list to the beautiful bones of the house, the hardwood that could gleam again, the crystal that could sparkle. It could still be the house I'd thought I'd inherited, before I'd seen it for the first time.

"Can I do one room at a time?" I asked hopefully.

He scratched his head in puzzlement. "It really don't work like that, Miss Hudson."

I guessed an interest-free loan for about twenty years wouldn't work either. No point in even asking. He was already looking at me with a deep pity that was embarrassing.

"Ten thousand dollars," I muttered. Might as well be fifty thousand, it felt so far out of reach.

"Miss Hudson? You got a minute?" One of my roofers stood on the upstairs landing in paint-splattered coveralls. Even from a distance, his discomfort was obvious. His had nothing on mine. "You should probably come see this," he added.

The only thing I wanted to see was a pot of gold, but I'd gotten myself into this mess. Well, technically, my great-aunt Kate had gotten me into this mess, but I'd kept myself in it by refusing to take Irene's suggestion to sell the house.

I glanced at Anthony. "Are we done, or do you have more good news for me?"

He seemed genuinely contrite. "I'm sorry, Miss Hudson."

I managed a weak smile. "It's not your fault. Thanks for coming out."

He nodded. "I'll give you a call soon as I can check my schedule so we can set up a start date."

Resolving not to answer my phone anytime soon, I saw him out before following the roofer upstairs to the master bedroom, which earned that distinction merely by its proximity to the single bathroom rather than through any actual amenities such as an en suite.

Rather unnecessarily, he pointed at the wood lathing visible through a gaping hole in the wall next to the gaping hole in the roof. A pile of crumbled plaster lay on the floor like a tiny snowbank. "I just leaned on it a bit, and this happened."

*This* was the death throes of my bank account. Repairing the wall wouldn't be nearly as expensive as rewiring the house, but it was the whole straw-and-camel's-back thing. The problems just didn't end, even when the money did. Maybe I could rob a bank. Or sell some blood. How much could you earn selling blood? How many liters of blood did the human body need, anyway? I could even throw in some plasma, or bone marrow. Or hair. People sold their hair, right? I could wear hats or scarves for a few months until it grew back. I'd be helping people and repairing my future home at the same time. It was a win/win.

I sank down onto the bed, my shoulders sagging. Who was I kidding? My hair didn't grow that fast. And I was fairly sure I needed more blood than I could sell. At the rate these repairs were adding up, I had *nothing* to sell that would put me in the black, other than the house itself. And that wouldn't even be worth the cost of repairs, the way things were adding up.

I sighed. As *inconvenient* as those pesky principles were, I did have one thing, and it could solve a few of my problems, if not all, with one quick endorsement. Maybe I should be *sure* I was working for a killer before snubbing my nose at a check waiting to be cashed…

# CHAPTER SEVEN

———

When I'd had all the good news I could handle from contractors, I took an Uber back to my apartment, where Toby greeted me with slobbery kisses and violent tail wags. While he crunched on his dinner kibbles, I heated a bowl of soup and made a grilled cheese sandwich, which I barely tasted since I was immersed in dreams of winning the lottery or stumbling onto sacks of cash fallen from a Brinks truck. I wasn't greedy; I didn't need millions and millions. Just one sack of cash would do the job.

When we were each finished eating, I washed all the dishes, gave Toby a dessert bone, and kept the cookie for myself because I needed all the comfort food I could get. Toby was sympathetic enough to my plight to spend the evening beside me on the sofa, although he did it sprawled on his back so that I could rub his belly while I watched television. We went to bed around eleven, and my dreams were filled with half a dozen contractors chasing me down the street, each clutching unpaid invoices.

The phone rang the next morning while it was still dark. Sometime during the night, Toby had swapped out his doggy bed for the real thing, and he lifted his head from the pillow beside me, looking at me blearily before sagging back into sleep. Toby's day didn't begin until the sun came up.

Although half asleep myself, I registered the delicious scent of peppers frying. Mr. Bitterman must have gotten to work early, this time with real food. My stomach growled faintly as I reached for the phone.

"Have you been online today?" Irene asked in my ear.

I glanced at the bedside clock. Five forty. "It's not today yet." I rubbed my eyes. "What time do you get up, anyway?"

"Oh, I've been up for hours. You know I don't need much sleep."

Yet she functioned like an astrophysicist. Life just wasn't fair.

"I've got a full day of VC meetings ahead of me," Irene continued. "This is my Zen moment."

Too bad her Zen moment couldn't happen at ten o'clock. "And you're calling me during your Zen moment because...?"

"We've gone viral!" she squealed, sounding positively delighted about it. "Well, Sherlock Holmes has, anyway. But we're the brains behind *him*."

"There is no *him*," I said automatically, fully awake now. I could think of several different reasons Sherlock would go viral, and none were good. "What happened? Did someone finally find out he's fake or something?" I suddenly thought of the reporter both Watson and PS Rossi had mentioned.

"You have so little faith in me," she said sadly. "It's just the opposite, actually. Ever heard of an alternative media blog called the *Irregulars*?"

"No," I answered, putting her on speaker while I googled it.

"Someone named Wiggins owns it."

"Last name or first name?"

"No clue. Anyway, he wrote a post about Sherlock Holmes. And it's gotten picked up by *everyone*."

The *Irregulars* didn't exactly sound like the ideal place to land publicity-wise. More like a self-fulfilling prophecy. "Define everyone," I said, hoping it didn't include Detective Lestrade. He didn't strike me as an internet surfer.

"Look for yourself," she said.

Resigned to the worst, I navigated to the site and its bold headline: *Case of the Disappearing Diva.*

"You've got to be kidding me."

"Isn't it great? Wish I'd thought of it." Irene sounded practically giddy.

A headache tapped at my temples as I scanned the article.

*New detective in town Sherlock Holmes*—he wasn't in town because he wasn't real, but okay, no damage there—*has been retained to solve the Case of the Disappearing Diva, also known as Rebecca Lowery, the coloratura soprano in the traveling company of* Ethereal Love, *which is set to open*—

"Who is this Wiggins character?" I demanded.

"Who cares?" Irene asked. "You can't buy publicity like this. Sherlock Holmes could be famous nationwide by noon. We could have a new case every week just from this one article!"

"I don't want a new case every week," I nearly moaned.

"Sure you do. It'd solve all your problems," she said. "I should send Wiggins a thank-you note. On behalf of Sherlock, of course. Since he's out of the country on another case."

"Maybe he'll have an awful accident there," I said. "He might even die."

She laughed. "Sherlock can't die. He's going to make us a lot of money."

"You already have a lot of money," I pointed out.

"When I said *us*, I meant *you*," she said. "Think about it. You can fix everything that's wrong with the house, and then you could actually move in there. No more 2B. No more Mr. Bitterman. Or Mrs. Frist, the geriatric peeping Tomasina."

"She peeps because she cares," I murmured, distracted once more by the possibility of a lot of money.

"She peeps because she's nosy," Irene said. "How'd it go with the contractors yesterday?"

My growling stomach did a slow roll over my appetite at the new topic. "My wiring might burn the place down, and it's going to cost ten thousand dollars to bring it up to code."

"You have to fix that, Marty." Her tone was stern. "That's too dangerous."

"On the upside, all the electrician should have to do to break through the walls is lean on them."

"What does that mean?"

I groaned. "It means I need money."

"Well then, lucky for you, Sherlock is gonna make you some," she said.

I hated to admit it, but she was right. I already knew my day job wasn't going to repair the Victorian. That was a given.

But finding Rebecca Lowery's body would be an awfully good start. And once we knew that Barbara'd had nothing to do with her death, we could cash that check with a clear conscience.

I only prayed that was what we *would* find.

After Irene and I agreed to talk later in the day, I managed to catnap for another forty minutes or so, intermittently listening to the building wake up around me. When it became apparent my sleeping was finished, I slipped out of bed, careful not to disturb Toby, and took a quick and gratifyingly warm shower. By the time I made my way into the kitchen, he'd transferred back to his doggy bed so that he could keep an eye on any breakfast morsels that might hit the floor.

Between two slices of toast and a semi-stale chocolate chip muffin, it occurred to me that while Barbara Lowery Bristol had a solid motive to have her sister killed, and Bryan Steele had the means and the temperament to do it, we had no real evidence against either one. As far as I knew, you still couldn't look up hitmen from some directory, and I was unaware of any connection Barbara might have to The City to facilitate any plot to kill Rebecca. Still possible…but Bryan Steele, on the other hand, *did* have that connection. Yet something told me he'd be harder to pin down. And Bryan Steele scared me a little.

And there were still those missed rehearsal days leading up to Rebecca's death. I had a hard time believing she'd just been calling in sick. The timing was too coincidental. So what had she been up to?

I decided it might be useful to reconstruct Rebecca's last day, to walk in her footsteps, and see where—or to whom—they led me. Although Irene would be tied up in her meetings, that plan seemed safe enough to go it alone, and I had plenty of time before I was due at work.

I pulled on a purposely nondescript outfit of jeans and a forgettable beige sweater, then gathered my hair into a low ponytail. I wanted to go unnoticed by Rebecca Lowery's neighbors. Keeping with that thought, I decided it wouldn't be wise to show up too early, either, so I clipped on Toby's leash and took him for a nice long walk, giving him plenty of time to meet and greet hydrants, fence posts, and trees as he saw fit.

When we got back to the apartment, I reviewed the notes from our meeting with Barbara. The logical place to start seemed to be Rebecca's apartment in the Hayes Valley section of The City. Only problem was, how to get there. I didn't want to use Uber in case I found myself hot on the trail of an actual lead. For the same reason, my bike was out. There was only one solution.

I called Irene back. "Can I borrow a car today?"

"Use the Prius," she said without hesitation, as if that wasn't a strange request at all. "I'll have it dropped off within an hour. What's your plan?"

"I thought I'd check out Rebecca's apartment building."

"Good idea. I've got to run now, but call me later, okay? Be careful, Marty."

The Prius arrived in just over a half hour. I forced myself to wait nearly another hour before threading my way through morning traffic to the address in the Hayes Valley neighborhood that Rebecca's sister had supplied us. Unlike my building, Rebecca's was filled with light and warmth and cheerful colors. The residents seemed quiet, the place was clean, and there were no toxic cooking fumes leaching from under any doors. I was instantly jealous of the dead woman.

Her apartment was on the fourth floor, just across from the elevators, which unfortunately would make it less likely for the neighbors to have noticed her coming and going. I knelt in the hallway, pretending to re-tie my shoe, while I studied her door. It was a perfectly ordinary door, with no crime scene tape or bulky lock affixed to the knob. Clearly this was still being classified as an accidental death. I wondered if Barbara had visited yet to begin cleaning out and boxing up the apartment's contents. Or if she even planned to. Maybe she'd just let the landlord deal with disposing of Rebecca's possessions.

I briefly thought about picking the lock to have a peek for myself, but at this hour it was all too likely someone would be stepping on or off the elevator or leaving their apartment at exactly the wrong time. Besides, if someone had killed Rebecca in her own home, chances were they'd been sure to clean up any evidence of it before leaving. My better bet if I wanted to know what Rebecca might have been up to in the days leading up to her death was to find a nosy neighbor like Mrs. Frist.

I started with the neighbor on her left. No answer. Ditto the one on her right. Four unanswered doors later, one finally opened to reveal an exhausted-looking thirtysomething woman with a toddler perched on her hip. A baby cried lustily in the background. Her free hand tugged her ragged ponytail free from the toddler's hand and flung it back over her shoulder where it belonged. The toddler immediately reached for it again.

"Michael, don't," she snapped. She looked at me. "What?"

I swallowed. "My name's Marty Hudson. I work for a detective named Sherlock Holmes." Why hadn't I brought any of Irene's fake-but-convincing business cards? "I'd like to ask you about your neighbor, Rebecca Lowery."

"Who?"

"Rebecca Lowery," I repeated. "She lived down the hall." I pointed, in case she didn't understand the concept. "The apartment by the elevators."

"Did she?" The woman frowned. "I wouldn't know. But I don't get out much. Did she get evicted or something?"

"No, she—"

"Stop it, Mike." She paused for a deep breath. "You got any kids?"

I shook my head.

"Don't." She pulled Mike's chubby little hand from her ponytail. "Rebecca Lowery. I don't think I know her. Like I said, I don't get out much."

"Did you ever hear any kind of fighting coming from down the hall?" I asked. "Maybe some unusual sounds, like banging or thumping?"

"Only unusual sound I hear is silence," the woman said. "I don't got to leave this place to hear banging and thumping. Michael Patrick!"

I said a hasty thank-you and moved on. Another "don't know her" and one shout of "go away—I'm not interested!" before I struck pay dirt across the hall.

"Rebecca? Sure, I know Rebecca." He was in his early forties, clean cut, neatly dressed, clean shaven. The sort of guy you'd see with an enigmatic smile behind the wheel of a luxury car in a television commercial. "Or I guess I should say I knew her." He stuck out his hand. "I'm Josh, by the way."

"Marty." We shook. "Why do you say that?"

"She's no longer with us, right? A friend of mine sent me a link to this *Irregulars* blog post about it. Some famous detective's been hired on the case, got a weird name. Hey!" His eyes widened. "You don't work for that guy, do you?"

Irene had been right; Sherlock Holmes was officially racing out of our control. Except in this case, Holmes's notoriety might work for us. "I'm one of his investigators," I admitted, fingers firmly crossed behind my back. "Did you know Rebecca? Can you tell me anything about her?"

"I've never talked to a PI. That must be interesting work, right?"

"It has its moments. Rebecca Lowery?" I prompted him.

"Right. Sorry. I can't tell you much," he said. "I only knew her as a neighbor. You know, we'd say hello in the lobby, ride the elevator, see each other at Buttercream. She was a singer, right?"

"Opera," I murmured. "Coloratura, to be precise."

"You don't need to be precise. I don't know much about opera." His grin became a self-deprecating smile. "I'm more of a reader. That's what I do for a living."

I frowned. "You read?"

"I'm a freelance editor," he said. "I work from home. In case you thought I was a bum or something, being here this time of day."

The thought hadn't occurred to me. "What's Buttercream?" I asked.

The smile fell away, replaced by a moue of astonishment. "You don't know the bakery, Buttercream? They have the best cupcakes in The City. You should check it out. It's only two blocks from here. Rebecca was in there all the time."

He didn't have to sell me on cupcakes. I was *so* there.

"Did you see Rebecca last weekend at all?" I asked.

He thought about it. "No, I don't think so. But when she wasn't rehearsing, she'd do a lot of entertaining. If you know what I mean."

"Men?" I asked.

He shrugged. "Rebecca was rarely alone. She was a beautiful woman."

"Any of these men in particular stand out to you?"

He looked up, as if trying to recall. "There was this one guy I saw go into her apartment a couple of times. Big. Not too friendly."

That sounded like Bryan Steele, alright.

"But I haven't seen him around much in the last couple of weeks."

"So he wasn't here last weekend?" I clarified.

"Honestly? I couldn't tell you. I hadn't seen her in a while."

"How long is 'a while'?"

He frowned, as if trying to remember. "Maybe a week? Week and a half? But you know these entertainer types. They keep odd hours, right?"

"And you didn't see anyone else go into her apartment this weekend?" I pushed again.

He shook his head. "Sorry."

"Thanks anyway."

"Sure." He shared another easy smile. "It's nice to talk to another human being during the week. It gets kind of lonely working from home."

Josh the Editor disappeared back into his apartment, and I moved on to the next door. No one home. After hitting half a dozen more doors, I only got one more neighbor—an older women—who said she knew a singer lived down the hall but she hadn't seen her in couple of weeks. Then again, she was wearing bifocals that looked thick enough to double as bulletproof glass, so I wasn't sure she'd seen much of anything lately.

After canvassing the entire floor, all I knew was that Rebecca kept odd hours, if she'd had a visitor last weekend he'd been stealthy, and the diva liked Buttercream cupcakes.

For lack of a better lead, I left the building and followed Josh's directions on foot to the bakery two blocks away. Ten minutes later, as I finished up a red velvet cupcake, I decided he'd been right. They were definitely the best in The City.

After two cupcakes, I licked cream cheese frosting from my fingers and wiped the crumbs from the screen of my cell phone, bringing up Rebecca's picture, and approached the counter girl again.

"Ready for another one?" she asked with a smile. "Red velvet, right?"

"To go, please." I held up the picture. "Can you tell me if this woman looks familiar to you?"

She looked at it. "Sure. That's that singer who died, right? I read about it online. I didn't know her name, but I recognized her face. She came in here all the time. Are you related to her or something?"

"Or something." I slid the phone back into my handbag. "I'm looking into her death for her sister."

Her eyes widened with newfound respect. "Cool! You must work for that Sherlock Holmes dude, right? I read all about him. Disappearing Diva." She giggled. "Sounds like fun. So you're, like, following her trail, right?"

I nodded. "Did she come in last weekend?"

She shook her head. "Sorry. I hadn't seen her in a while. I know she had a big show coming up, so I just figured she was laying off the baked goods, you know?"

I resisted the urge to suck in my own gut. "Did she ever come in with anyone? Meet anyone here?" I fished.

She shrugged. "Sorry, I don't really remember." She paused. "But I know she talked to Carlos, like, all the time."

"Carlos?"

She nodded and pointed out the front window. "He owns the newsstand over there. She bought the trades every week when they came out, to read the reviews."

Someone cleared his throat behind me. I glanced over my shoulder at the thirtysomething guy waiting in line. His shaggy sandy blond hair fell low on his forehead over light brown eyes behind wire-rimmed glasses. Not bad looking, if you were into geek chic. He met and held my eyes in a *hurry up, before the double chocolates run out!* kind of way.

I thanked the counter girl for the information, bought a couple of doughnuts to go along with the third red velvet cupcake (purely for research purposes), and left Buttercream, headed for the newsstand across the street.

My cell phone chimed with an incoming text. *Looking forward to chatting more about your celebrity boss at dinner.* Watson.

I let my head drop back as I blew out a sigh. Was there anyone who *hadn't* seen the *Irregulars* post? Didn't he have better things to do than read blog posts about fictitious characters all day? Didn't he have enough official duties to keep him busy? Worse, what if that post prompted Lestrade to look into the credentials of Sherlock Holmes? What then? It was against the law to pretend to be a police officer. Was it against the law to pretend to be a private investigator too? I wondered how many times we could get away with saying Holmes had been called out of the country.

I should just forget about Sherlock Holmes, sell the Victorian, and resign myself to living in a dilapidated apartment building next to Mr. Bitterman and across the hall from 2B. There were worse things in life.

"Help you?"

I just couldn't think of them at this moment.

"Lady?"

I realized that was directed at me. I recalled Rebecca Lowery's photo on my cell phone and showed it to the newsstand clerk. "Can you tell me if you remember seeing this woman last weekend?"

Carlos ignored it. "What, you think I take names? You gonna buy a paper or what?"

I dug for some change. "Let me have a *Chronicle*."

He handed it over with an impatient snap. I paid him and showed him the screen again. "Please have a look. It's important."

He gave an impatient shake of his head but glanced at the picture. As soon as he did, his eyes widened in recognition. "Yeah. That's Miss Lowery."

"You knew her?"

He shrugged. "Just to say *hi* to. It's not like I *knew* her. You know what I mean? She bought the papers all the time. Read all about the other singers and shows in town, you know?"

"When did you see her last?" I asked.

"Maybe a week ago? Week and a half?" He paused. "Wait. I know why you're asking me these questions."

I froze. "You do?"

His head bobbed up and down in sudden realization. "I read about her on this online thing my wife showed me this morning. They're calling her the Disappearing Diva. You must be one of them Sherlocks that I read about." He regarded me with open suspicion and maybe a little hostility, making me wonder what he had against "them Sherlocks." Regardless, I wasn't making the same impression here that I'd made with Josh back at the apartment building. Might be best if I nudged things along.

"You said you last saw her here a week ago?" I asked.

He shook his head. "No, not here."

I raised an eyebrow his way. "Not here?"

"I seen her outside Lucky's Deli, over on Leavenworth, in the Tenderloin. Between Golden Gate and Turk? I was picking up some pastrami for the wife. She's pregnant, and she's got the cravings, you know? Some days she—"

A man in a business suit interrupted that train of thought, hurrying toward the clerk with some change for a newspaper. They made the exchange, and then he hurried away with it folded under his arm.

"What were we talking about?" he asked, turning back to me.

"Rebecca Lowery."

"Oh, right, yeah. Like I said, I saw her outside Lucky's. Weird, no? I don't know what she was doing there when there's, like, lots places to eat around here."

"Weird," I agreed. "Was she alone outside the deli?" I asked, thinking of Bryan Steele.

"Oh, she was with someone alright. Arguing."

This was getting good. "Can you describe the man she was arguing with?"

"Woman," he corrected.

"Woman?"

He nodded. "She was arguing with some redheaded broad, with big..." His hands moved outward from his chest, then froze, his cheeks going red. "*Tetas. Grande tetas.*"

My mind went immediately to Tara Tarnowski, Rebecca's understudy and now star of the show.

"What were they arguing about?" I asked.

"See, that's the thing. I don't know." He scratched his chin. "I heard it clear as day, but I didn't get it. They were arguing about a fluffy bunny."

I blinked. "Excuse me?"

"That's what I thought too." He nodded. "That's why I remember. It was so weird, no? She say she was going to buy a fluffy bunny at the deli. Don't ask me. I been going there for years. I never seen them selling bunnies, fluffy or otherwise."

"Did the two of them go inside?"

"Your Disappearing Diva did. She wasn't having none of what that redhead was saying. I could tell 'cause I've seen it before, with my wife. When the hands go on the hips, you know it's over for you, and you might just as well do what she wants you to do, because—"

"The redhead didn't go inside?" I clarified. "Did she leave?"

"Don't ask me," he said. "I don't know nothing from there. Don't know what the redhead did. Don't know how long your girl was inside. I had to get over here to work. I got five mouths to feed, you know what I mean?"

I knew what he meant. I had two mouths to feed, one of them mine, and it was problematic. Still, he *did* have a pregnant wife, and he *had* given me another lead, so I felt I owed him some token of gratitude. I dug for some more change. "I really appreciate your help. I'll take an *Examiner* too."

He handed it over. "All my customers appreciate me that much, I'll have that mansion in no time."

You just couldn't thank some people.

\* \* \*

I walked back to Rebecca's apartment building to pick up the Prius and drove to the Tenderloin district, munching on my research cupcake. I found Lucky's Deli on Leavenworth without too much trouble, but I wasn't sure I'd want to shop there, let alone park a Prius in the open. While Hayes Valley was an up-and-coming neighborhood full of trendy bars, boutique restaurants, and high-rise apartment and condo buildings, its neighbor, the Tenderloin, was full of drug dealers, overflowing dumpsters, and crumbling tenements and liquor stores. And Lucky's Market and Deli didn't look like the exception. I tentatively parked on the street and beeped the car alarm on, glad I was making this visit in broad daylight. Not that I was sure that meant the Prius would still be there when I got back. I crossed the street and pushed through the glass doors of Lucky's. The same pungent smell of cold cuts and dill pickles that perfumed every deli in America hung thick in the air, but this one had an underlayment of something else. I sure hoped it was garden variety dust and grime, and not dead bunnies.

The interior was one narrow aisle. On the left was a floor-to-ceiling shelf full of dusty canned goods—mostly dented—and a variety of ethnic foods ranging from jars of kimchi to pickled jalapeños. On the right sat a glass deli case featuring gray-looking chorizo and sliced meats along with a variety of cheeses growing mold that spoke of long past expiration dates. As icky as it was, I couldn't imagine how anything about this place would incite an argument between Rebecca and Tara. Unless Tara had refused to eat here.

I stepped up to the counter and was met with burly crossed arms and attitude from a fireplug of a man in a filthy white apron, his stare openly suspicious. Maybe he thought I'd come to steal a can of Cheez Whiz. His face had the bloated, flushed look of an experienced drinker. The hair missing on the crown of his head had moved to his arms and the open collar of his shirt. A soggy toothpick protruded from the corner of his mouth.

Suddenly I lost all appetite I might have had.

Knowing Irene's Prius was on borrowed time, I pulled out my most friendly smile and shoved it his direction. "Would you mind if I asked you a few questions?"

"Yeah, I'd mind," he snapped. "This ain't no information booth. Order something or get out."

With customer relation skills like that, he'd go far.

My smile dissolved. I took a deep breath. Might as well go for broke…

"I'll take a fluffy bunny, please."

His eyes narrowed and raked across me with excruciating slowness. Just when I'd decided that the newsstand clerk had played some kind of weird joke on me, he said, "Stay there," and stomped off into the back.

Where did he think I would go? I stood there inhaling mingling scents of pungent cheese and sliced salami, wondering what I'd just ordered. Could it be they really made sandwiches out of bunnies? I shuddered, the cupcakes in my stomach lurching.

I didn't have to wait long before the guy came back with a brown bag in hand. "A hundred bucks."

I tried to hide my surprise. I think I failed.

"Cash," he added.

I could buy a warren of rabbits for a hundred bucks. Or pay my phone bill. I dug in my purse. Normally, that number was way more cash than I carried around. Luckily, I'd emptied my coffee can savings this morning on the off chance I'd need to grease some palms. I just hadn't expected them to be *this* greasy. Reluctantly I counted off twenties until I had enough to hand over. He traded me the bag for them, and I hurried outside, anxious to escape from his gimlet-eyed scrutiny and to breathe fresh air again. I practically dove into the Prius (Still there. Yay!) and squealed off down the street, forcing myself to wait until I was well out of sight a few blocks away to reach into the bag.

Inside was a clear baggie containing four little pink pills.

I stomped on the brake, and the car swerved to a stop at the curb. I sat there staring at the baggie.

Pills? *Drugs?* Fluffy Bunny was code for some sort of drugs? Rebecca Lowery had been buying drugs. Barbara was right about her sister. If the diva had gotten clean in the past, she'd clearly fallen off the wagon again. Had her sister found out and killed her for it? Had Rebecca had some falling out with Tara over her use…and had Tara killed her over it? Or had her death been about a drug deal gone wrong after all?

A guy walking his dog moved down the sidewalk toward me, and I shoved the pills back into the brown bag, suddenly feeling guilty. I rolled up the bag again and stuffed it deep under my seat, out of sight of the dog walker or any police officer who might pull me over for reckless driving or speeding or running a stop sign or driving while petrified.

It took me almost half an hour to drive the three miles back to the Bayside Theater, since I drove at about ten miles per hour, obeying every light, stopping at every stop sign long enough to eat a three-course meal, and wondering the whole time what exactly I'd brought along with me for the ride.

# CHAPTER EIGHT

———

Unlike my first visit, when I'd been to the Bayside with Irene, this time PS Rossi greeted me with open suspicion mixed with the slightest hint of hostility. "Miss Hudson, you're here. Again."

"Don't look so happy to see me."

He shook his head. "I'm sorry. It's just…this whole unpleasantness is making our backer very nervous. We open in less than two weeks."

"I understand," I told him.

He nodded. "What is it I can do for you?"

"Actually," I said, "I'd like to speak with Tara, if she's available."

"I'm afraid she's not here. She's left for the day already."

I checked the time on my phone. It was just past one. "Short day."

"We're rehearsing the male lead's part this afternoon," Rossi explained. "Can I help you with anything?" he asked, looking as if the only thing he wanted to help me with was finding the door.

I hesitated, unsure if I wanted to cast aspersions on his new prima donna. But I needed information that he wasn't likely to give without good reason. "You'd mentioned suspecting Rebecca of dealing with substance abuse in her past," I said slowly, watching his reaction.

He nodded. "Yes, but as I said, it was only a guess."

"Do you think it's possible she might have relapsed?"

A frown formed between his eyebrows before he shook his head. "No. Absolutely not. She was a professional—she never would have done anything to jeopardize this tour."

"I have reason to believe that might not be totally accurate."

The frown deepened. "What do you mean?"

Again I hesitated, not sure how much to say before talking to Tara. "We have received information that leads us to believe Rebecca was using again." I paused. "And we believe Tara might have been aware of it."

His whole body was suddenly tense, a flat coldness hitting his eyes. "That's a serious accusation, Miss Hudson. Are you sure about this?"

I nodded. "My source is credible."

He traced both hands across his jawline. "Are you telling me that Tara is using—"

"No," I said quickly. "I have no reason to think Tara is on any substances. None of my information suggests that. Just the opposite, actually."

His arms dropped to his sides. "Then why do you say she was aware of it?"

"The two of them were seen together outside a location where…" I paused, choosing my words carefully so as not to incriminate myself. "Where we're fairly certain illegal pills are being sold. And Tara was heard arguing with Rebecca before she went inside."

"To buy drugs," he said grimly.

"It looks that way."

"Did Tara go inside with her?"

"I don't think so."

His eyes narrowed. "You don't think, or you don't know?"

"My source didn't specify. Only that Tara was overheard arguing with Rebecca about the pills."

"This is just great." Rossi punched a fist into his palm, squeezing his hands together so tightly his knuckles whitened. "My backer is already angry at the delays. The last thing he needs to hear about is some drug scandal with my diva."

"It may not become public knowledge," I told him. "If it's any reassurance, there won't be a leak coming from our office." There weren't enough leakers. Or an office. Of course, the wild card just might be if that enterprising *Irregulars* reporter caught wind of a potential drug correlation to Rebecca Lowery's death and disappearance. If that happened, the whole sordid story would break overnight, shining an even brighter spotlight on Sherlock Holmes and potentially dropping the final curtain on *Ethereal Love* before it had even opened.

"It's important that I speak with Tara as soon as possible," I said. "To clear this whole matter up quickly," I added.

He nodded, clearly liking that idea. "As I mentioned, she's gone for the day, but I can give you her number." He scrolled through his contacts list and read it off as I entered it into my phone. "I appreciate your discretion in this matter," he implored.

"I'll do my best," I promised him. Which wasn't saying all that much, but I could hardly tell him that my grip on the case was as tenuous as my ability to pay my rent.

We exchanged a few rote pleasantries, I assured him again of Sherlock Holmes's discreet reputation (hard for the guy to talk to the press when he didn't exist), and he disappeared backstage, muttering to himself, clearly burdened by the information I'd imparted.

Once I'd returned to the relative privacy of the lobby, I dialed Tara's number. After a few rings, the call went to voicemail, and I left a message. I jumped into my car and waited a full twenty minutes before sending her a vague text about needing to ask a few quick questions, leaving out any reference to fluffy bunnies and grungy delis.

No reply. Maybe her phone was dead, or turned off, or buried in her purse. I was sure she'd get back to me.

* * *

I sent Tara two more messages as I grabbed lunch and picked up my mail at the Victorian while ignoring the holes in both the ceiling *and* wall that I could not afford to fix. I also did not turn on the lights, figuring I wouldn't tempt fate with my ancient wiring. Instead I pulled back the musty curtains in the guest room (thankfully, one room that was fully intact, if dark) and set about trying to remove some of the floral wallpaper while trying not to check my phone. Which remained silent. I was beginning to think Tara was ignoring me.

A thought echoed by Irene that evening as I stood inside her cottage-sized walk-in closet looking for something I could wear to my dinner un-date with Watson.

"She's probably ignoring you."

"Gee, you think?" I asked. "I don't know why though."

"Unless she's guilty," Irene pointed out.

"Of buying drugs or killing Rebecca?"

"If we're lucky, both. Here, try this on." Irene held up a designer dress made for seduction, or at the very least, a night of slow dancing. "You look fabulous in black," she added.

While the *dress* was fabulous, I was fairly sure neither seduction nor slow dancing was in my future. This was a business meeting. And the hem of the fabulous dress was just a couple inches short of business. "It's a little short."

"That's the point." Irene waggled her eyebrows at me.

"Next," I said as I ran my fingers down an exposed silky red sleeve wedged in on the packed rod. Irene's closet was less actual closet and more department store. Twenty outfits for every occasion, with fifty more thrown in for good measure along with handbags and shoes and scarves and belts. It was the only thing in the whole house that carried a vibe of excess. The rest of Irene's house was a monument to simplicity and high tech at the same time: open and bright, with lots of glass and marble, the house was a smart home in every way. Sometimes I swore all I had to do was just *think* about a grilled cheese and some hidden wireless smart device would make it appear from her pristine kitchen.

"You're thinking red?" She yanked at the sleeve, and a whisper-soft silk blouse slid off its hanger. "I've got a pencil skirt that'll look great with this."

"I don't know. It's pretty, but..." I shook my head. "Too risqué."

"It's a blouse with long sleeves, Marty." She shook it at me like a threat. "How can a blouse with long sleeves be risqué?"

"I need something bland." I kept looking. "Brown, maybe."

"Oh, yawn."

"Okay, blue."

"You're a real wild child," she muttered. "Just put yourself in my hands, okay? I promise, you'll look fabulous."

"I don't want to look fabulous," I protested. "I want to look professional. Dignified."

"And sexy. Sexy never hurts." She held up a cobalt blue wrap dress. "I've got Louboutins that'll be killer with this."

"I feel like such a phony wearing your clothes." I took the dress from her anyway and held it up to myself. It was soft and gorgeous and would cling in all the right places. Plus the hem was long enough to almost qualify as dignified.

Irene rolled her eyes. "You're not a phony by any definition of the word."

I could think of one definition. The one that included Sherlock Holmes.

She cocked her head, assessing. "You'll look like a million bucks in that." She looked over her expansive shoe display and selected a pair with distinctive red soles. "Try these."

"He's seen my apartment," I reminded her. "He knows I can't afford Louboutins."

"He's a guy," she said. "He doesn't know Louboutin from Payless. Try it on. I've got a little silver clutch that'll go great with this outfit. I'll be right back."

I stepped out of my jeans, shucked my sweater, and let the dress float over my head and across my skin like a warm spring breeze. Twisting and turning to appraise my reflection from every angle, I had to admit Irene was right. This was the dress.

"So, you said you had a line on the fluffy bunnies?" Irene called from the depths of her handbag collection.

"I do," I agreed, happy to shift the conversation away from my wardrobe. As soon as I'd come to the conclusion that the wallpaper in my guest room was the only thing actually sturdy in my house and it would take much more than sheer determination to pull it from the guest room walls, I'd abandoned home improvement projects for a little research project instead. I'd grabbed the bag of pills from my car and done some digging online to see what, exactly, I had purchased. It had taken the better part of the afternoon, but I'd finally hit upon something that looked similar.

"Fluffy Bunny's the nickname for this new synthetic amphetamine created by the replacement of a hydrogen atom with a fluorine atom on the aromatic ring to facilitate passage through the blood-brain barrier."

Irene pulled her head out of Handbagland to stare at me. "In English, please?"

I grinned. "Basically, it's a designer stimulant drug."

"Stimulant—like cocaine or meth?"

I nodded. "The user gets a similar high."

Irene pursed her lips as she turned back to the bags. "So, useful for someone who, say, has a hectic rehearsal and performance schedule?"

"I would imagine it would have been very tempting to Rebecca. Especially if she had a history of drug abuse in the past."

"The name's too cute for such an ugly thing," Irene said. "I wonder what made Rebecca fall off the wagon this time. I mean, with the lead in the opera, it seems like she had everything going in the right direction for her." She appeared in the doorway holding the clutch. "What do you think?"

I nodded my approval. "They say appearances can be deceiving, right?"

"That's true." She grinned. "Mr. Bitterman looks like an innocent grandfatherly type. You'd never know he's a culinary assassin."

I laughed. "His cooking's not *that* bad."

"His vichyssoise made your spoon melt," she reminded me. "And didn't his stink bomb cabbage dish destroy your microwave?"

Alright, so maybe his cooking *was* that bad.

"I get your point," I said. "And I agree, Rebecca's life did seem to be in a good place. But that's just on the outside. You know she'd had her problems in the past."

"She had a problem in the present, too," Irene said. "Its name was Bryan Steele."

"Two problems," I said, thinking of Fluffy Bunny. "Which just goes to show, you never really know what people are dealing with."

Irene cocked her head at me again. "That dress looks better on you than it ever did on me."

I doubted that. Irene would look better than I did wearing a steel wool bathrobe.

"So, where do you think Tara fits into all of this?" she asked. "I mean, the fact that she and Rebecca were fighting outside of Lucky's Deli implies that she was *against* the idea of Rebecca buying drugs?"

I nodded. "Maybe Tara confronted Rebecca about the use again later, like at her apartment. They fought, things got out of hand, and Rebecca winds up dead."

"That sounds more like an accident than a murder you'd steal a body to cover up," Irene reasoned.

"If Tara was afraid it might jeopardize her new lead status, she might have been desperate."

"Or, maybe Tara was into the drug scene herself," Irene offered. "We don't even know if it was Rebecca or Tara who was the regular at Lucky's."

"Or maybe Tara was just in the wrong place at the wrong time, and Rebecca's death was all about a drug deal gone wrong." I thought back to the hairy stump of a man at Lucky's and could easily see *him* disposing of an incriminating body.

"Well, one thing's for sure," Irene decided.

"Yes?"

"We need to talk to Tara."

I groaned and checked my phone for the umpteenth time. No messages. "You know, I could always cancel with Watson, and we could take a little trip to Tara's place and—"

"No way!" Irene shook her head. "No way you're getting out of this date, missy."

"Business dinner," I shot back lamely.

"Look, you go schmooze Watson, and I'll look into the Lucky's angle. Maybe I can find out who owns it. If we can get a name to go with the place, maybe we'll have a lead on who might have wanted Rebecca out of the way enough to dispose of the body."

"You're not going down there?" The place was slimy enough in the daylight—I couldn't imagine what manner of creeps came out at night.

Irene shot me a look. "Online, Marty. I'll look into it online. Geeze, what do you take me for?"

"Oh. Right." Of course she meant she'd dig into the place on the computer. In fact she'd probably find out more in five minutes online than I had all day.

"Want to use the Porsche tonight?" she offered.

"Thanks, but Watson's picking me up."

She pinned me with a look and a sly smile. "You know, business associates don't usually *pick you up* for a date."

"Good thing this is a dinner and not a date then."

"Right. Call me after," she said. "I don't care what time it is. I'll be up. Unless Watson spends the night. Then you can wait till the morning."

I rolled my eyes. "I'll call you before midnight," I told her.

Her nose wrinkled. "That would really disappoint me."

\* \* \*

When I looked at Watson, I saw stability, reliability, predictability. I also saw *yummy*, but that was just my left brain talking. Either way, I liked looking at him. He'd gone the Casual Stud route with gray slacks and a lightweight black sweater, both of which displayed his athletic build to perfection without being obvious about it. With a body like that, he didn't need to be obvious.

"I hope you like jazz," he said, opening my door for me at the curb in front of a very cool looking club. We found an open table draped with crisp white linen, and Watson pulled out my chair. "I thought it might be nice to have some uninterrupted conversation."

Only if that conversation had nothing to do with my fictitious employer. I had high hopes the intimate setting, complete with deep, plush chairs, flickering votive candles under cut-glass globes, low lighting, and the soft music of a jazz trio, would keep his mind off Mr. Holmes and on more pleasant things. My mind, for instance, was wandering all over pleasant territory as I stared into his clear blue eyes.

Watson repositioned his seat for a clearer view of the stage, which brought him closer, allowing me to bask in the subtle musky scent of his aftershave. I felt my stomach flutter and gave myself a mental *down girl*. I was here on business. My mission: don't blow Sherlock's cover. Or Irene's and mine, as the case may be.

After a waitress took our drink orders and left, Watson sat back with a smile. "That color suits you."

I smiled. "Thanks. It's Irene's." Now why did I go and ruin a perfectly nice compliment with a line like that?

He raised an eyebrow. "The color?"

"The dress." And the shoes. And the purse. But thankfully I was able to keep *those* thoughts to myself.

"Well, it looks nice on *you*."

"Thanks," I said again lamely. Good God, what was it about an attractive man that suddenly made my IQ plummet twenty points?

"So," he asked, watching me closely. "How is Mr. Holmes taking to his newfound notoriety?"

So much for pleasantries. "Uh…notoriety?"

"The *Irregulars* article."

I suppressed a groan. "So you *did* read that, too, huh?"

"Wiggins had the nerve to send me a link, thanking me for my help."

"Yeah, well, the publicity is good for our business, I guess," I hedged, wondering where that server was with our drinks.

"I would think so." He studied me for a second, and I prayed he was only enjoying how good I looked in blue.

"It's strange," he said. "No one seems to know much about Mr. Holmes."

So much for the power of prayer.

"That's by design," I said. "He's very private."

"Not even a photograph," he said.

"He's a little insecure about his looks."

"And no mention of where he's from, other cases he's worked, what college he attended."

"He moved around. Client confidentiality. He wasn't a very good student."

We looked at each other.

"I get it," he said. "You don't want to talk about Mr. Holmes."

I laughed nervously. He had no idea.

"Okay," he acquiesced. "How about we switch topics."

No arguments from me there!

"Have you made any progress in finding Rebecca Lowery?"

Oy! From one sore spot to the next. Suddenly I was really wishing I'd ordered a shot of tequila instead of a dry white wine. "I'm not sure," I told him. "Maybe. Some. We, uh, are looking into several leads at the moment."

"So she's still missing then."

I nodded. "We know her body made it safely from the morgue to Gordon's Mortuary, but it seems to have disappeared from there."

His lips tightened. "You talked to the mortician." It wasn't a question.

I nodded again. "Although I'm not sure I believe him. Setting foot in that place makes you want to take a bath with bleach."

"That doesn't surprise me. I've heard it's not exactly a class operation."

"You wouldn't recommend it to anyone then?"

He looked at me. "I don't make those kinds of recommendations. That's not my business."

"I thought maybe since our client is from out of town…" I let the thought trail off.

Watson stepped into the silence. "When you do find whoever is responsible, he'll face serious charges." Anger and disgust sharpened his voice to a knife's edge. "No one deserves the indignity of this treatment. Rebecca Lowery should be properly laid to rest."

My heart went pitter patter at the passion mixed with compassion in his voice. "We'll find her."

"I know you will."

Then he knew more than we did. Still, I appreciated his confidence in us, even though I wasn't at all sure of its origin.

I nodded to the band. "They're really good."

To my relief, his expression brightened. "Aren't they? The Matt Bernard Trio. They perform here a few times a month."

Was that an oblique invitation?

*Focus, Marty.*

The server *finally* arrived with our drinks, and I took a grateful sip of my wine, hoping it didn't go straight to my head. I hadn't eaten since lunch, and that had been a drive-through burrito.

"I apologize," Watson said.

My eyes shot up. "For?"

"For getting a little heated just then." The corner of his mouth ticked up in an adorable little half smile. "I can't help taking it a bit personally that one of my cases is missing."

"No apology necessary," I told him, waving it off with my free hand. "I totally get it. A missing body is disturbing any way you look at it." I paused, thinking about our current theory as to why she might be missing. While I was 99 percent certain Watson hadn't missed an obvious sign of foul play, I had to ask…

"I'm curious…nothing stood out to you as odd during your examination of her, did it?"

The apologetic smile disappeared. "What are you suggesting?"

"Nothing, nothing," I assured him, taking another fortifying sip of my wine. "I guess I'm just grasping for why someone would want her body." Or want it out of the way.

He relaxed a little. "No. Nothing seemed out of the ordinary about her. And nothing was incongruent with a slip and fall," he added, clearly knowing where my line of questioning was headed.

"You said you ran a tox screen?"

"What does Mr. Holmes suspect?" he asked instead of answering.

Mr. Holmes? Nothing. But Irene and I had all manner of harebrained theories.

"I'm not entirely sure what his working theory is." I blinked at him, hoping the color of my dress looked good enough on me for him to buy the dumb blonde act I was currently selling.

It might have been the dim lighting, but I could have sworn his eyes narrowed just *that* much at me.

I took another sip—oh, who was I kidding? It was a gulp—of wine, cutting my own eyes to the stage so that Watson couldn't see the deception that was surely imprinted in them. I hated this charade. I couldn't pull it off as smoothly as Irene. And when it came to Watson, I really didn't want to.

I slid a glance at him, at his startling blue eyes with their tiny laugh lines, at his mouth, with its pouty lower lip just begging to be kissed. If only I wasn't lying to him about, well, everything. I wasn't even wearing my own clothes. Or carrying my own purse.

"I'm hoping to meet him some day. He seems like an interesting man."

I set my glass on the table with an unladylike thud. "Excuse me?"

"Your boss," he said.

Him again. "Yes, he is," I agreed. "Interesting and very busy. That's why he lets Irene and me do much of the legwork. In fact, lately he's been mentioning bringing someone else on board too. You know, to run background checks and things like that. The mundane work."

*What?* What was I saying? I was worse than I thought at this lying thing. I had to stop talking, right now.

Watson's smile reached beyond his eyes straight into my fantasies. "I'm not complaining, Marty. My life would be much less interesting if he kept you behind a desk. And you can tell Mr. Holmes that the tox report was negative for all illegal substances."

The second most important thing he'd just said almost slipped right past me unnoticed, thanks to the first most important one. "Negative?" I repeated. How could it have been negative given Rebecca's purchase of Fluffy Bunny?

"You sound surprised." Watson frowned. "What's going on, Marty? Do you have information I should know?"

Probably. But the truth was if I told him about Fluffy Bunny, I'd have to tell him where Rebecca had gotten it. And how I knew about it. Which just happened to be from yours truly purchasing it. I was no lawyer, but I was pretty sure the law frowned upon buying illegal drugs.

I shook my head. "Nope. Not a thing."

"Hmm." He didn't seem to believe that any more than I did. Thankfully, though, he let it go, his attention focusing on the Matt Bernard Trio.

We listened to the band for a few minutes while I waited for my heart rate to normalize and my suffocating guilt to dissipate.

"You should probably be aware of something," Watson finally said, breaking the silence. "When Detective Lestrade came in to observe an autopsy this morning, he told me that Barbara Lowery Bristol has been calling him every day about her sister. Sounds like she's demanding he put the entire department on the case."

"I don't blame her," I said. Even though I did, just a little bit, because it meant she didn't have faith in Sherlock Holmes's ability to do the job. On the other hand, if she'd hired us solely as a red herring, it was possible her badgering of Lestrade was the same thing. Did she really expect Lestrade to divert resources away from his murder caseload to find a missing accidental death? Or was she playing a game with us—hiring Sherlock Holmes and badgering Lestrade to solve the case that she knew neither of us would in order to deflect suspicion from herself?

My throat felt dry. I didn't want to think the worst of people, but I had the feeling that it just might be a consequence of the job. No wonder police officers always looked suspicious. They had to deal with deceitful people like Barbara Lowery Bristol every day. And I'd only been doing this for a few months. At this rate, I'd come to only trust my dog Toby, and there were a few times I'd seen *him* look at me sideways when his dinner hadn't met expectations.

My phone chimed at the same time that Watson said, "You know, Marty—"

I held up one finger with an apologetic smile and pulled my phone from Irene's clutch to read the text.

It was from Tara.

"Would you excuse me?" I pushed back my chair and stood. "I should take care of this."

He stood reflexively. "Of course. Take your time."

I hurried into the ladies' room, bypassing the counter to huddle beside the wall-mounted hand dryer.

*Got your messages. All of them.*

Okay, so maybe I had gone a little overboard there.

*What do you want to know?*

So many things. How I'd gotten myself involved in chasing another killer. How Rebecca's toxicology screen had come up clean. How women could stand to wear stilettos for more than thirty minutes at a time. I shifted on aching feet.

I typed, *It would be best if we could meet.*

A stall door swung open, disgorging a plump middle-aged woman who hustled over to the sink then waved her hands beneath the dryer, keeping her eyes fixed on the floor. I slid a step to the right. She left before the timer had expired, leaving the dryer running noisily.

My phone chimed with another text. *I don't have much free time tonight.*

I typed, *I only need fifteen minutes.*

Another few minutes passed before her reply. Reading it, I could practically hear her impatience. *Fine. Meet me at Lampley Park in half an hour. Northwest corner. Do you know it?*

I knew the park. I'd have to figure out the Northwest corner part of it, but that was doable. That's why there were compass apps. My bigger issue was meeting outside on a foggy evening (but weren't they all in San Francisco?) in Irene's skimpy dress. And in these killer heels.

*Are you sure about that location?* I asked her.

*I want privacy. I don't want to be seen talking to a detective.*

That was a little insulting, but I sort of understood it. PS Rossi had been practically apoplectic at the though of bad publicity to the show. As a recent understudy-turned-lead, Tara was most likely a bit gun-shy of bad press herself.

Of course, if she'd had something to do with Rebecca's death, did I really want to meet her at Lampley Park, alone, in the dark, in Irene's thousand dollar shoes? I wasn't sure which of those three might be worst.

I briefly thought of taking Watson with me but quickly nixed the idea. If Watson went with me, I feared it wouldn't take long for him to realize I was no detective. I wasn't prepared for the big reveal. Besides, Tara might not be willing to talk to me if I brought company, especially if privacy was her chief concern.

I typed *I'll be there*, tucked the phone into the clutch before I could change my mind, and went back to the table.

"I'm sorry," I told Watson. "Something important has come up. I have to go."

The look on his face made me *really* sorry. If I didn't know better, it was genuine disappointment. "Duty calls?"

"Something like that." The last thing I wanted to do was have him tempt me into second-guessing my decision not to bring him along.

He stood, dropped some bills on the table, and touched a gentle hand to my lower back, escorting me to the exit. "Maybe I can take a rain check."

Be still my beating heart. "I could be persuaded."

We stepped outside into a chilly evening. Low fog had rolled in thick and heavy, threatening an actual rain.

"Where can I drop you?" he asked.

I'd forgotten I had no car. "Thanks, but I can take an Uber," I told him.

"You don't have to do that," he said. "I'm happy to take you wherever you need to go."

A couple brushed past us on their way into the club, holding hands, relaxed and casual. We stepped away from the door.

"No. Really. It's fine."

A frown formed between his eyebrows again, and I resisted the urge to reach out and smooth it down with my fingertips. And brush that gorgeous blond hair away from his eyes. And kiss those pouty lips, and…wow, the wine had definitely gone to my head.

"I, uh, I'm meeting a potential witness. In another case," I quickly lied. "But I have to protect my sources. I'm sure you understand."

"Sure." Nothing about his tone said understanding.

"I'm sorry," I said again. Truly meaning it.

Irene was going to be so disappointed in me when she heard how this non-date had gone.

# CHAPTER NINE

———

Privacy was one thing. Invisibility was another. Lampley Park had the benefit, or drawback, depending on your perspective, of both. After I figured out where it was, thanks to my newly installed compass app, I picked a careful path to the Northwest corner of the park, practically feeling my way along in search of a bench where I could sit and wait. They were few and far between, as were the old-fashioned replica gaslights that for some horrifying reason brought to mind London's East End in the days of Jack the Ripper. Best to put *that* right out of my head. I had enough problems trying to walk on the uneven pavement in the heels meant for fashion editorials and nothing else. The trademarked red soles had threatened to slip me right into dewy grass more than once.

But it was more than the footing that had me slowing my steps. It was the *other* things I couldn't see out there. My eyes hadn't yet adjusted to the darkness. For all I knew, Tara was standing just off the path, watching me. A light mist had begun to fall, largely trapped in the canopy of trees overhead, sprinkling glistening diamonds across the black landscape.

What had I been thinking, agreeing to meet a potential killer in a dark, secluded spot? Why had I been in such a hurry to talk to her? Tomorrow in the nice, safe daylight would have been soon enough. I had no self-defense training and no weapon, unless you counted the stiletto heels, which I'd be only too happy to take off for any purpose. I did have a cell phone, but having the 9-1-1 app didn't make me feel any more protected out here. It had taken me roughly twenty-five minutes to reach the park and at least ten more to make my way to the Northwest corner. Tara should have been waiting. But she wasn't, as far as I could tell, which made me wonder if I'd been stood up.

Or set up.

A twig snapped, sounding like the crack of a rifle shot in the silence. I froze, squinting into the blackness. I couldn't see anything, but I could *feel* that I wasn't alone. My adrenaline spiked, making me hyperalert to the point of dizziness. Blood roared in my ears, nearly deafening me. I was afraid to move. And afraid not to.

A shadowy, hooded figure stepped out of the darkness to my left.

Reflexively, I screamed and lashed out with a kick, hearing a startled yelp when I connected with shin. But that wasn't enough. I went into human windmill mode, throwing more kicks and fists, wishing I had a larger handbag so I could swing that too. One full of bricks.

The figure stumbled back, causing his hoodie to slip from his head, revealing a shaggy mop of sandy hair and a pair of light brown eyes behind wire-rimmed glasses. Recognition hit me like a slap to the face. I'd seen him before. He was the same guy who'd been in line behind me at Buttercream bakery early that day as I'd tracked Rebecca's last movements. Icy fear stabbed me in the gut. Was I being followed? Or worse yet, stalked?

"Are you following me?" I demanded, taking on a very menacing karate pose that I envisioned looking like a female Chuck Norris. But probably fell more toward Sandy the Squirrel from SpongeBob.

He took a step back, eyes going wide. Either with fear I'd hit him or fear I was crazy, I wasn't sure.

"Who are you?" I yelled again. "Answer me. I'm trained in Bokator!"

His big brown eyes blinked behind his lenses. "What is that?"

"It's an ancient Cambodian martial art based on animal techniques and sheer brutality." Totally true. "And I know every technique." Totally false. I'd sat in on a lecture once about Asian battle styles in the anthropology department. All I knew about

Bokator was that it sounded menacing. At least, I hoped it did to the stalker.

"Look, take it easy, okay, girl?"

I narrowed my eyes at him and deepened my fighting stance. "Did you just call me *girl?*"

"Lady! Woman! Cripes, just back off, okay?"

"Who are you?" I demanded again.

He straightened his clothing, restored his hood, and pushed up his glasses. "Look, I'm not here to hurt anyone. My name is Wiggins."

I froze. Oh no.

"I'm a reporter for the—"

"*Irregulars*," I finished for him.

"Yeah. The *Irregulars*." He grinned. "You've heard of us?"

I gave him a *get real* look and dropped the fighting stance "Yes, I'm familiar."

His grin widened, looking absurdly pleased. Great. An egomaniacal stalker.

"What do you want?" I demanded.

"Mind if I ask you a few questions?"

Anger surged through me at the realization that he *had* been following me. Not only here but at the bakery as well. "Yes, as a matter of fact, I do mind."

He shrugged. "Okay, maybe I can speak with your employer, Sherlock Holmes?"

Ha! Fat chance of that. "He's out of the country," I said automatically.

"When will he be back?"

"Indeterminate."

"Surely he has a phone wherever he is?"

"It's hard to catch him. Time difference, you know."

He paused. "And how much exactly *is* that time difference?" he asked, clearly fishing for a more exact location.

I narrowed my eyes at him. No way was I falling into that trap. "What are you doing out here anyway?" I asked, turning the interrogation tables on him. "You scared me half to death. I thought you were a mugger!"

"Good thing I'm not," he shot back. "Because you're a pretty easy target in a place like this." He pointed at my feet. "How are you supposed to maneuver in shoes like that?"

If I didn't fear assault charges, I'd have hit him again. "My shoes are none of your business," I snapped. "I can't believe you thought it was okay to follow me. Twice!" I paused. "It was only twice, right?"

He shrugged instead of answering. "I do what I have to do to get the story. And people seem to enjoy it. The first post in my Disappearing Diva series got over a million hits in twenty-four hours."

My mind glossed over the staggering number of a million hits and latched on to another important word. Series? He was doing a *series*? Where did he think he'd get the material? Even if I wanted to, I couldn't provide enough information on Sherlock Holmes to fill a tweet. And I was supposed to actually know the guy.

I shook my head. "No. No series. This…it's an open case."

"Making any headway on it?"

"Some, but I—" I caught myself falling into his conversational tone. "No! No story. No series."

He shrugged again. It was beginning to get annoying. "I've given your employer a lot of free publicity."

"Yeah, I wish you'd stop that."

"You'd think he'd want to help me out. I mean, I could tell the public a lot about the guy."

I doubted that.

"Like, how many cases has he closed so far?"

Bit my lip. "Lots," I lied.

"Where's he from?"

"He's from none of your business," I told him.

Rudeness had no effect on him at all. "Where was he trained?"

I glanced around, although I was unable to see much of anything, wondering just where Tara was. Standing in the shadows enjoying the show? Had she even bothered to show up? Had something happened to her?

"I have no idea," I said levelly. "I never asked him."

"Funny thing." He put a contemplative finger on his chin. "Sherlock's picture isn't anywhere online—not on his website, no social media, zilch. And he's got two babes as his wing men."

"Women," I said sharply.

"Okay, wing women," he said.

"No." I rolled my eyes. "We're not *babes*. We're *women*."

"You can be both." He smiled, looking me up and down in a way that suddenly made me shiver. Or maybe that was just the fog. Granted, when he wasn't shooting off smart remarks, the geek-chic thing he had going on was kind of cute. You know, if you were into the nosy reporter type. Which I so was not.

"What is your point exactly?" I demanded of him, ignoring the way my body responded to his appraising gaze.

"My point," he said, "is that every time I call the number on his website, I get a recording. And he never returns my calls. Why is that?"

"Maybe he doesn't like reporters." I knew I, for one, didn't like where this was going. Wiggins asked questions as if he knew the answers. Even if he didn't, he was much too curious for comfort. "Listen, I don't want to catch you following me again," I added, as if I had actually caught him the first time. "I have connections to law enforcement, you know."

"Who, that ME, Watson?"

My anger swelled again. "You followed me on my…" I paused, searching for the right word. Un-date didn't seem very dignified.

"Date?" Wiggins grinned.

"Business dinner."

"Right. At a jazz club."

I stabbed my finger at his chest. "Just leave me alone. You've been warned." Sure, it sounded good, but it had no teeth, and we both knew it. Still, I knew a good exit line when I said it, so I turned and stormed off, hoping the darkness would conceal me from him. I didn't want to be followed by anyone, let alone a reporter. It felt like a gross invasion of privacy. Besides that, I had no answers for him.

A few minutes later, I realized the night *had* hidden me, and I realized something else. Wiggins had the stubbornness of a toddler and the night vision of an owl, because I heard him scuffling along behind me. At least it seemed like behind me, although the darkness was disorienting. It was possible he was just keeping his distance as he left the park along with me. It was also possible he was still on the story and hoping to follow me to his next breaking news.

Well, I wasn't going to stand for *that*. I wheeled around to confront him.

But before I could say a word, something struck my temple.

Caught completely off guard and unable to gain my equilibrium on the stilettos, I immediately went down, with just enough time to realize I'd fallen face first into mud before everything went black.

# CHAPTER TEN

———

"Marty? Can you hear me?"

I cracked open an eye to discover two things. First, I was no longer facedown in mud but lying faceup staring into the lacy mist, my head cushioned by something soft. Second, Watson knelt beside me, lightly stroking my hair, concern etched on his face.

"Thank God," he muttered.

I opened the other eye and tried to smile, but it hurt, so I gave up. "Watson?" I managed.

"Just relax. Do you know where you are?" He was staring intently at my eyes, checking my pupils for signs of a concussion if I had to guess.

"I'm at the park," I croaked out. I paused. "What are *you* doing here?"

"I followed you here. How many fingers am I holding up?"

"Three. Wait—*you* followed me?"

He nodded. "Your story was shaky at the club. I was worried, so I followed you."

Honestly, if anyone else followed me, I'd have to hire a marching band and some floats. I sat up, touching my head gingerly. "It wasn't a story. I really was meeting an informant."

"An informant who did this to you?"

I shook my head. Ouch. Bad idea. I took a deep breath, waiting for the world to stop spinning. "No, she never showed."

"*She*?"

I moved to nod but thought better of it. "Yeah. Women have information too, you know," I muttered. What was with men today?

Watson's jaw clenched. "I'm aware. I was just surprised that two women would choose a dark, deserted park to meet in."

Oh. Right.

"Whose idea was it to meet here?"

"Hers," I admitted.

"It was a bad one."

"No argument here," I said, running a hand along my cheek and feeling mud begin to cake there. "Do you have a tissue or something?" I couldn't imagine how I must look. Even my hair felt stringy with mud. Irene's dress needed an emergency dry-cleaning intervention. I was afraid to look at the shoes.

Watson found some tissues in his pocket and handed them over. "So you and your partner never saw the informant?"

I froze, tissue midway to my face. "Partner?"

"The man you were with. I saw him bending over you on the ground. Only, when I called out to him, he took off toward the parking lot. I assumed he works for Sherlock as well." He paused, suddenly looking embarrassed. "Or perhaps he was a social acquaintance."

I snorted. Which coupled with my mud-caked appearance must have been highly attractive. "You mean Wiggins? You think I'm dating *Wiggins*?"

Watson's eyes shot up to meet mine. "Wiggins? The reporter?"

I nodded (with slightly less pain this time). "He followed me here." I glanced at him. "You know, before you did."

"Did *he* do this to you?" Watson had gone from looking adorably jealous to angry in seconds flat.

I thought about that for a moment. Had he? It was possible. In fact, I'd thought it was Wiggins following me a second time just before I'd blacked out. Only I couldn't come up with a reason the reporter would want to harm me. Hound me for a story—yes. Bash me over the head—doubtful.

"I don't think so," I said slowly. "He doesn't seem the type."

"You know him well?"

Did I detect that jealousy edging into his voice again? "Not really," I admitted. "But he didn't strike me as the violent kind. Plus, why would he knock me out?"

Watson shrugged. "Why would anyone waste time reading his blog drivel, but a thousand hits later, there you have it. People do odd things."

"Million," I corrected, still marveling at the number. "But no, I don't think it was Wiggins."

"Then your informant?"

I pursed my lips together. I could feel the next question forming in his mind even before he voiced it.

"Who is she?"

I thought about lying. But I just didn't have the energy at the moment. "Tara Tarnowski," I told him.

His blank face told me the name meant nothing to him.

"She was Rebecca Lowery's understudy. *Currently* the lead in *Ethereal Love*."

"And you're thinking her change in career status might have something to do with the missing Rebecca?"

"Possibly even her death."

"Her *accidental* death?"

I worded the next bit carefully. "You know, a fall and a push would look a lot alike."

Watson shook his head. "Look, maybe you better start at the beginning," he said, helping me up off the ground and grabbing the folded and now muddy jacket he'd placed beneath my head.

Against my better judgment and Irene's screaming voice in my head, I did. I laid out the details of how Rebecca's body had been taken and not just lost, our theory that it had been done to cover up evidence of a crime, and the few suspects we'd cobbled together so far. I even told him about Fluffy Bunny, though I might have glossed over a few felonious details of my own purchase.

The more I said, the more granite-like Watson's jaw became, grinding and clenching until I was pretty sure he could create diamonds with his back molars.

"...and that's why I was meeting Tara here. I wanted to know what the argument was about," I finished.

He was silent, eyes staring me down with some unidentifiable emotion behind them.

I cleared my throat. "But the meeting didn't go quite as planned. Clearly."

"Clearly."

I bit my lip. "But, I'm fine, so…"

"Fine? You were knocked out cold!"

"Just for a second…" I mumbled, not sure why I was suddenly defending myself.

"You could have a concussion. You could have been killed!"

"But I wasn't?" Only it sounded more like a question.

"This is completely irresponsible of him."

I blinked, wondering if it was the bump on the head making me slow. "Him?"

"Sherlock Holmes," he spat out.

Right. That *him*.

"I can handle myself just fine," I said, sounding a lot more confident than I felt.

"No, you can't."

I felt my spine straighten.

But before I could respond, Watson continued. "Marty, if drugs played any role in Rebecca's death, you need to let the authorities handle it. Synthetics are big business, and these aren't the kind of people who just let things go. If they have a problem, they eliminate it."

I swallowed hard, feeling the night send a chill down my spine. "I'll talk to Lestrade in the morning," I promised, only slightly mentally crossing my fingers behind my back.

But it seemed to placate him, as his jaw finally softened. "Come on. Let me take you home."

Since I was muddy, tired, and broke, I agreed.

It was a quiet ride back to my apartment, the silence between us filled with questions I didn't want to answer and he probably didn't want the answers to anyway. I occupied myself with wiping the remaining mud from my face and exploring the lump on my head with tentative fingers. Watson spent the time seething on my behalf. I could tell by his white-knuckled grip on the wheel.

When we reached my apartment building, I turned to face him. "Thanks for the ride—"

"I'll walk you in."

He was out of the car before I could protest. Not that I wanted to. Truth was, I was feeling a little shaky, and having Watson next to me was much more comforting than I wanted to admit.

I used his ready arm for support as we climbed the stairs to my apartment, moving awkwardly because the front of my dress was stiff with dried mud. No sign of 2B. No scent of Mr. Bitterman.

Mrs. Frist, however, was hunched at my door, trying to peer through the keyhole. Not an uncommon position for Mrs. Frist, although she usually did it in the other direction, at her own place. I couldn't imagine what she hoped to see in mine. Or how she hoped to see it.

Clearly she didn't hear us coming, because she didn't budge even when I cleared my throat gently from the last step. Her concentration was complete and impressive and misdirected, unless she and Toby had something weird going on.

I tapped her on the shoulder, hoping I didn't startle her into a coronary. "Can I help you find something, Mrs. Frist?"

"Oh!" She straightened up. "I didn't hear you coming."

I would have been mortified if I'd been caught in her position, but not Mrs. Frist. She was shameless enough to look annoyed at the interruption. "Is he in there?"

I glanced at Watson. "Is who in there?" I asked, puzzled. "Toby?"

She sniffed at me. "Is that what he wants you to call him? Toby?"

I rested my hand on the doorknob. "I'm sorry, Mrs. Frist, I'm tired and cold—"

"And dirty," she said, staring at me. Since her glasses were hanging on a chain around her neck, it was possible she was trying to focus on me. "No wonder you're not married, if that's the way you look when you go on a date."

"I wasn't on a date," I said wearily.

She pointed at Watson. "Isn't that a man?"

His neutral expression melted away into a bemused smile.

"That's a man," I agreed. "Excuse me."

"Men want a lady to look like a lady," she informed me. "Hair that's combed, clothes that are clean. Not…" Her gesture swept the length of my body. "*That*."

"I'll make a note." I unlocked the door, and Toby came scrambling out of the bedroom to conduct his routine inspection, devoting extra time to the mélange of scents I'd brought home in my clothing, before trotting off to the kitchen to await his bedtime snack.

Mrs. Frist crowded in behind me, trying to see over my shoulder. "Is Isaac in there?"

"Mr. *Bitterman*? Is that who you were looking for?" I dropped my purse on the occasional table by the door. "Why would he be in my apartment?"

"Because the old coot is hiding from me. That's why. He *knew* I was cooking him dinner."

Her mistake. Mr. Bitterman didn't eat anyone else's cooking, and he didn't date. Marriage had cured him of that.

Mrs. Frist turned to Watson. "If you're not a date, you must be the landlord. Can you open his door for me?"

My cheeks did a slow burn. "He's not the landlord, Mrs. Frist. He's the medical examiner."

"The medical examiner!" She pressed a hand to her chest. "Am I dead?"

Watson chuckled. "No, ma'am, you're not dead. You're still a beautiful woman in her sixties."

I'd never heard Mrs. Frist giggle before, and I silently thanked Watson for the experience. Mrs. Frist wasn't a day under eighty-five.

She edged up beside him, leading with her bony little shoulder, batting her lashes, a regular femme fatale in support hose. "Are you hungry, young man?"

"Thank you, but we had dinner earlier," he told her, only bending the truth a little. We'd been *at* dinner, but the one lonely glass of wine I'd ingested rolled in my empty stomach, which was crying for a gooey slice of pizza to go with it.

"The two of you?" Mrs. Frist asked with disappointment.

"It was a business dinner," he added quickly.

Right. Just business, I reminded myself.

Mrs. Frist looked at me. "You took her out with that dirty face?"

Oops. I'd thought I'd taken care of that in the car. "I had a little accident," I said.

"In fact," Watson added, "I'm just about to examine her, and then she'll need to get some rest." He smiled down at her. "You'll excuse us?"

She practically swooned. Granted, Watson's smile had that effect on me as well.

"Keep me in mind if you're ever in the mood for pickled pigs' feet, young man."

"I promise you'll be the first one I think of," he assured her, guiding her out into the hall with a gentle but firm hand on her arm. He closed the door behind her and turned to me with a wry smile "Pickled pigs' feet?"

"She'll be the first one you think of, alright," I told him.

"Is she always like that?"

I shook my head. "Sometimes she's man-hungry."

He chuckled. "Can I make you something hot to drink?"

"You don't have to do that," I said. "I can make myself a cup of tea."

"I'm sure you can." His smile faded as he looked down at me. "Indulge me. You've been through a real ordeal tonight, and I'd like to know you're okay before I leave you alone."

"I'm fine," I told him. "But if you insist, I guess I can put up with being catered to. First I'm going to get out of this filthy dress, if you don't mind."

He was much too polite to offer his help with that task, which was a shame, so I did it myself, leaving the heap of dirty clothes on my bedroom floor and slipping into a thick, fluffy robe and warm woolen socks. I pulled my hair up off my neck, securing it with a tortoiseshell clasp, all too aware that my hair, too, was dirty. It would just have to wait until I was alone.

I chose to believe it was Watson's medical training that led him to have no reaction to my wardrobe change when I led him into the kitchen, where he insisted I take a seat while he found a spoon, a teabag, and a few sugar packets I'd squirreled away in the utensil drawer, setting them in front of me before putting a mug of water into the microwave to heat. While the timer ticked down, he gave Toby a treat from the bag on the counter. "How are you feeling?"

I shrugged. "I'll be alright. I'm not sure I could say the same if you hadn't come along."

"I can't imagine…" His voice trailed off without finishing the thought.

Neither could I, and I didn't want to.

He reached out a hand, his fingers gossamer soft as he felt the bump at my temple. I sat very still, barely breathing, although my heart rocketed into the red zone. His practiced fingers gently explored the lump on my head while I was distracted by his nearness and his warm, enticing scent. My eyes fluttered shut, basking in the sensory overload. If I'd have known this was coming, I would have wandered alone at night in a dark park in ridiculously high heels long ago.

The microwave let out its jarring beep. I opened my eyes in time to see him retrieve the mug of hot water and place it on the table. "Need anything else?"

I shook my head. "Thanks. You've been great."

He stood there looking at me, saying nothing, his expression thoughtful. I'd never wished so hard that I could read minds.

"You should get some rest now," he said finally. "I'll give you a call tomorrow to see how you're feeling."

Leaving my tea to steep, I got up to see him out, ignoring the throbbing ache in my head and the dull disappointment in my heart, which I couldn't understand. It wasn't like I'd expected him to stay. I wasn't even sure I wanted him to. I planned to do just as he suggested and go to bed after I soaked in a nice hot bath. Assuming I had some nice hot water, which was never a given.

At the door, he turned to me. "Marty, promise me you'll let Mr. Holmes handle the heavy lifting from now on."

A little sexist, but I was too tired to argue with him at the moment. "I'll talk to him about it."

"Thank you." He gave me another mind-melting smile that faded when our eyes met and held.

Again I tried to decipher his thoughts, but a second later, I no longer had to. He leaned forward to brush his lips against mine, so softly I wasn't completely sure it wasn't a figment of my imagination. Then he was gone.

And so was I.

\* \* \*

I had a restless night—due more to thoughts of Watson than the unrelenting aching from my head—and woke up angry—due more to the unrelenting aching from my head than thoughts of Watson. The idea that Tara might have set a trap for me at worst, or at best, left me alone and vulnerable in the park when she'd stood me up, put my blood in a low simmer. I might have been inclined to be gentler with her under different circumstances, but no more. Now I wanted answers, and I wasn't willing to wait for them. I planned to be at her front door before she could even think of heading for the Bayside Theater.

But first I needed to know where her front door was. I reached for the phone and called Irene. "Can you find out where Tara Tarnowski lives?"

"Sure." As usual, she was wide awake and unfazed by the request. "Something come up?"

I touched my head, where at least the throbbing had stopped even if the growth of the lump had not. "You could say that." I gave her a CliffsNotes version of my night, minus that insomnia-producing kiss and Mrs. Frist putting the geriatric moves on Watson. "I'll have your dress dry-cleaned right away," I finished. "I don't know if the shoes can be saved. I think I chipped a heel when I fell."

"Throw them out," she said. "Shoes aren't important."

"I'm sorry," I said. "Shoes aren't important? I must have the wrong number. I meant to call Irene Adler."

"Seriously, Marty, I'm with Watson on this one. Why on earth would you go to that park alone at night to meet Tara Tarnowski?"

"I didn't pick the place or the time," I said.

"You could have called me."

"It would've taken you too long to get there."

"Then we would have set it up for another time."

"And risked Tara changing her mind."

Irene sighed. "Fine! But just don't go alone to any more late-night meetings with possible killers, okay?"

Well, when she put it that way, I had to admit it did sound a little foolish. In my defense, I'd only thought Tara would be at the park—who was smaller than I was, slimmer, and hardly threatening—and not an entire parade of people following me.

"Okay," I agreed.

"Thank you." Irene was quiet for a second. "You think Tara set you up?"

"I haven't ruled it out."

"Or maybe it was Wiggins," she said.

"That was Watson's first thought too."

"It's pretty creepy that he's been following you around like that. Who does he think he is?"

"He's convinced he's on the trail of a hot story," I said. "Apparently he's doing a whole series on Sherlock Holmes's latest case."

"I don't like that guy. Even if he wasn't the one who attacked you, he sure didn't show up to help you, did he?"

I paused. "Watson said he saw Wiggins kneeling over me."

"What?! As in, after he knocked you out?"

"Or, to try to help me," I said, wondering why I was defending the guy. "I think all he wants is a story. And I don't plan to give it to him," I added.

"I'm glad to hear that," she said. "Did you go to the hospital?"

I shook my head even though I knew she couldn't see me. "I'm sure Watson would have taken me if he thought I needed to go."

"Marty." The single word was a rebuke.

"Honestly, besides the lump on my head, I was just muddy and cold and mad. Besides, Watson examined me when he brought me home."

"I bet he did."

"Not like that," I snapped. "He was"—*tender*—"very thorough. He even made me tea before he left."

"Oh, he left?"

"Sorry to disappoint you," I said. "But yes, he left."

"Oh. Well, there's always next time," she said.

I wasn't so sure there'd be a next time after that disaster of an *un*-date. "Got Tara's address yet?"

"Here it is." She read it off while I wrote it down. "If you want me to come with you, you'll have to wait until after eleven. I've got a meeting with a baby entrepreneur at ten."

"What is it this time?"

"A couple of guys in San Jose with a Chinese takeout business."

I frowned. "That doesn't sound like your usual investment."

"They deliver the takeout via drones."

There it was. "Thanks, but I'll be alright by myself," I assured her.

"That's what you said last night."

I rolled my eyes. "It's broad daylight. And I'm guessing Tara lives near other people. Aka witnesses."

"Fine. But keep me in the loop," she said. "And remember, you've always got Wiggins as backup."

I hung up on her.

A half hour later, after sharing a toasted English muffin with Toby, I grabbed my purse and Irene's muddied dress, hoping I wouldn't be waylaid by Mrs. Frist, 2B, or Mr. Bitterman on my way out.

Instead, I was waylaid by something else: a note taped to the outside of my door.

*Check with Mrs. Frist.*

I didn't want to spare the time, and I *really* didn't want to listen to any more lectures about my grooming, but if she had some information for me, I was definitely interested. Maybe she'd spotted someone lurking around my door, like Wiggins. If that was the case, I'd want to know about it for the restraining order I'd file. Besides, this morning, my clothes were clean and my hair was brushed. If that didn't make her happy, there was no pleasing her.

I locked up and hurried down the hall to her door. She answered as quickly, as if she'd seen me coming, and she probably had. It was a wonder she didn't just drag a chair into the hallway and sit there with a clock and a notepad.

Subtle as always, her eyes flicked to the dress draped over my arm. Maybe I imagined it, but I thought her nose wrinkled slightly.

I held up the note. "I found this taped to my door this morning."

She squinted at it, and her nose unwrinkled. "Oh, yes. That nice young man left it last night."

Nice young man? Wiggins? There was nothing nice about Wiggins. Why was he still following me? Did he think Sherlock Holmes lived in my apartment? How fast could I get that restraining order?

Mrs. Frist dug a key ring from her pocket and waved it at me. "He said you should use his car. He said it has GPS tracking so he can keep an eye on your whereabouts. He said to make sure you knew he meant that in a good way. He told me to smile when I said it." Her lips stretched obediently over her teeth.

Not Wiggins. Watson.

Conflicting emotions warred in me. While the thought that Watson was so concerned over my safety that he'd lend me his BMW, made a flood of warmth pool in my belly. On the other hand, the idea that he had "to keep an eye on me" was insulting enough that I almost wanted to tell him where he could stick that key ring, *with a smile* when I said it.

Almost.

No matter the circumstances, having free use of a BMW for the day was much better than Uber. Plus, I was broke.

I took the key ring from her. "Why didn't he just leave it with me last night?"

She shrugged. "He said he thought you'd think it was sexist and refuse. That's why the smile." She flashed her forced grimace at me again.

I couldn't help grinning back. Watson was a smart man.

"Besides, he saw my light was on. I'm a bit of a night owl, you know. Three hours of sleep, that's all I need."

That explained a lot.

"I enjoy those infomercials they show in the wee hours," she went on. "You can get some real deals at two a.m., in case you didn't know. Anyway, he said he didn't want to disturb you.

That you needed your rest. If you ask me, that young man's a keeper."

One had to *get* a man before she could keep him.

"Is Isaac awake yet?" she asked me.

I dragged my thoughts away from Watson. "I wouldn't know, Mrs. Frist. Why don't you knock on his door and see?"

"I did. He didn't answer. But I know he's in there." She narrowed her eyes at Mr. Bitterman's apartment.

I had a brief moment of concern. Mr. Bitterman hadn't answered his door? I tried to remember if I'd heard the rattling of pots and pans or other signs of life coming from his place.

"I thought he might have invited you to breakfast," she added. "I hear you favor his cooking."

She'd heard wrong, but given how Mrs. Frist liked to talk, I wasn't about to tell her that. I was too fond of Mr. Bitterman to risk hurting his feelings. I made a note to set aside some time later to check on him, even though the chances were good he was just hiding from Mrs. Frist.

"I'm running a little late." I held up the key ring. "Thanks for holding on to this for me."

"You can return the favor," she said. "Put in a good word for me with Isaac."

I was too fond of Mr. Bitterman for that too.

\* \* \*

When the door to Tara Tarnowski's tiny row house in the Outer Mission opened forty-five minutes later, I thought Irene had given me the wrong address. The woman in front of me wore a knee-length terry robe and fuzzy pink slippers. Her hair hadn't yet seen a flat iron or hot rollers but was pulled back in a ponytail, with frizzy tendrils haloing her head. The absence of makeup betrayed dark shadows smudging her eyes. Hard to reconcile this mere mortal with Rebecca's glamorous understudy we'd seen onstage.

She sent me a flash of recognition followed immediately by surprise. If she'd answered the door expecting a visitor, she clearly hadn't expected it to be me.

"What do *you* want?" she asked, glancing around as if checking to see if I'd brought an entourage with me.

"I want to talk to you about last night. Can I come in?"

"No." She stepped out onto the porch, pulling the door shut behind her.

"Fine. We can chat out here in front of all of your neighbors."

She crossed her arms over her chest, clearly not caring about that threat.

"Do you have any idea what happened to me last night?"

She clutched the robe tightly around herself, as if warding off my anger. "Hey, what you do at night is your business. Why would I care?"

"I was attacked."

If she was surprised, she didn't show it. "Sucks for you."

"In the park. Where *you* were supposed to meet me."

"You should be more careful. We done here?"

"No, we're not. I still have some questions to ask you about Rebecca Lowery."

"Sorry, not interested." She turned to go back into the house, but I sidestepped to the right to block her way.

"Listen, you're going to answer some questions, or I'm going straight to the police station to file an assault charge against you for attacking me last night." It was a total bluff, of course, since I hadn't even seen my attacker, but I was willing to gamble that she didn't want the negative publicity. I knew PS Rossi certainly didn't.

"Assault charge," she repeated. "Are you joking?"

I tightened my lips and squinched my eyes into my best I-am-dead-serious expression. The same expression I used whenever Toby stole food off my plate, only hopefully to better effect.

We stared at each other—well, she stared; I squinted—while I could practically see the do-I-or-don't-I-cooperate battle warring in her eyes.

Finally, she relented with a dramatic huff. "Fine, but I haven't got all day. What do you want to know?"

Gracious in victory, I unsquinched my eyes. "Tell me about Lucky's Deli."

"Don't eat the knockwurst."

I ignored the sarcasm. "So you know it."

She shot me a murderous look. "So I know a deli. So what?"

"It's a deli that sells illegal drugs practically next to the bologna. And you were seen with Rebecca Lowery. Shall I connect the dots, or would you rather do it?"

"I don't do drugs," she said.

"That's not the way it looks from here," I told her.

"I don't know where you get your information," she said with a sniff.

"But you do know it would be damaging for your reputation if my information got out, don't you?"

She shot me a look of pure venom. "*Fine.* Yes, I was with Rebecca at Lucky's. I overheard her on the phone talking about something that sounded shady, so I followed her. But I told you, I don't do drugs."

"Then why follow her?" I asked.

"Haven't you ever heard the saying 'information is power'?"

"But you already had the information," I said. "You overheard her on the phone."

She didn't say anything.

"Did you think you could stop her?"

Her stare was incredulous. "Do I look like Donna Do-Gooder to you?"

Hardly. And she didn't sound like her either. Suddenly an ugly realization struck me. "You were blackmailing her, weren't you."

Her chin lifted in defiance. "You don't have to say it like that."

The woman was shameless. "How should I say it?"

"I was executing a career plan," Tara said. "I'm no different than any other performer. I want exposure and publicity, the kind of publicity you can only get during opening week, when all the reviewers are in the house. I simply suggested that she call in sick just for one night so the world could discover Tara Tarnowski, the next great talent."

Great ego was more like it. "Or?"

"Or I'd go to Rossi about her unfortunate little drug problem." She shook her head with bogus sympathy. "A thing like that might have even cost her her career."

I thought about the newsstand clerk's claim that he'd seen the two women arguing. "That's what you and Rebecca fought about? She didn't want to give in to your blackmail?"

She didn't even have the grace to flinch. "Rebecca just laughed at me. She was selfish enough that she didn't want to give up any performances. Not even one! She told me to go ahead and try it."

"Except you didn't have to," I said slowly. "Because she conveniently died."

Her smile was humorless. "Good word, convenient."

A shiver ran up my spine at her coldness. Considering her obvious thirst for fame, it wasn't hard to imagine she'd been involved in Rebecca's death. She could have removed her competition and ignited her career at the same time. It was despicable but conceivable, given her complete lack of remorse.

But why would she have stolen the body? It was hard to imagine her slinging a corpse over her shoulder like a handbag and spiriting it away to its hiding spot. Tara didn't seem like a heavy lifting kind of girl. But the obvious answer was that if she was capable of murder, she was capable of anything. Once you got past the…what was the phrase, *moral turpitude*—it would have been just a matter of the mechanics.

"Why didn't you show up at the park last night?" I asked her.

"Oh, that." Her hand fluttered dismissively. "My driver was late. By the time I got there, you'd already hooked up with some hot blond guy. I figured you weren't interested in talking to me anymore, so I went home." She paused. "Actually, it's too bad I didn't see him first. I could have used the entertainment. Be a doll. When you're done with him, let me have his number. He looks like the type of man who'd be able to handle me."

Anger flared deep in my belly, along with maybe just a little jealousy. First off, I'd never *hooked up* with anyone in my life. Second, it was too bad *she* hadn't taken the knock on the head. The way I felt about her, I could have done it myself. And not just for that last comment either.

"Is there anything else? I'm due at rehearsal in ninety minutes."

She didn't wait for an answer before slipping back inside and all but slamming her door shut in my face. I hurried back to Watson's car and slid behind the wheel. I sat there looking at the row house while I thought about what I'd just heard. I didn't like Tara one bit. More than that, I didn't trust her. But did that mean she'd killed Rebecca? She had motive. She had means. It seemed to me she could have easily created the opportunity. Reluctantly, I wondered if my perspective was skewed by that comment about Watson. I had to admit it hadn't helped.

While I was busy staring at the house, actively disliking Tara, her front door opened again. I expected to see the redheaded diva, yelling at me to quit spying on her. But instead I saw a man slip out and head for a pickup parked at the curb three doors up.

I raised my eyebrow. No wonder Tara hadn't wanted me to come in—she'd had a guy in there.

And as he turned his body toward me to angle himself into the truck, I realized it was a guy I already knew.

Bryan Steele, Rebecca Lowery's boyfriend.

Before I could fully comprehend what I was seeing, the pickup rolled away, disappearing with a flash of brake lights around the corner at the bottom of the hill.

Suddenly, the idea of Tara stealing Rebecca's body didn't present as much of a problem. What if Tara was the brains behind the killing and Bryan Steele was the muscle? I wondered how long Tara had been sleeping with Rebecca's boyfriend. Was Tara what they'd been arguing about at the theater just before Rebecca's death? Or was this a new relationship…a role Tara had stepped into as soon as Rebecca died, as neatly as she had the lead in *Ethereal Love*?

I was still contemplating that when my phone chimed with a text. It was from Irene.

*Got info on the deli owner. Meet me at the Victorian ASAP.*

# CHAPTER ELEVEN

———

"Tara and Bryan Steele?" Irene echoed.

I nodded. "I know. I couldn't believe it either."

"Are you sure it was him?"

"It was him." I paused. "He was probably listening just inside the door to our entire conversation."

"Yet the tough guy didn't have the guts to show his face." Irene's mouth twisted in disgust. "Can't say much for Rebecca's choice in men."

"Or Tara's," I agreed.

She made a face. "Those two deserve each other. Not exactly two class acts. She's got to be hiding something."

"She was hiding *him,*" I said. "Obviously they didn't know I was still outside when he left."

"Wonder why she cared whether you knew about them," she mused. "She seems completely shameless about everything else."

"Maybe *he's* the one who cared." Although I couldn't imagine why. It wasn't like he was married, hiding an affair from his wife. "What'd you find out about the deli, anyway?"

She brightened. "It wasn't as easy as I thought to figure out who owns the business. I had to wade through a ton of boring corporate records. A company parenting another company, parenting another company. The trail was a mile long and not a straight shot by any means."

I raised an eyebrow. "Sounds like a lot of work to go to just to hide your ownership of a simple deli."

Irene grinned. "Right. It if *were* just a simple deli."

"So, did you get a name?"

"Yes, ma'am, I did. You ready for this?" She paused for effect. "Vincent Gordon."

I looked at her. "Who's Vincent Gordon?"

"Gordon? Name doesn't ring any bells?" She shook her head. "I knew I was right about that creep. He's in this up to his pale little neck."

"You mean Dominic Gordon?" I asked. "Of Gordon's Mortuary?"

Irene nodded.

"I don't know. That's a pretty common name. They might not even be related."

"Oh, they're related, alright," she said. "Vincent Gordon not only owns Lucky's Deli but also Gordon's Mortuary."

"I stand corrected."

She grinned. "I know, right?"

"It *is* coincidental," I mused, shoving mental puzzle pieces around to fit in this new information.

"It's more than coincidental. It's downright diabolical."

"There's that word again," I said, feeling another harebrained theory coming on.

"Think about it—Vinny gets people hooked on his Fluffy Bunny pills, they overdose, and then they end up at Gordon's Mortuary. It's an ideal business model. He profits on both ends. They live—he has an addicted client. They die—he profits from the funeral."

"That's pretty cynical."

"These aren't Boy Scouts," she said. "We're talking about drug dealers and probably worse."

I wished talking about them was *all* we were doing. I had a bad feeling that this case had just gotten exponentially worse. "But Rebecca didn't take the Fluffy Bunny," I said. "According to Watson, her tox screen came back negative."

She waved me off. "That's not important right now. They sold it to her, didn't they? Well, Vincent's minions did, anyway. But maybe something with the deal went sideways. Maybe Rebecca can't pay or decides to rat them out. They follow her home, kill her, then—believing she has the Fluffy Bunny they sold her in her system—they steal the body so no one can trace the designer blend back to them."

As much as I hated to admit it, it made as much sense as anything else we'd come up with so far.

I glanced at Irene. Her eyes had that dangerous look in them. Like she was either about to initiate a hostile takeover or drag me into another Sherlockian moment.

"We're going back to Gordon's Mortuary, aren't we?" I asked.

She nodded. "I think we have to."

"Fine. I'll drive." I pulled out the car keys.

Irene immediately snatched them from me. "These are BMW keys! Where did you get these?"

"They're Watson's," I reluctantly admitted. "He left them for me last night."

"Oh, did he? Did you properly thank him?"

"I was asleep," I told her.

"That happens," she said. "Only usually it's the man who falls asleep."

I rolled my eyes. "Will you stop it? He left his keys with Mrs. Frist so I didn't have to Uber around today." I left out the part about keeping an eye on me, as I wasn't sure Irene would be as forgiving about the insult as I was. She, unlike me, had a fleet of cars at her disposal.

"That man," Irene said, "is a geyser of surprises."

"Yeah, well, I'm returning the car as soon as we get back from the mortuary," I told her as I made my way toward the door.

Only as soon as I opened it, I found Barbara Lowery Bristol standing on the other side, her hand raised as if ready to knock.

Surprised, I took an inadvertent step back, bumping into Irene, who immediately took the lead. "Please, come in, Barbara. Did we have an appointment today?"

Barbara stepped into the foyer, clutching a handful of tissues to her reddened nose. "I hope this isn't a bad time."

Not if it kept us away from Gordon's Mortuary, it wasn't.

"Not at all," I assured her. "How can we help you?"

"I hadn't heard anything from Mr. Holmes, so I thought I'd stop by for an update on the case. I can't bear the thought of my sister being out there..." She sniffled, and her lower lip caught between her teeth while she struggled to maintain her composure.

"We completely understand." Irene steered her into the living room while I followed behind, wishing we could delay an update until we actually had one. Especially now that I knew she was lobbying Detective Lestrade to take over our job. We couldn't compete with law enforcement. After all, what did we have so far? Everything but Rebecca's body.

"The not knowing must be just awful," Irene continued. "I can't imagine. Can we get you anything?"

I didn't *have* anything except dry dog food, for those times when Toby paid a visit. There was no point in stocking a kitchen in a house where I didn't live.

Thankfully, Barbara shook her head. "I won't take up your time. I really would just like to know if you've learned anything that might help find my sister."

I expected another expression of solicitude from Irene, but that's not what I heard.

"We've learned that you're claiming 100 percent of your parents' estate," Irene said.

Barbara recoiled at the bluntness, the tissues halting partway to her nose. "Yes, I-I-I suppose that's true. But I told you I hadn't spoken to Rebecca in years. I mean, yes, I'm living in our parents' home, but I knew Rebecca had no intention of doing so."

"Was it Rebecca's intention to sue you for her half of the value?" Irene asked.

"My parents weren't wealthy people," she said. "We're not talking about millions of dollars. Just so you know."

"That's not an answer," Irene said. "Was your sister going to sue you?"

"I don't…" Barbara swallowed. "I really don't know."

I got the feeling she really *did* know but didn't want to say. Whether it was because she didn't want to speak ill of her dead sister or for more nefarious reasons, I wasn't sure.

"So, who inherits your sister's half now?" I asked.

Barbara licked her lips. "I do."

"Your *estranged* sister left you her half?" Irene asked.

Barbara looked distinctly uncomfortable. "Not exactly. It was a provision in our parents' will that if one sister outlived the other, the estate reverted to the living sister. At least, for a certain period of time after their passing."

"And how long was that period?"

Again with lip licking. "Five years."

Irene and I shared a look. By Barbara's own admission her mother had died almost five years ago. That provision was almost up. Fortunate timing for Barbara.

"I'm not sure where you're going with all these questions," she said, gathering her purse close to her chest in a protective gesture.

Since I was distinctly interested in learning what was in said purse, I switched gears to calm her nerves.

"Tell us how you chose Gordon's Mortuary," I said.

She seemed relieved at the change of subject. "You could say they chose me. Mr. Gordon contacted me and offered me a generous discount on his services. I guess they were having a sale of sorts."

A Blue Light Special on funerals?

"How did he even know about you?" Irene asked. "Did he say?"

She shrugged. "I assume he got the information from the morgue or something. To be honest, I didn't ask. I was just grateful for the kindness in my moment of need." Her voice caught at the end of that sentence, and she put the tissue up to her nose again.

Watson had specifically said he hadn't referred Gordon's to Barbara. I couldn't imagine it would go the other way. And I had to believe the staff would follow his standard of practice. Something felt off. Well, *everything* felt off. I didn't want corpses and drugs and criminal masterminds taking up space in my brain. Yet here I was, and here they were.

"I wish none of this had happened," Barbara murmured.

None of what? Her sister dying? The body disappearing? Or her complicity in all of it? I had to agree: I wish it hadn't happened too. Looking for a dead body wasn't my idea of a good time.

"I hope our questions didn't offend you," I said. "We're just following the process." As if we had one. "We never know what might lead to useful information," I added.

She nodded her understanding. "I just want Rebecca to be found."

It took another few minutes to assure her we were doing everything possible to that end, and then she packed up her tissues and left. We locked up and followed her out. A few minutes later we were on the road in Watson's BMW, with Irene rooting through the papers in the glove box.

"Barbara was pretty broken up back there." She pulled out the registration. "This baby isn't a lease. Watson owns it. Nice."

"Stop being so nosy," I told her. "Do you think her grief was genuine?"

"Hard to say. She could have taken sandpaper to her nose, right?"

"You think I'm being overly suspicious."

She glanced up from the pile of receipts in her lap. "There is no such thing. Especially with the timing of her sister's death."

"Convenient, right?" I asked.

"Too convenient." Irene shoved the receipts back into the glove box and slammed it shut. "But I'd still like to know how she got connected to Gordon's."

"Agreed."

I rolled to a stop at a red light and glanced in the review mirror at the gray sedan behind us.

"No way," I said, more to myself than my passenger.

Irene spun in her seat. "What?"

Shaggy sandy hair, big brown eyes behind clear glasses, and a self-confident smile that made me both want to be in on his little joke and smack the grin off his face all at the same time.

"It's *him*," I hissed.

"Him who?"

I squeezed the wheel, imagining it was his neck. "I told him to stop following me!"

Irene opened her visor mirror to take a more surreptitious look. "That guy behind us, cool glasses, needs a haircut?"

I nodded grimly. "That's him. Wiggins."

"Marty, you didn't tell me your stalker was cute!"

I shot her a look that could freeze a volcano. "Let's focus on the *stalker* part and not the *cute* bit, okay?"

The light changed. I fought the urge to stomp on the gas, instead letting the car accelerate gently, as if I hadn't noticed him on my bumper. "What should we do?"

"I have an idea. Keep driving, but don't go to the mortuary yet." She tapped a number into her phone. "I need an intervention," she told someone on the other end.

I mouthed *intervention?*

She held up a *one second* finger. "Tell me where you are, and I'll deliver the target."

Target? A frisson of alarm shivered through me.

Irene glanced at her watch. "Give me ten minutes. Thanks." She disconnected. "Head toward the Westfield Centre mall."

"Why? That's in the opposite direction from Gordon's."

"Because we need to shake Wiggins." She crossed her arms. "And he has to learn to respect boundaries."

I liked the sound of that. I headed toward the mall, remembering my conversation with Wiggins. "You know, he asked me about Sherlock Holmes. Details like where he went to school, where he lives, why there are no photos of him."

She waved it off. "I'll shore up Sherlock's bio. No worries."

I had worries, alright. Plenty of them. To begin with, what did Wiggins think he already knew that had him tracking us? Had he followed me to Tara's house? If he thought she was a suspect, would he make that public? How far would he go to uncover the details of Sherlock Holmes's life?

"There it is up there." Irene pointed. "Slow down a little. See that black Challenger?"

I saw it, crouched on the side of the road like a snarling jaguar.

She smiled. "This should be fun."

"Should I pull over?" I asked.

"No. Drive right past him. Be casual about it."

I cruised past the waiting Challenger with Wiggins following—not exactly tailgating us but making no effort to be discreet either.

As soon as we'd passed, the Challenger leaped into action, a blue light flashing on the dash. While I watched in the mirror, Wiggins' sedan slowed, pulled to the curb, and stopped. The Challenger nestled up behind him, and a hulking muscleman swaggered up to the driver's window.

"There." Irene sat back, pleased. "That'll keep him busy for a while. Now we can go talk to Dominic Gordon."

"Who is that?" I asked. "He's not going to kill him, is he?"

She laughed. "Not unless we want him to."

"Are you serious?"

"Marty." She touched my arm. "Relax. He's an actor friend who owes me a favor, that's all."

"Then what was with all that 'intervention' and 'target' stuff?"

She shrugged. "Okay, so maybe he's an actor who I met during a Jericho spy mission."

I blinked at her. "Spies? More explanation please."

She grinned again. "It's an urban gaming adventure. The game master gives you a 'mission' to track down a defective spy. Then you're outfitted with all kinds of cool spy gear and take off in teams around The City. Shinwell was on my team."

"Shinwell?" I asked. "Sounds like a prison nickname."

"Relax. Shinwell's harmless." She paused. "At least I'm pretty sure."

"Very comforting," I mumbled, gripping the wheel again as I pointed the car toward Gordon's Mortuary.

We drove on in silence the rest of the way while I gauged how comfortable I was with Irene's actor-slash-spy-games friend pulling Wiggins over under false pretenses. As long as he didn't really hurt the reporter, I decided I could live with it. In fact, I wouldn't mind putting him on the payroll if it kept Wiggins away from Sherlock Holmes and our investigation.

By the time we arrived at Gordon's, a brooding black cloud had snuffed out much of the day's light, threatening more rain. I chose to believe it was purely nimbostratus and not a prophetic omen. We had our choice of parking slots in the empty little lot and stepped out of the car into a stiff breeze scraping off the bay.

"Do you have the same weird feeling I do?" I asked.

"You mean kind of like a tingly electrical thing?" Irene asked. "Nope."

Just for that, I pushed her ahead of me into the foyer, where there was, once again, no sign of life. No phones ringing. No Muzak playing. Presumably the pink-cheeked old lady in Viewing Room Two had come and gone.

"How can this place afford to stay open?" I whispered.

"It's probably Vincent's money laundromat," Irene whispered back.

That tingly electrical feeling was back, fizzing through my veins.

The office door across the lobby flew open, and Dominic stuck his head out. "Can I—oh."

How could he have heard us whispering?

"Mr. Gordon." Irene grabbed my arm and pulled me over to him before he could duck back inside. You'd think he'd have been happy to see anyone who was vertical. "We'd like to ask you a few more questions."

"I'm busy right now," he said.

I looked over his shoulder into an empty office, with its empty desk and silent phone. Then I looked at him with raised eyebrows.

"Maybe I can spare a few minutes," he said, stepping aside so we could enter.

We sat on the lumpy cousins of the lobby furniture while he situated himself behind his desk with a lot of minute, precise adjustments. Watching him, I wondered again if he ever saw sunlight. His skin was so pale that it practically glowed. And not in a good way.

"How can I help you?" he asked when he was finally satisfied with the placement of his clenched hands on the crosshatching of tiny time-worn lines and divots on the desk blotter. For the first time, I noticed the wheeled microwave stand in the corner, repurposed as a computer stand holding an ancient looking ink-jet printer coated in a thin layer of dust.

"I'd like to ask you about Vincent Gordon," Irene said.

His fingers tightened into a white-knuckled prayer position. "And why's that?"

"Because he's an interesting guy," she said. "For instance, I find it interesting that he owns this mortuary."

"My brother's an entrepreneur," he said. "He has a diverse portfolio of businesses in several sectors, this being one of them."

"He owns other businesses too," I added.

Dominic cleared his throat loudly. "Yes. As, as I said, his portfolio is very diverse."

I was about to press when my phone chimed in with a text. I surreptitiously checked the screen. Watson. *What are you doing at Gordon's Mortuary?*

For a brief second I thought maybe Watson had a hidden camera in the room. Then I remembered—the GPS in his car. This was his idea of "keeping an eye on me."

*Planning my life celebration*, I shot back. Then I shut off the ringer.

"—public records of your brother's holdings," Irene was saying. "Which are fun to sift through, believe you me. Your brother has a lot of companies that own companies that own companies."

No reaction from Dominic.

"For example, the company pyramid was several deep before I found out he owns Lucky's Deli."

Again Dominic maintained his Vampire poker face. Not even a flinch.

"Care to discuss what goes on at Lucky's?" Irene prodded.

"I wouldn't know," he said through unmoving lips. "It's my brother's business."

"Really?" Irene pushed. "I would imagine you've met a fair amount of Lucky's customers. Or, should I say *former* customers? I bet you get a lot of ODs come through these doors."

Dominic's demeanor suddenly changed with that one. It was subtle, but his poker face went from nervous to on the offensive—eyes more intense, breathing slower, the hint of a sneer tugging at his lips, which told me he was envisioning us coming through his doors in a much more horizontal and professional capacity.

I slid my suddenly wet palms up and down my thighs, willing Irene to abort the conversation before she said something *really* insulting. Vincent Gordon was hardly up for citizen of the year, and the way Dominic was looking at Irene, I didn't think his brother was a whole lot better. If they'd made Rebecca disappear, what would they do to a couple of nosy pseudo detectives?

Dominic leveled unnervingly flat black eyes on her. "People from all walks of life come to us. Old. Young. Singers. Jane Does. Even detectives," he added.

"Is that a threat?" Irene asked, leaning forward.

My palms stopped sliding. My heart might have stopped for a second too. I had a bad feeling we were one question away from a contract on our heads. And I liked my head just where it was—attached to my very living body. I nudged Irene in the leg. No response.

Dominic's tiny smile was as chilling as the possibility that he went outdoors only after sundown. "Speculation is the orphan child of intellectual deficit."

Oh, great. Now the vampire was going all philosophical on us.

Irene's eyes narrowed. "Spock said that, right?" She smiled.

He stared at her. "I think it's time for you to leave. My family has got nothing to do with your...investigation." The word lingered between us, laced with disdain.

Irene uncrossed her legs and stood. "Yes, that's probably true. Unless you consider the fact that Rebecca Lowery's body was taken from your facility, on your watch. But that's got nothing to do with you either, right?"

He stood from his seat, stomped around the desk, and yanked open the door, his face finally showing some color. "I'll thank you to direct any future communication to my lawyer."

"Happy to," Irene shot back, marching to the outer door.

I followed a step behind, only pausing for a quick glance back over my shoulder at Dominic. He was seething, a total shift from the slimy, creepy guy we'd seen so far. His jaw was clenched, the veins in his neck bulging, hands balled into fists at his sides, and his knees were locked tight as if he was purposely forcing himself not to chase after us.

But as my gaze went lower, I felt a breath catch in my throat. Dominic's black outfit was spotless…except for his highly polished wingtips. Dried mud was spattered across the glossy surface of each. Soft, crumbling clay mud. There was no mud at the mortuary, just a small asphalt parking lot, a tiny patch of grass landscaped to perfection, and a two-bay garage to house the hearse and flower car.

But I knew where there was clay mud exactly like that. I'd been picking it out of my hair all the previous evening.

Lampley Park.

# CHAPTER TWELVE

———

Back in the parking lot, I yanked at Irene's sleeve. "Did you see his shoes?"

"Those muddy Bruno Magli knock-offs? So what?"

"Exactly!" I speared the air with my finger. "Muddy! There was mud all over them!"

"Probably from playing in cemeteries," Irene said. "Notice we never see any employees around? I bet this mortuary is a one-man operation. Creepy could be the mortician, the gravedigger, and the guy who knocked off the victims to begin with."

I tugged on her to keep her moving. "It's not a one-man operation. Vincent is part of it."

"Vincent." She snorted. "I'm guessing he's not a hands-on kind of guy."

I wouldn't be, either, if I had minions like his friend at the deli. We got into the car.

"The mud on Dominic's shoes is from Lampley Park."

Her eyebrows shot up. "Are you sure? I mean, it rained last night. There's mud all over."

I bit my lip. "True. I'd have to have the silt to clay rations of each analyzed to be certain. But I'm telling you it looks exactly the same. The same pale color, the same viscosity. Trust me. I got up close and personal with that mud last night."

"So you think Dominic Gordon is the one who attacked you?"

"I admit, he looks more like the blood-sucking type," I said. "But yes, the thought occurred to me."

"Well, he does have a temper," she said, thoughtful. "It's hidden beneath a few layers of pasty skin and moth-riddled suits, but we just saw that it's there. You just never know about the creepy undertaker types, do you."

"Be serious," I told her. "I think he was there." I pulled out of the parking lot, enjoying the smooth acceleration of Watson's car. Before we'd reached the traffic light, the ominous black cloud overhead slid away, revealing an afternoon awash in pastel watercolors. If I'd believed in omens, the timing would have freaked me out a little.

"Seems like a lot of people were there," Irene pointed out. "Watson, Wiggins, Tara." She paused. "You really sure Tara didn't hit you?"

I shook my head. "No, I don't think so."

"Why? Because she's a woman? This is the twenty-first century, Marty. Anyone can be a criminal these days."

I couldn't argue with that, since we seemed to be meeting a lot of them. "Granted, she won't win any personality contests," I said, "but I don't know if I see her whacking me over the head. That feels like more of a brute-force move."

"Okay," Irene said, "so, let's say it was Dominic who hit you. Why?"

"Maybe he didn't want me questioning Tara about Lucky's."

"So, you think Dominic Gordon hid Rebecca's body to conceal evidence of the Fluffy Bunny his brother peddles along with the coleslaw and dill pickles?"

I bit my lip. "Except there was no trace of drugs in Rebecca's system," I reminded her. "And she died from a fall, not an overdose."

Irene and I both fell silent, neither of us having a good theory to take that tidbit into account.

"What about Bryan Steele doing the walk of shame from Tara's place this morning?" Irene finally said, breaking the silence.

"What about it?" I asked.

"You know it's entirely possible we have two sets of bad guys here. Maybe Rebecca found out Bryan was cheating on her, they had an argument that got physical, and he pushed her into the counter."

"And the other set?"

"Recognizing Rebecca when she comes to the mortuary, and thinking someone might look for traces of Fluffy Bunny, the Gordon brothers dispose of the body."

I nodded. "It's possible."

"Let's face it—no one is getting a gold star for honesty in this case," Irene reasoned.

*Case* might be stretching it, but she had a point.

"Maybe we should talk to Steele again," I reluctantly suggested. Not that I wanted to talk to Steele. Steele scared me almost as much as the idea of Vincent and Dominic Gordon and their well-oiled body disposing setup.

"I don't have any meetings for another hour," Irene agreed.

"But maybe we should check the trunk for a tire iron first," I said as I headed for Bryan Steele's place. "Steele's a big man with a gun."

"Don't worry. We have the truth on our side."

"No offense," I said, "but I'd rather have the gun."

\* \* \*

I hadn't expected Bryan Steele to open the door to us, let alone invite us inside. A half hour later, he surprised me on both counts. Once inside, I half expected to find dorm room furniture or a bare mattress on the floor, but he had oddly good taste. The place was tidy, done in soft grays and blues. Four matching chrome and leather chairs were pushed against the wall, bringing to mind a small-scale poetry reading waiting to happen, with two plush leather recliners arranged in homage to a giant curved screen television accessorized with every electronic component known to man. And to Irene. She practically drooled as she took it all in.

Steele separated one of the bare bones chairs from the herd and sat facing us, his ankle crossed over his knee, his hands resting casually on his shin. He wore jeans and a long-sleeved green T-shirt, and he was barefoot. His buzz cut was damp. Once you got past the severe haircut and the square-jawed, suspicious-eyed face beneath it, he wasn't exactly bad looking. I could sort of get what women like Rebecca and Tara might see in him, especially if they were into men with testosterone overload. Looking at him, I tried to envision him in a fury shoving Rebecca into the granite countertop. It wasn't all that hard.

"You two have got to stop coming over here," he said. "My neighbors are going to think there's something kinky going on."

"Really?" Irene asked, tearing her gaze away from his home theater. "And what would Tara Tarnowski think?"

I'd hoped that he would register surprise like an ordinary human being. But he had the no-reaction cop face down pat.

"Don't try denying it," I added, although he hadn't. "You were seen leaving her place early this morning."

"Oh, golly gee, was I?" He had sarcasm down pat. "Well, isn't that embarrassing." He cocked his head, appraising me. "You should've said something when you saw me. It might have gotten interesting."

Just as I'd thought, he'd been eavesdropping on my conversation with Tara. My already shallow opinion of him drained a little bit more. "I might have," I shot back, "if you hadn't been *hiding* in another room."

"Look." He pushed up his sleeves, the better to intimidate us with his Popeye forearms. "It's not like either one of us is married. No animals were harmed. No laws were broken."

"Did Rebecca know you were cheating on her?" Irene asked.

"What is it with you two?" This time he couldn't hold a neutral face. He couldn't hold a neutral anything. It was like he suddenly deflated, all the rebellion gone. "*I* cheated on *her*?" He snorted. "That's rich."

I frowned at him. "What are you saying?"

"I'm saying you got it way wrong." He lowered his head, preoccupied with the cuff of his jeans, quiet for a moment before he cleared his throat and spoke in a more subdued voice. "Rebecca was seeing someone behind my back, alright? *She* cheated on *me* first."

Despite his obvious discomfort, that seemed convenient to me. "How do you know that?" I asked.

He looked up. "I'm a cop, remember?"

I just stared at him. In the kitchen, the hum of the refrigerator fell silent, as if eavesdropping. Beside me, Irene remained motionless, waiting.

"I know it, alright?" He sighed. "I thought we had a good thing going. An exclusive thing, you know? Finding out I wasn't enough for her wasn't great for my ego. I've got my pride. I'm like any other guy."

Any other guy with a badge, a gun, and a temper.

"Did you confront Rebecca?" Irene asked.

"Worse."

Irene and I exchanged a glance. What could be worse? Murder? Was he about to confess to murdering Rebecca?

Steele was back to picking at his cuff, his face expressionless, which made him impossible to read. He might as well be working from a script he'd prepared ahead of time in case he'd be facing questions. "I'll admit it wasn't the mature thing to do," he said, "but I kind of lost it when I found out. I wanted to hurt her the way she had hurt me…" He hesitated, regrouping. "Rebecca had complained to me plenty about Tara, so hooking up with her seemed like the best revenge."

"Yeah, that's much better than talking it out with Rebecca," Irene said.

His eyes lifted slowly to bore into hers. "Guys don't *talk it out*. We take action."

I was still chewing on the casual *wanted to hurt her* remark. "So you knew Tara and Rebecca couldn't stand each other," I said. "You were deliberately trying to upset her."

"That's the point of revenge, Sister Theresa," he snapped. "It's supposed to be *hurtful*."

But had it gone beyond hurtful to homicidal?

"If Tara was just for revenge, why are you still seeing her?" Irene asked. "Now that Rebecca's dead, I mean."

He shrugged. "Turns out Tara's not so bad, actually. I kinda like her."

Having seen Tara's generous cup size, I could guess what it was he liked.

"Who did Rebecca cheat on you with?" I asked. While I still wasn't sure I 100 percent believed him, it felt like another party was suddenly thrown in the mix. If Rebecca had been seeing someone on the sly, maybe that someone didn't want anyone to find out and killed her.

He scowled at me as if he'd caught me doing a hundred in a school zone. "Don't know, and it doesn't much matter. When I found a pair of boxers at her place, she couldn't very well deny it."

Okay, that bordered uncomfortably on TMI.

"You said you slept with Tara out of revenge…I'm guessing that means you didn't hide it from Rebecca."

He narrowed his eyes at me. "That would kinda defeat the purpose, wouldn't it."

"Is that what you were arguing about with Rebecca at the theater the week before she died?" I asked.

Bryan turned his gaze on me. At first I thought he'd deny it, but finally he nodded. "She was pretty pissed." Instead of looking pleased, he looked almost sad.

"Well, what did you expect?" Irene asked

"Sue me," he said, turning on her. "I've got feelings too. Haven't you ever had someone cheat on you?"

Irene shook her head. "No. But if he did, I'd break up with him. I wouldn't play juvenile games with him."

His smirk was taunting. "What's it feel like to be so perfect?"

"One last question," I cut in before Irene could answer that. I could feel her hackles going up. "Where were you when Rebecca died?"

"As if it's any of your business, but I was with Tara."

Convenient. Our two best suspects just happened to be each other's alibis.

\* \* \*

I dropped Irene off in the Mission for a VC meeting to back a restaurant that served only gluten-free, fat-free, casein-free, cruelty-free, sustainably farmed, organic raw food. Then I made my way to Stanford for a shift of serving caffeine-laden, fatty, buttery, chocolaty, creamy coffees and pastries at the coffee bar. The afternoon crowd was relentless, being close to midterms, which gave me little time to think about the case. I wasn't sure if that was a good or bad thing, as my mind ran circles around the sparse facts we knew so far. The truth was, Rebecca hadn't seemed particularly loved by the people in her life. And any one of them could have had a potential reason to want her dead.

"Hey, Marty," Pam said, coming up behind me as I knelt behind the counter, restocking the bakery case during a much-needed lull mid-shift. "Guess what? I'm in love."

I took the tray of muffins she handed over. "Mr. Leather?"

Her nose wrinkled. "No. I'm totally over him. Turns out he's too old for me. He's almost thirty."

"Wow. Ancient," I mumbled, calculating the precious months I had left before I became "too old."

"Anyway, he came in yesterday, and I think he was flirting with me."

"Really? Can you pass me the doughnuts?" I asked. "What's his name?"

She paused. "You know, I forgot to ask." She slid the tray into the case herself, her fingers flying like hummingbird wings as she arranged the pastries.

"He a student here?"

She shrugged.

I narrowed my eyes at her. "Do you know anything about him?"

She bit her lip. "I guess I did most of the talking. He was a great listener. He wanted to know all about the bookstore, the coffee bar, you, Alberta…"

"Wait—me?" I stood, my internal radar pricking up.

She nodded. "Like I said, he was a great listener."

"What did you tell him?"

She gave me a blank look. "I dunno. Just stuff."

"You told a stranger 'stuff' about me?" I loved Pam, but *too trusting* was like her motto in life.

"Don't worry. He was, like, totally a nice guy."

"What did this *nice* guy look like?"

Pam's face broke into a grin, and she pulled out her phone. "I took a selfie of us."

I took one look at the screen and thought a really dirty word. I'd know that self-confidant grin, taunting me from next to the image of Pam leaning over the pastry case, anywhere. Wiggins.

"That is *not* a nice guy, Pam," I told her.

"You know him?" She blinked at me.

"I know he's bad news."

She looked at the photo. "Come on. He's so cute. How could he be bad news?"

I thought about telling her, but knowing Pam, it was best to just let this crush play out. Chances were by nightfall she'd be in love with another guy anyway.

"Just do me a favor. If he comes back, don't talk about me." I paused. "And don't tell him where I live!"

She grinned and rolled her eyes. "Give me some credit, Marty."

I tried on a daily basis, but it usually boomeranged back.

While she took over refilling the napkins and swizzle sticks, I took the moment of quiet to check my phone. Five more texts from Watson had silently come in since I'd shut off the ringer. Two telling me to stay away from Dominic. Two had come in while we were at Bryan Steele's place, asking what was in the Richmond District. And one asking me if I was ignoring him. The boy caught on fast.

As much as I liked having wheels—and precision performance ones at that—it was time to ditch the GPS babysitter.

I sent off a text to Watson. *Car is at Stanford.*

A minute later his response came in. *I know.*

Duh. GPS monitor. *I can drive it to you after work.*

It took a couple of minutes for the response to pop in this time. *Don't bother. I'm already here.*

Here? As in, *here* here?

That question was answered as I looked down to find Watson on the ground floor of the bookstore, making his way up to the coffee bar. And, from the looks of the tension in his shoulders and set of his jaw, he wasn't happy.

I did a little one-finger wave in his direction as he approached.

"Hey," I said.

"Why have you been ignoring me?"

Wow, cutting right to the chase, huh?

"I haven't been ignoring you. I've been…busy."

He glanced around at the empty coffee bar and raised an eyebrow my way.

"Well, I was busy. You know, investigating stuff. And then here. When there were customers here. But there are not now, clearly. Which is why I got back to you." I held up my phone, as if the text thread proved my point.

Watson sighed, running a hand over his jaw. Unshaven, I noticed. As if he'd been up too late last night thinking about a certain blonde who kept getting herself into trouble and making him hot under the collar. Or maybe I was reading too much into it.

"What were you doing at Dominic Gordon's mortuary again today?" he asked.

I bit my lip. "Investigating."

"I thought we agreed to leave that up to Sherlock Holmes."

"*We* didn't agree on anything. You asked me to leave it to Sherlock. I said I'd talk to him."

"Did you?"

"Yes?" Only it sounded more like a question.

He shot me a hard look. "Did you at least call Lestrade to report the attack?"

"Sort of?"

"How do you sort of call someone?"

"Fine." I threw my hands up. "No, I did not call Lestrade, and, no, I did not talk to Sherlock Holmes," I said, spitting the hated name out a little harder than I'd meant to. "And you want to know why?"

Watson crossed his arms over his chest. "Why?"

"Because I'm not some damsel in distress. I am a private investigator. And I know what I'm doing." Big words from someone who (a) was not an investigator and (b) had no idea what she was doing. But I stood my feminist ground anyway, matching his crossed arms with a mirrored posture of my own.

"Marty, you're being ridiculous."

"Really? My job is ridiculous?"

Watson shook his head. "No, I'm not making any comments about your job or your abilities. And," he added as I opened my mouth to protest, "before you get the wrong idea, I'd be giving the same speech to you if you were a man."

I snorted. "I doubt that."

Watson frowned. "Okay, fine, I probably wouldn't be quite as personally invested in your well-being if that were true."

I paused. Was that a roundabout way of saying he liked me?

"But, I'm just asking you to be careful," he added. "Take proper precautions. Don't go running around town accusing people of crimes that may or may not even exist."

I bit my lip again. He had a good point. We were running down a supposed killer for a death that very well might have been an accident after all.

"Fine," I conceded. "I'll be careful."

"Thank you," he said, his voice softer. More tender. He took a step toward me, and suddenly all I could focus on were his pouty lips inching toward mine

"Hey, Marty!"

Watson took a step back, suddenly creating a void between us. I reluctantly swiveled to find Pam hailing me from behind the counter, where a line had formed.

I turned an apologetic gaze back to Watson. "I have to go."

He nodded. "Duty calls" was his rueful reply.

"Thanks." I paused. "But take your car back. I'll be fine."

The look on his face said he didn't 100 percent believe that. Truth be told? Neither did I. But I wasn't about to confess that to him.

# CHAPTER THIRTEEN

———

After my shift, I grabbed an Uber to 221 Baker Street. Not that I was looking forward to hanging out in the cold, dark death trap, but the sky looked like it was threatening rain again, and I wanted to make sure my tarp had held after last night's downpour. The last thing I needed was a swimming pool in my master bedroom. I'd just tossed my bag down on the Victorian's entry table, when my cell vibrated with a call. I fished it out of my pocket, expecting to see Watson's name again, but when I checked the ID, I did a surprised double take.

"Mr. Bitterman? Are you alright?" I asked, quickly answering it.

"Martha Hudson?" He was using the senior citizen whisper, which was loud enough to be heard in the next room at Windsor Castle. "Where are you? You have to come rescue me."

Fear ran an icy hand down my spine. I'd meant to check on him earlier. Had something happened? "Did you fall? Are you hurt? You need to call 9-1-1."

"I'm not going to die in some hospital," he whisper-shouted. "All they want to do with us old folks is give us pills and enemas. I've got some good years left in me, as long as I stay away from doctors."

"But if you fell—" I began.

"Martha Hudson, will you listen to me?"

Like I had a choice. If I put my phone on speaker, the whole block could listen to him.

"It's that old bat, Edna Frist," he said, his so-called whisper now tinged with irritation. "She's gone and parked her liver spots in front of my door like some dusty traffic cop. She's got me trapped in my own home!"

"Is that all?" I felt my shoulders sag with relief.

"Is that all?" he shouted. "I'm supposed to be taking my fish eye casserole up to Mrs. Streelman's for dinner. It's a dish that can't be served cold!"

My eyes closed, my nose wrinkled, and my stomach turned all at the same time. "Fish eye…?" I swallowed the bitter taste that crawled up my throat. "You just call it that, right? You don't mean real fish eyes."

"Sure I do," he said. "I just discovered them. It's amazing what you can find in Chinatown. It doesn't smell too good, but with all those eyes looking back at you, you hardly notice that."

I was fairly sure I'd notice.

"What do you want me to do?" I asked. *And please don't let it be taste testing the casserole.*

"I want you to dial Edna's phone number," he said. "When she leaves to answer it, I'll be able to make my escape."

This almost made me wish I was home, with a front row seat. "Two problems," I said. "What if she doesn't hear it, and what if she doesn't want to answer it?"

"She'll hear it," he said. "She's got the darned thing set so loud that Abe Orgeron hears it downstairs. And she'll answer it because she can't stand not knowing something."

"What am I supposed to say to her?"

"Don't ask me," he said. "Talk about your fingernails or brassieres. You know, girl talk."

No wonder all the old ladies had their eyes on him.

"Okay, give me the number," I said. "And just so you know, I'll do my best to stall her, but I won't be held responsible if she catches you."

"I'm way ahead of you there," he said. "I can move like quicksilver in these new running shoes. I got gel insoles. Hold on. Where'd I put it?" I heard papers rustling. "It's 1-800-Old Biddy," he said and let out a cackle that dissolved into a coughing fit.

"Your casserole is getting cold," I told him.

"What? Oh." More rustling. "Here it is." He read it off. "Give me three minutes to pack up the casserole. I owe you, Martha Hudson."

Just so long as he didn't pay me back in food.

I disconnected but kept my phone out as I made my way upstairs to the master bedroom, praying my tarp had staved off most of the recent rains. The room was damp but not bad. The ceiling looked a bit soggy, but the wood floors seemed to be damage free. It wasn't as if the plaster walls could get any flimsier. I gingerly touched the far one. It crumbled in my hand like papier-mâché. Okay, I stood corrected.

I checked my phone and saw that five minutes had passed since Bitterman's call. I dialed Mrs. Frist's number. It rang, and rang some more, and just when I was ready to give up, her impatient voice shrilled in my ear. "Yes, who is it?"

"Mrs. Frist, it's Marty Hudson."

"You can come out of there now," she said. "I heard him talking to you."

"I'm not in the building," I said. "I'm not even in the neighborhood. I wanted to ask you—"

"He thinks I don't know what he's up to," she groused. "When I heard him perfectly well. He's making fish gut stew for you."

Somehow, that sounded even worse than the real thing.

It suddenly dawned on me I had nothing to say to keep her on the line while Mr. Bitterman and his gel insoles sneaked up two flights of stairs to Mrs. Streelman's apartment. Until I had a sudden stroke of inspiration. "Mrs. Frist, could I ask for your help with Dr. Watson?"

That knocked her right off her rant. "You mean that handsome young man who gave you his car? Is he coming to call on you again?"

"Around seven o'clock," I said, fingers firmly crossed. "And I may be late. Do you think you could entertain him until I get there?"

"Well, this is awfully short notice, but I suppose I could." She sounded pleased, and maybe a little excited. "I know. I'll bake some cookies. What kind does he like? Never mind. Everyone likes sugar cookies. But you do know this is very bad form. It's rude to be late when a gentleman calls on a lady."

"I'm having my hair done," I said. "And I have to pick up my clothes at the cleaner's." I glanced at my watch. By my calculation, Mr. Bitterman had had a nine-minute head start. If she caught him on the landing, he had no one but himself and Dr. Scholl's to blame.

"…will teach the old goat," Mrs. Frist was muttering, mostly to herself.

Uh-oh. I had the feeling I'd just missed something important. "What will you teach the old goat?" I asked. "I mean, Mr. Bitterman?"

"Seeing me on the arm of a younger man. *That* will teach him not to take me for granted."

My romantic life flashed before my eyes, and it was less exciting than Mrs. Frist's. If she were sixty years younger, I'd have a real fight on my hands for Watson.

"Please don't go out of your way," I told her. "It's possible Dr. Watson will have something come up at work and have to cancel at the last minute. He has a very demanding job."

"You young people." She *tsked* in my ear. "You never slow down. We're not here forever, Martha. Stop and smell the—what was that?" A beat of silence pulsed through the line. "I hear voices in the hallway. The old goat might be trying to give me the slip. Don't worry. Your young man will be in good hands." She hung up on me.

That was what I was afraid of. While I was standing there wondering if I should ask Watson to avoid my apartment for the foreseeable future, a text buzzed through my phone. Irene had finished her meeting.

Perfect timing. I couldn't take much more of the humiliation of not measuring up against an octogenarian in the romance department. I told her to meet me at the Victorian.

\* \* \*

"You look worried," Irene told me as she sank down into a wooden chair in my kitchen twenty minutes later. "What's going on?"

I handed her a cup of tea (I was proud to say I'd acquired tea bags in my kitchen!) and gave her the abbreviated version of my participation in Mr. Bitterman's great escape. "I'm afraid he didn't make it," I said.

She laughed. "Worried you'll get home to find Mr. Bitterman missing and fish eyes all over the stairs?"

"Or Mrs. Frist trying to seduce Watson with sugar cookies," I said.

Irene snorted. "I'd almost pay to see that."

I shot her a look. "What I want to hear is Barbara Bristol *paying us* for finding her sister." I paused. "If it rains inside my house again, I'm afraid the walls might just give up in surrender."

Irene cast a glance at the ceiling above her. "Comforting," she mumbled.

"Look, I agree there were people in Rebecca's life who might have wanted her dead."

"A *lot* of people," Irene mumbled again.

"A *few* people. But right now they're all irked at us, and we're no closer to finding Rebecca's body. Which is what we were really hired to do."

Irene nodded. "Agreed. Okay, so where do we look?"

I looked down into my teacup. "Well…"

Irene narrowed her eyes. "Oh no. Don't say it."

"Gordon's *is* the last place she was seen."

Irene closed her eyes and said a bad word. "I told you not to say it."

"It only makes sense," I argued. "Trust me. I do not want to go back there any more than you do—"

"I doubt that."

"—but the Gordons are definitely crooked—"

"That I don't doubt."

"—and she definitely disappeared under their watch." I paused. "Plus, there's something else that I've been thinking about since we left Bryan Steele's place."

"What?" Irene asked, toying with her teabag.

"Well, Bryan said he knew Rebecca was cheating on him. What if the guy she was seeing was Vincent Gordon?"

Irene blinked at me. "Wow. That would be a twist."

"But it's possible. I mean, we know she was at Lucky's Deli. Maybe it wasn't for the Fluffy Bunny after all but to see Vincent."

"So, she gets in an argument with Vincent at her place," Irene said, following my train of thought. "Maybe over her ex, Mr. Bad Cop."

"Or Vincent's drug dealing," I added.

"The argument gets out of hand, and Vinny pushes her into the countertop. To make sure it goes down as an accident, he gets his brother to contact the next of kin and plans to cremate the body."

"Only when he finds out Rebecca wanted a real viewing, he panics, worried some evidence of his crime might be on display."

"And he has Dominic switch her out," Irene finished.

"So where is the body now?"

Irene pursed her lips together. "You know, we never actually searched the mortuary for Rebecca's body."

I was loathe to admit it, knowing where she was going with this, but…"No, we didn't."

"I doubt Barbara Bristol did either."

"Why would she? At the time she believed the worst thing Dominic could have told her was that her sister was missing from the mortuary. She had no reason to suspect he was lying."

"Neither would the police," Irene reasoned. "I mean, Barbara said they didn't sound like this was a high priority for them. Chances are, not high enough to do more than call and take Dominic's word for it."

"Everyone has been relying on his word," I mused.

"Which doesn't seem all that reliable to me."

"Agreed." I paused. "But please don't tell me you're thinking what I think you're thinking."

Irene cocked her head at me and frowned. "Hey, you're the one who said it was the last place she'd been seen."

"Me and my big mouth."

"And what better place to hide a dead body than among dead bodies?"

I hated to admit she had a point. "How would we even get in?"

She grinned. "Leave it to me."

"Breaking and entering a mortuary." I shook my head. "How has my life come to this?"

"Relax. It's really just an office building."

"With dead people in it!"

"Think of them as sleeping."

"This just feels wrong."

"Lots of things feel wrong until they feel right," she said. "Look on the bright side. We could earn Barbara's check tonight."

As if on cue, I felt raindrops start to come down from that threatening sky. Only I was inside. And on the first floor.

Irene and I both looked up to see a new leak had formed around the glass light. Well, that couldn't be good for my ancient electrical.

I sighed. "Fine. You win. Pick me up at ten?"

"Just think—it'll be a story for your kids someday," Irene said.

As if I'd ever speak of this night again.

\* \* \*

Surprisingly, there were no fish eyes scattered on the landing when I got home to change into what Irene had called "inconspicuous black." The lack of fish parts could only mean Mr. Bitterman and his toxic casserole had made it safely up to Mrs. Streelman's apartment. And the hallway outside his apartment was clear, which could only mean Mrs. Frist had packed up her folding chair and gone home to bake sugar cookies for Watson. I managed to slip into my apartment without alerting her or attracting 2B, which seemed like a promising start to the night.

I rummaged in the near-bare cupboards and managed to find bread and peanut butter, which coupled with a diet Coke (for me) and a can of Alpo (for Toby) made for dinner. I tried to watch a couple of DVRed shows to pass the time, but all I could find were crime dramas, which only managed to ratchet up my nerves even further.

By the time ten o'clock rolled around, I was strung more tightly than the Union Square Christmas tree as I assessed my reflection in the mirror. Black jeans, black sweater, and black low-heeled boots. I looked ready for a hipster coffeehouse or a breaking and entering. I really wished my evening plans included the first one. I might talk a good Sherlock game, but I wasn't sure I could walk it. Especially if that walk included lock picking. I swept some blusher on my cheeks and a single coat of mascara, just in case I had to look presentable for a mug shot. I considered the flat iron before deciding to go full-on ninja with a black knit cap, pulled down low. Hat head wouldn't be the worst thing in the world. Besides, a hat meant less chance of shedding hairs whose DNA could later be used to identify me. That sort of thing happened all the time on TV. *It would have been the perfect crime, if it hadn't been for that single dog hair found at the scene, tracked back to the perpetrator, whom witnesses reported seeing walking her dog in the vicinity.*

I cast a suspicious eye on Toby. He went utterly still, staring back at me with eyes that said *I've never been anywhere near that sweater. I swear it.*

Just in case, I found a roll of tape in my kitchen junk drawer, ripped off a length, and pressed it over every reachable inch of myself to remove all hairs of any origin. Possibly I was taking things a little too far, but people had gone to prison for life due to some small overlooked detail. I didn't know the sentencing guidelines for what we were about to do, but I didn't intend to find out.

I poured some dry food into a bowl for Toby, gave him some fresh water, slipped my smallest cross-body bag over my head, and headed for the door, unable to put it off any longer.

As soon as I opened my door, my heart jumped, and I let out a little yip.

Wiggins leaned against the wall in the hallway, munching on a sugar cookie, the very picture of the casual stalker. He still had that windblown, slightly-too-long hair, curling at the ends as it brushed the shoulders of his black hoodie. Broad shoulders, I noticed. Wider and stronger-looking in the light than they had appeared as shadows in the park the day before. Geek Chic frequented the gym?

"Good," he said, ignoring my surprise at seeing him. "You're home. Got a minute?" He brushed past me into the apartment without waiting for a response.

Toby stuck his head around the corner, growling low in his throat.

"Good boy," I told him.

Toby gave me a *no problem, I got your back* look and went back to his snack.

"Nice building. Love the neighbors." Wiggins popped the last of his cookie into his mouth. "Lady down the hall said she baked these cookies for your date tonight, but he never showed." He paused. "You get stood up?"

I glared at Wiggins. "What are you doing here?" I demanded. "I told you to stop following me. How did you find out where I live?"

He grinned. "You're not exactly hard to find." He glanced around. "I've got to be honest, though. I figured your place would be a lot nicer. Sherlock doesn't pay much, huh?"

"What do you want?"

"What's that smell?" he asked, ignoring me.

Mr. Bitterman. I hadn't even noticed the aroma seepage through the wall or under the door or however it had oozed into my apartment.

"Never mind," I snapped. "I'm not giving you a story."

Wiggins cocked his head at me. "You know, I'm having a hard time figuring why."

"'Why?'" I blinked at him, not understanding the question.

"Yeah, why doesn't Sherlock Holmes want the press? I mean, the guy *is* taking on new clients, right?"

"Um, I guess…" I hedged.

"And I haven't exactly given him bad press in the past, have I?"

"Well, not exactly…"

"In fact, I'd venture to guess his name is a whole lot more well known now than before my article."

"Maybe…"

"So, why doesn't he want the world to know more about him?" Wiggins crossed his arms over his chest, the last sentence more of a dare than a question.

I licked my lips, choosing my words very carefully, lest they go viral by morning. "He...uh...doesn't like to comment on a case before it's closed."

Wiggins stood very still, and I couldn't tell if he believed me or was waiting for me to crack and spill more. "You mean the Disappearing Diva?" he finally asked.

I nodded. "Yep. We're, uh, still working on it."

"So, when it's finished, he'd happily give me an interview then?"

"Oh, wow, well, gee, I'd have to check his schedule..."

He pursed his lips together, arms still crossed. "Huh."

I swallowed hard. This guy had a way of saying a thousand words with just his myopic stare.

"Alright," he finally said, pulling out a chair at my kitchen table and sitting himself down. "Sounds like we better solve this case quickly so I can get my story then, huh?"

"Uh...we? No, no, no. We are not a *we*."

"We could help each other."

"I work alone."

"What about Irene?"

"*We* work alone."

"With Sherlock Holmes."

"Right. With him too." I paused. Why did I always feel like I was saying more than I meant to around this guy? "Look, I'm on my way out," I told him.

"Yeah, you look nice." His eyes drifted from my head to my feet. "Black looks good on you."

I blinked. Was that compliment or another dare?'

"Uh, thanks. It's slimming."

He grinned. "Too much fun at that Buttercream bakery?"

"No!" Hey, I'd only had two muffins today, and they'd both been banana walnut. Fruit and nuts were healthy, right? "Look, I'm late," I lied.

I walked to the front door and opened it, hoping he'd get the clue.

He stood and shrugged, a self-satisfied smile still on his face. "Where are you off to?"

"None of your business."

"That hot date?"

"No."

"I bet it's with that ME."

"I'm not going on a date!"

"Secret spy stuff then?" he mocked as I locked the door behind us.

"Yep. Lots of it."

"You know I'll just follow you and find out anyway, right?"

I did, which was incredibly unnerving considering what we had planned.

A noxious smell wafted our way as Bitterman opened his door.

"Martha Hudson, I thought I heard you out here! Just in time for a late dinner." He paused, taking in Wiggins. "And you brought a man along."

"I did!" I responded enthusiastically, seeing a way out. I pushed the reporter forward. "This is Wiggins. He's…a friend."

I heard a snort from behind Mrs. Frist's door.

"Well, lucky I made extra!" Bitterman said. "Come on in."

Shoving Wiggins ahead of me, I made it as far as Bitterman's foyer before I smacked myself on the forehead dramatically. "Oh my gosh, I'm so sorry, Mr. Bitterman, but I completely forgot. I have an appointment to get to."

Wiggins shot me a look. "Yeah, and I have to—"

"*He* has to tell you how much he's been admiring the smells coming from your place," I jumped in. "Right, Wiggins?"

"Actually, I—"

"Well, I gotta run. Enjoy the meal, Wiggins!" I jumped back across the threshold before either man could stop me. As I closed the door behind me, I could just make out Mr. Bitterman's voice.

"You're in good hands," Mr. Bitterman told him. "My fish eye casserole didn't go over so well, but I came up with a new recipe, and you can be my first taste tester. Do you like eel?"

Poor Wiggins. I almost felt bad.

Almost.

* * *

"Why did we have to do this in the middle of the night when it's so dark?" I whispered, kneeling at the mortuary's back door, beneath the unnecessary added shade of a portico. The chill of the damp fog curled around me like tentacles. While I'd been dressing myself up like the angel of death hipster, I'd forgotten a jacket.

"It's barely eleven o'clock, Marty." Irene glanced over her shoulder. She'd gone with black sweats and running shoes and still managed to look chic. Her hair was pulled back in a ponytail. No earrings or makeup. She looked stunning. "But you're right," she added. "It *is* dark."

"Unnervingly dark." We'd been afraid to turn on our flashlight apps, for fear of nosy neighbors calling the police about prowlers. Which made it all the more difficult to pick the lock. Not that I was an expert in the field, but I had sat in on a locksmith training seminar last year after accidentally locking myself out of my apartment for the third time. If the mortuary had a more sophisticated model, I'd have given up and broken a window. Lucky for me, their security was about as outdated as their decor.

"How much longer," Irene asked, dancing from foot to foot in the damp.

"Almost there…" Something clicked, and the door cracked open. Relief surged through me. "Got it."

Irene entered ahead of me, quickly moving to the alarm keypad, where she used her phone and some fancy app to run a set of numbers on her screen. Then she punched in a key code, and the alarm went into sleep mode. She turned and grinned at me. "Told you this place's security was child's play."

"I never doubted you for a moment."

"Come on. I don't want to be here all night," she said, shutting the door behind us.

I didn't want to be there at all.

I rested my fingertips against Irene's back as I followed her inside, not breaking contact as we moved through a plain galley kitchen, down a hall beneath the eerie red glow of an *Exit* sign, and into the foyer, thinking that nothing ever looked the same in the dark. That grandfather clock, stately in the daylight, now loomed as a menacing silhouette. An ordinary coatrack, with its multitude of spindly arms, was now a malevolent *War of the Worlds* creature.

My swallow was audible. "I don't think I can do this," I whispered. "This place is spooky."

"Don't be silly," she said. "Remember, it's just an office. Now where does he keep the dead people?"

That made me feel much better.

We left the foyer for another even darker room, one without windows and (maybe it was just me) oxygen. It felt increasingly harder to fill my lungs with anything other than dust and mustiness.

"Listen," Irene said suddenly. "What is that?"

A spear of panic shot through me. "What? What do you hear?"

"I think it's the *Addams Family* theme."

"Seriously?" I snapped. "Is this situation not ridiculous enough for you as it is?"

Irene giggled. "Lighten up, Marty. It could be worse."

"We've broken into a *funeral home*," I told her. "How could it be worse?"

"It could be a cemetery."

I didn't even *want* to go there.

"I can't see a thing," I whispered. Irene had moved beyond the reach of my groping fingers, so I stretched my left arm to the side and touched a cold, hard surface. With…was that a lock?

Oh. No.

"Irene!" I hissed. "There are *caskets* in here!"

"There *are*?" Her voice was disembodied, floating from somewhere ahead of me. "That's really strange—caskets in a funeral home."

I rolled my eyes, not that she could see me.

"Don't worry, Marty. They're empty." She paused, shining the flashlight app on her cell phone under her chin, transforming her face into a ghoulish mask. "Or are they?"

I looked away. "Very funny."

"Hey." Suddenly she was next to me. "You're really spooked, aren't you."

"Let's just get this over with, alright?"

She swept the light from side to side, revealing a nightmare. We were in a casket showroom. They ringed the walls, sitting both on the floor and on biers. Just looking at them made me shiver, even if they did come with sanitized curb appeal names like Bronze Eternity Cushion and Platinum Slumber Pillow. I didn't want to even think about my earthly remains spending eternity in a box named after a cheap mattress set.

Suddenly Irene doused the light. "Did you hear something?"

"No, I don't hear the *Addams Family* theme," I said impatiently.

"I'm not kidding this time," she whispered.

I strained to listen, hearing only oppressive silence. Except for…what was that exactly?

"There it is again!" she whispered. "It's really faint. Hear it?"

"A kind of scratchy sound? I think it's coming from the kitchen. You don't suppose Gordon *lives* here, do you?"

"There's apartment space upstairs," Irene said. "But…"

But? But what? But it was vacant? But it was soundproofed?

A very faint tinkling sound came from the hallway. The sound of keys, or loose change in a pocket?

"It's getting closer," Irene hissed. "Hide!"

Hide where? Where did she think we were? There was nowhere to hide.

"Do it!" She gave me a shove before leaping into the nearest casket and lowering the lid.

Oh, no. Oh, no, no, no. There was no way I was…

Another tinkle, this time just outside the room.

I dove for the Bronze Eternity Cushion, pulling the lid down after me. It was surprisingly comfortable, if not exactly roomy. I didn't move and barely breathed, eyes squeezed shut because even though I couldn't *see* the casket around me, I was all too aware it was there. I lay frozen in the utter darkness, listening, picturing Dominic Gordon creeping around in the dark. Imagining him casting his black Prince of Darkness eyes around the room, deducing the significance of the two lidded caskets in a room full of convertibles, and fastening the locks so he could easily deliver us to the police. Or worse. Right at that moment, the police were the best-case scenario. I didn't want to think about the worst.

Another few seconds passed during which the only sound I heard was my hammering heart. Could I get a signal on my cell phone from inside this— From where I was? I could text Irene, ask if she heard anything. Admittedly, texting wouldn't be the easiest thing to do, since I couldn't lift my arms more than a few inches. Could you text 9-1-1? Maybe it would be better to confess to breaking and entering than to spend the night inside this— Where I was.

Suddenly a terrible thought came to me. What if caskets were airproof? I remembered an anthropology class I'd ducked into about burial customs and practices, during which I'd learned that people used to be buried with bells extending from within the casket to above the ground, to forestall the possibility of being buried alive. But what about the air supply for the inhabitant of the casket then awaiting exhumation? How long might that last before the bell ringing became a moot point?

Oh, boy. That line of thought wasn't doing me any good. In fact, it was making me panic. My heart pounded, and my breathing shallowed, barely expanding my chest with each inhale. If I wasn't careful, I would hyperventilate. I had to think happier thoughts. Warm summer days. Soft cuddly kittens. Sexy hard-bodied medical examiners.

Well, *that* wasn't going to slow my breathing.

I gave myself a mental shake. If I was going to pretend to be a detective, then I was going to have to pretend to be brave. I had no choice. We couldn't stay where we were. If Dominic

Gordon was waiting us out, so be it. We'd just have to deal with the consequences.

Besides, I was uncomfortably hot, which probably meant I was running out of air. These things weren't designed for occupancy. If I didn't do *something*, Dominic Gordon was going to find two new clients when he got to work in the morning.

I shoved the lid open with all my force and sat up, gasping.

A fat black and white cat sat on top of Irene's closed casket, batting a jingly toy mouse around. It paused to turn luminous green eyes on me.

"Meow," it said.

*   *   *

"A cat," I grumbled as we made our way down the hall. "I jumped into a coffin to hide from a *cat*."

"Seriously!" Irene said. Then she paused. "Though, some cats can be really ill-tempered."

I shot her a look, not sure if she was trying to be funny or save face after I found her nearly hyperventilating in her Platinum Slumber. Clearly the brush with the near afterlife had affected us both. I could still feel the oppressive weight of impending suffocation in my chest. After scaring us half to death, the cat had casually trotted off, toy mouse firmly clenched in his little cat teeth, laughing under his breath. At least, I imagined it was laughing.

"We were fine," I assured Irene with confidence I didn't feel and was pretty sure I wasn't exuding. "We were nowhere near death. We had plenty of air."

"So long as we didn't breathe," she mumbled. Then she stopped short. "This door must lead to the basement."

"Move on," I told her. "Who knows what might be down there."

"Dominic Gordon told us what's down there, remember?" She sounded suddenly uplifted. "Mortuaries keep all the good stuff in the basement, away from poor old Aunt Lulu, who might stumble into the embalming room by accident when she's looking for the restroom."

I froze. "Embalming room?"

"Think of it as a science lab."

"With dead people!"

Irene put her hands on her hips. "Do you want to find Rebecca Lowery or not?"

Less and less with every passing moment.

"Fine," I huffed. "Let's go. You first."

We descended the stairs into a stygian basement that grew no more welcoming when Irene shined her flashlight app on it. It *was* the embalming room, evidenced by the stainless steel table, the drain, the reek of formaldehyde, the...

"I think I'd rather be in the coffin," I said.

"This is life, Marty." Irene glanced around. "Pardon the pun. Hey, your Watson deals with this every day."

"*Day* being the key word here. He's not sneaking in to disturb the dead at night." I paused. "And he's not *my* Watson."

"Yet."

I opened my mouth to protest, but Irene shouted, "Look!" She pointed to a metal cabinet in the far corner. "What's that? It looks like...an oven." She whispered the last part with a wrinkled nose that said she was thinking about what might be cooked down here.

I shook my head. "No, not an oven. A freezer."

She bit her lip then whispered, "Like that's better?"

"Slightly?" Nothing about this was what you'd call good. I had the heebie-jeebies big time. And all I wanted to do was get out of here.

We stood in front of a large metal unit with six drawers. It almost looked like an oversized metal dresser, but I had a feeling this season's latest styles weren't being held inside. I grabbed the handle of the first drawer and glanced at Irene. "Here goes nothing."

I closed my eyes and pulled. I did a two count before opening them and looking inside.

Empty.

I let out a big breath I hadn't realized I'd been holding.

"One down and five more to go," Irene said on an exhale that matched mine.

We did a repeat on drawer number two and came up with the same results.

I did a quick eeny-meeny-miney-mo to pick the next drawer and opened.

"Eww!" Irene jumped back.

I'll admit, I might have jumped as well. In drawer number three lay an older gentleman with wispy white hair and a serene smile on his face. He might have just been dreaming peacefully had I not just pulled him from a human Sub-Zero.

"Not Rebecca," I said, quickly closing the drawer again, feeling like I'd interrupted the mother of all naps for the poor guy.

"This is freaking me out," Irene admitted. She held her phone in front of her as if to ward off spirits with her power of technology.

"We could leave now," I offered, kinda liking the sound of it.

But Irene took a deep breath, steeled her spine, tossed her ponytail over one shoulder, and said, "No. I can take it."

That made one of us.

I cracked my knuckles, shook the nervous energy out of my hands, and grabbed the handle of cupboard number four. I gave it a yank.

And both Irene and I gasped as one.

In the metal drawer lay a thirtysomething blonde woman who exactly matched the picture Barbara Lowery Bristol had shown us in my living room four days earlier.

Rebecca Lowery might have been missing in action, but one thing was certain—she'd never left Gordon's Mortuary.

# CHAPTER FOURTEEN

———

After indulging in a couple of really girlie screams, a few near-hyperventilation deep breaths, and running from the scene of our sorta crime as fast as our black-boot-clad feet could take us, Irene and I huddled in her car a block down the street, still checking the rearview mirror, as if expecting Rebecca Lowery to come loping after us, *Walking Dead* style.

Once we had our breathing under control, Irene pulled out her phone and dialed 9-1-1 on speaker. After semi-coherently telling the dispatcher that we had a body we needed to report to Detective Lestrade, and waiting on hold for so long that any real emergency would have passed (or killed us), we were finally connected to a bored sounding desk sergeant at the local precinct.

"This is Sergeant Claiborne. How can I help you?"

"We'd like to report a body," Irene told him.

"A body?" I could hear papers rustling on the other end as he grabbed a pen. "You have a deceased person?"

"Yes." Irene nodded emphatically in the dark car interior. "A missing body."

"Wait—a body's missing?"

"Well, no. We found the missing body."

"So, a body was missing, but it's found." He paused, the edge of urgency leaving his voice as he tried to process our situation.

"Right. We found her," Irene repeated, a hint of pride in her voice.

I had to admit, I was a little surprised we'd actually done it too.

"Where did you find this body?"

"At Gordon's Mortuary."

"You found a body at a mortuary." He paused. "Gee, how odd." All concern had left his voice, now replaced by pure sarcasm, as if he was being prank called.

"Look, it was missing from the mortuary. And now we found it."

"At the mortuary."

"Right."

"So, it's not missing. It's exactly where it should be."

"Um…I guess…kinda…"

"Look, kid, I have real calls to take."

"Wait! This is a real call! I'm not kidding. Ask Detective Lestrade."

"Detective Lestrade is gone for the day."

"Well, call him at home!"

"You want me to bother the detective while he's at home with his wife to tell him that a missing body isn't missing and it's right where it should be?"

Well, when he put it that way.

"Can we leave him a message?" I jumped in.

Irene shot me a look like I was giving up too quickly. I shrugged. Clearly Sergeant Claiborne wasn't sending the cavalry tonight.

"Sure. I can take a message."

"Can you tell him to call Martha Hudson first thing in the morning?"

"He has your number?"

Regrettably. "Yeah, he does."

"I'll leave him the message."

I was about to offer a halfhearted thank-you when the dial tone in my ear told me he'd hung up.

"Well, that was a bust," Irene huffed, shoving her phone into the holder mounted on her dash and turning on the car.

"It's the best we can do tonight," I sighed. I briefly thought about calling Watson. But since our last conversation was about me being more careful and this one would be about breaking into a mortuary, I wasn't totally sure he'd be more receptive. And, the truth was, he had no reason to take the body back to the morgue. The cop was right—Rebecca was right where she was supposed to be.

"Let's hope Lestrade has more sense in the morning," Irene said.

"So, what do we do now?" I asked.

Irene pulled out onto the deserted street. "Call Barbara Lowery Bristol and tell her we solved the case."

Technically we had. But something didn't feel right about it.

\* \* \*

"Definitely get the roof fixed first," Irene said the next morning. We stood in the Victorian's master bedroom, staring up at the ugly yellow-brown water stain on its ceiling. "There's no point in doing anything else if it's just going to rain indoors."

"Roofers are coming by tomorrow," I informed her. "And, I've got my electrical guy meeting me here this afternoon to finalize his estimate."

Irene raised an eyebrow my way. "A roof *and* wiring that won't burn the place down? How decadent, Miss Hudson."

I laughed. "Right? Next thing you know, I'll be buying furniture without moth holes in it."

"Maybe we should let the check clear first," Irene suggested.

"Trust me—an estimate is all I'm getting." At least for now.

Downstairs, the front doorbell rang. Toby gave a sharp bark and ran around my feet in circles in case I hadn't heard.

"Speak of the check…" Irene said, heading to the front door.

I followed reluctantly. While the idea of a payday wasn't a terrible thing, that niggling feeling that something just wasn't right hadn't dissipated any overnight. And when morning had come and gone without a call from Lestrade, it had maybe even grown a tad.

Once Irene and I had gotten back to her place last night for a calm-the-nerves pitcher of margaritas, we'd called our client and informed her that we'd found her sister—right at the mortuary where she should have been all along. Talk about an awkward conversation. I wasn't sure how much we could charge her for basically finding something that wasn't missing. Only, clearly someone at Gordon's Mortuary had wanted her to *appear* missing. Which was why the next call on our list was to Haley's Mortuary—which had the highest Yelp rating we could find for a mortuary in the area *and* was open 24 hours—and we arranged to have them pick up the untagged body in cupboard number four first thing in the morning. Then Irene texted her pal Shinwell, and sent him Rebecca's picture, and asked him to accompany the people from Haley's just to make sure they got the right body this time. All of which had gone off without a hitch, as Shinwell had reported to us an hour ago. Now all that was left was to collect our payment from Barbara Lowery Bristol and close the case of the Disappearing Diva.

At least that was what I kept telling that niggling feeling.

I caught up to Irene downstairs as she met Barbara Lowery Bristol at the front door.

"I know I'm early," she said, stepping into the foyer. "Is that alright?"

"Perfectly fine," I told her, meaning it. "Would you like to sit down?"

"No, thank you," she said. "I don't have much time. I've got another appointment, actually."

Toby moved in to give her shoes a thorough sniffing, wagged his tail in approval, and wandered off into the living room to take up his usual post at the window.

Barbara's glance encompassed both of us. "I just wanted to thank you for finding my sister. I can't tell you how much peace of mind it will give me to see her laid to rest before I head home tomorrow."

"You're not taking her back to Iowa?" Irene asked.

She shook her head. "I wish I could, but I want to honor Rebecca's wish to stay here in San Francisco. I owe her that."

I nodded my understanding before it struck me. "Wait—tomorrow? Will they be able to complete a full autopsy by then?"

"Autopsy?" Another headshake. "There's not going to be an autopsy. In fact, she's due to be laid out and buried tomorrow morning."

"Tomorrow," I repeated. I'd been sure someone would have insisted on a full autopsy now. I mean, didn't a missing body speak to some sort of foul play? I narrowed my eyes at Barbara Bristol. And even if the police didn't request an autopsy, why wouldn't *she*? While it was a given at this point that the Gordons had hidden Rebecca, was it possible someone else had put them up to it? They seemed the type to do just about anything for money. Wasn't Barbara just the least bit curious why someone would want to hide her sister's body?

Unless, of course, that someone had been her all along and she already knew.

"The police didn't request an autopsy?" I pressed.

Barbara blinked at me. "Well, that detective—Lester?"

"Lestrade," Irene supplied.

"Yes, Lestrade. He called me this morning and suggested it. Just to be thorough, I suppose."

So he *had* gotten our message last night.

"But I declined," Barbara went on.

I shot a look at Irene. Her eyebrows were raised in a way that made it clear she was thinking the same thing I was.

"You declined," I repeated slowly.

Barbara nodded. "Yes. Look, I didn't want my sister taken all the way back to the morgue again. I mean, they already determined she died of natural causes. What more is there to see? I just want to lay my sister to rest and put all of this unpleasantness behind me."

"When is the service?" Irene asked. "We'd like to pay our respects."

"I appreciate the thought," Barbara said, "but there really won't be a formal service. Just Rebecca and me, a few prayers, and some quiet reflection. You understand."

Irene's smile was warm with compassion. Or at least fake compassion. "Of course. I hope you'll accept our condolences."

We spent another few minutes chatting and accepting praise that now rang hollow to me, before Barbara wrote us a check and made her exit.

As soon as the door closed behind her, Irene turned to me and frowned. "She's hiding something."

With a sinking feeling in my stomach, I agreed. "I know. She's in a big hurry to get rid of that body again. Without an autopsy." I shook my head. "How can Watson sign off on that?"

"*If* Lestrade even consulted him, I'm sure it's not like Watson has much choice," Irene reasoned, flopping down on my sofa, raising little shimmers of dust that danced in the cracks of sunlight coming through the windows. "I mean, if there's still no indication of foul play in her death, he has no official reason to investigate."

"Stealing a body isn't indication of foul play?"

Irene shrugged. "I suppose that's all in how hard Lestrade looked into Dominic Gordon, and what kind of story he spun about the missing corpse in his refrigerator," she mused, looking like she really wanted to hear that story.

I, on the other hand, didn't. I knew whatever he was telling the police was pure fiction. For all we knew, Vincent Gordon could have offed Jane Doe just to have a substitute for Rebecca.

"Surely someone else is curious why the body was taken?" I pressed. "I mean, you can't tell me that it's just going to be swept under the rug? What about justice for Rebecca Lowery?"

Irene let out a dramatic sigh. "We're not cashing Barbra Bristol's check, are we?"

I looked to the peeling paint, the electrical waiting to go up in flames any minute, and the second story that was just one good rain away from melting like the wicked witch of the west. "Not yet," I decided. "Not until we know for sure she didn't hurt her sister."

"Your conscience is so inconvenient."

Tell me about it.

* * *

We left Toby dozing at 221 and headed to the police station. As soon as we got out of the car, we saw Lestrade leaving the building. I'd like to think it was coincidence and not a sixth sense that told him we were approaching to harass him. His shoulders were hunched against the stiff breeze, eyes hidden behind aviator sunglasses as they turned our way. He wore a different suit and tie than the last time I'd seen him, but his attitude hadn't changed. He still wasn't pleased to see us, a reaction I was starting to think he reserved for humanity in general.

"What are you two doing here?" he demanded.

Irene planted herself squarely in front of him. "You got our message about Rebecca Lowery?"

He nodded. "Yes, and I followed up with the next of kin."

"Who refused an autopsy," I added.

"And?"

"And we think there should be one."

"Sherlock Holmes thinks there should be one," Irene added.

"Sherlock Holmes," he repeated. A gust of wind rearranged the thinning hair across his scalp and pried opened his suit jacket. He gathered it with an impatient snap. "Then why doesn't he call me himself?"

I cut a glance toward Irene, hoping she had a story for that one.

"He tried. Your line was busy," she easily lied. The woman should have been an actress. Her ability was either Oscar worthy or pathological.

"Why didn't he leave a message?" Lestrade ground out.

"He's hard to get a hold of. He'll call again."

"When?"

"Soon."

"Right." He stepped around her to descend the steps to the street. "Well, if there's nothing else, ladies?"

"There is!" Irene said. Glancing my way, she did a *come on* tilt of her head before following him at a speed walk. "About the autopsy."

"I told you. The next of kin refused it."

"And you're just going to give in to her?"

"There's no basis to force one," he snapped. "Look, Watson did an examination. No crime has been committed. There's no evidence of foul play."

"Except that she's dead," Irene said. "A woman in her twenties with suspicious connections."

"*Suspicious connections*?" Lestrade eyed us both.

I paused. It was one thing to tell Watson I suspected Rebecca of buying drugs. It was another to admit to a police detective that the suspicion was based on my own drug buy.

"She has a boyfriend with a temper who was cheating on her with her understudy who is now the lead in her opera," Irene jumped in, saving me.

"Great. Her love life's a mess. Join the club," he mumbled, taking the steps two at a time. "That's not evidence of a crime."

I hurried to keep up with him, fighting against the wind in my face and Lestrade's long stride. "We believe she may have been involved with drugs. Synthetic designer drugs," I added against my better judgment.

"I don't care what you *believe*. Her tox screen was negative."

"What about the fact Gordon had hidden her in the mortuary this whole time?" I asked, just slightly out of breath. "That's got to be some kind of crime. Isn't that called abuse of a corpse?"

"That's called an honest mistake," he said. "A mix-up. I talked to Mr. Gordon this morning, and he was very apologetic."

Yeah, I bet he was.

"I'm sure her sister was relieved to hear it was just a mix-up," I said tartly. I didn't buy it. No reputable mortician would mix up or lose track of bodies. Dominic Gordon was up to *something*. Possibly for *someone*.

"Well, if this is all above board, why would someone hit Marty on the head?" Irene asked.

Lestrade spun abruptly to face us. "What did you say?"

"You heard me," Irene said. "She was hit on the head while she was following a lead in this case."

Lestrade turned to me, something akin to actual concern in his eyes. "Did you file a report?"

I shook my head. "But I think it was Dominic Gordon."

"You 'think'? Did you see him?"

"I was attacked from behind."

"Recognize his voice?" he asked.

"He didn't say anything."

"Did you see or hear anything that indicated who hit you?"

"Well, not exactly." I felt foolish admitting it.

"Then what makes you think it was Gordon?"

"His shoes were muddy." As soon as the words left my mouth, I realized how thin they sounded.

Lestrade crossed his arms over his chest. He stared down at me over his hawklike nose, the expression on his face the same one a parent would use on a child who just blamed the crayon covering the walls on her imaginary friend.

"He had muddy shoes," he repeated.

Irene stuck her fists on her hips. "Marty knows what she saw, Detective."

Lestrade shook his head. "Tell me, why is Mr. Holmes so invested in an autopsy anyway?"

Irene and I shared a glance. This was our one chance. It was now or never to make our case. "We don't think the bodies were accidentally switched. If that had been the case, Rebecca would have shown up where Jane Doe was supposed to be."

"So maybe Gordon is really bad at organization," Lestrade argued, laying on the sarcasm.

"So, who is Jane Doe?" I asked.

Lestrade blinked at me, his eyes blank.

"And how did she die?" Irene pressed.

"And who arranged for her to be buried with Gordon's?" I added.

"And who was *paying* for Jane Doe's burial?" Irene jumped in.

"And why did—"

"Enough!" Lestrade cut in. He sighed and put a hand to his temple, as if we were giving him a headache. "You two aren't going to let this go, are you?"

Irene and I shook our heads as one.

"Alright. I'll make you a deal."

That sounded promising. A deal was better than the cold shoulder we'd been getting.

"I promise I'll talk to the ME about an autopsy. Just *talk*, mind you. If"—he held up a warning finger—"you promise me I'll get a call from Sherlock Holmes by the end of the day."

I opened my mouth to protest, but Irene was quicker.

"Done," she said. She gifted him with a smile that would have made lesser men hand over their wallets. Lestrade only planted himself in the unmarked car and drove away without another look. Clearly Mrs. Lestrade had nothing to worry about in the fidelity department.

"Just how are we going to produce Sherlock Holmes by the end of the day?" I asked as we headed back to our car.

She shrugged. "We'll think of something."

"You'd better think fast. It's already noon," I told her.

She grinned. "Ye of little faith."

"Me of little bank account for bail money if Lestrade finds out the truth."

"You worry too much, Mar," she said. "Besides, the ends justify the means, right? He's going to talk to Watson about the autopsy, and—"

I grabbed her arm, stopping her midsentence. "Irene, look."

A man leaned against the side of her car, legs crossed casually at the ankles as he studied the cell phone in his hand. He wore tan khakis and a white button-down shirt under a tan windbreaker, which struck me as a deliberately forgettable outfit. In fact, I almost couldn't describe him even while I was looking at him. Almost...

"Hey!" Irene yelled. "Get away from our car!"

He lifted his head. And recognition dawned.

"Wiggins!" I muttered.

"Again?" Irene. "Dang, he's persistent."

"That's one word for him," I muttered, power walking toward the car.

Irene jogged beside me to keep up with my anger-fueled determination. "Marty, take it easy," she warned. "There are police everywhere."

I didn't want to take it easy. I wanted to cash Barbara Bristol's check, forget this Sherlock lie had even been started, and go back to happily slinging coffee and crashing college classes. But as long as Wiggins kept poking around, I had a bad feeling that wasn't an option.

Irene touched my shoulder as we approached. She must have seen the look in my eyes as she said, "No hitting."

"No promises," I told her. I glared at him from a foot away. "What are you doing here?"

He pushed his glasses up his nose with one finger and grinned at me, showing off a dimple in his left cheek that might have been adorable had he not been stalking me. "Hi, Marty. Nice to see you too."

I clenched my fists at my sides. Something about how calm and jovial he was made me all the more angry.

"Down, girl," Irene mumbled to me.

"And this lovely creature," he said, turning to Irene, "must be the famous Irene Adler. Charmed to make your acquaintance."

"Did he just call me a *creature*?"

"No hitting," I told her.

"No promises," she said.

"Look, you, there are laws against stalking, you know," I told Wiggins, wagging a finger at him.

"Oh, come on. You can do better than that, Marty. I'm just doing my job as a member of the fourth estate."

"Come off it. You're a blogger. You're one step up from a meme," Irene shot back.

Wiggins put his hand over his heart in mock pain. "Ouch." Though the self-satisfied grin stayed firmly in place.

"What do you want?" I asked again.

"You know what I want, Marty. A story."

"Not interested."

"Not even if I were willing to trade for it?"

I paused, ashamed that he'd piqued my interest. "What do you mean, trade?"

"The Disappearing Diva. I know you're looking into her death."

"We were only hired to find her body. We did. Case closed," I lied. The less Wiggins knew, the better I felt.

"Right." He winked at me. "Then why are you here?"

I opened my mouth to try my hand at lying again, but Irene jumped in first.

"We're here to see Watson. Marty's dating him."

I blinked at her. "I'm not dating—*ow!*" I rubbed my arm where she'd elbowed me.

"So you *are* dating the ME." Wiggins turned his gaze on me, and for the first time I saw that smile falter a bit. "Pity."

I felt my spine straighten. "What's that supposed to mean?"

"You're hot. You could do better."

I froze mid-mental comeback. That was so not what I'd expected him to say.

"I'll have you know that Dr. Watson is the finest ME on the West Coast," Irene defended.

"Really." Wiggins finally turned his attention away from my shocked face and toward Irene. "Then how did he miss the fact that Rebecca Lowery was murdered?"

Irene's turn to look shocked. "How on earth do you know that?"

Wiggins shrugged and leaned back against her car again, ankles crossed. "I have my sources."

Oh brother. I barely resisted the urge to roll my eyes.

"Look, clearly you know something about the case. Enough with the coy stuff—what is it?" I said.

"I'd be happy to share." He paused. "*If* I get my exclusive story out of it."

I glanced at Irene. She had the same look of mild disbelief I was feeling. It was *possible* Wiggins did know something. It was also possible he was bluffing and would play us for fools before breaking the story that Sherlock was a myth from the start. I bit my lip. Wondering which was worse—complete public humiliation or working with Wiggins?

"How do we know you're not bluffing?" Irene asked, narrowing her eyes at him as she voiced my thoughts.

"You don't. But I can tell you her death involved a Vincent Gordon." He paused for dramatic effect.

Irene gave me a look. I nodded.

"Fine," she conceded. She glanced behind her toward the uniformed officers coming and going from the building. "But we're not doing this here. Follow us to my house, and we'll see what we can work out. And you'd better not be wasting our time."

"I wouldn't dream of it," he assured her. "Uh. I won't have to worry about your actor friend waylaying me this time, will I?"

"We'll see how things go," Irene called over her shoulder.

Once we were in her car and pulling away from the curb—with Wiggins in his gray sedan close behind—I turned to Irene. "We aren't actually going to share info with him, are we?"

Irene shook her head. "But if we agree to work with him, we can spoon feed him the information we *want* him to have about Sherlock Holmes and not what he might find if he keeps digging on his own."

I hadn't thought of that, but it made sense. Irene could probably concoct an entire life framework around Sherlock Holmes, right down to an ex-wife and estranged kids, and every bit of it would be utterly believable. But if we left Wiggins to his own devices, Sherlock Holmes's unmasking would likely go viral overnight, and our complicity right along with it. I'd lose my dignity. I'd lose my reputation.

I'd lose Watson.

"He is cute though," Irene said, cutting into my thoughts.

"Who, Watson?"

She frowned at me. "No, Wiggins. Where was your brain at?"

I shook my head. "Nowhere good. You sure you want my stalker knowing where you live?"

She shrugged. "That's what trespassing laws are for."

As if a member of the fourth estate would obey those.

# CHAPTER FIFTEEN

---

"Nice place," Wiggins said a half hour later as he looked around Irene's smarter-than-most-PhDs house. "I'm impressed. Sure beats Marty's place."

I stuck my tongue out at him.

"Thanks," Irene said, tossing her keys on the counter and grabbing a trio of water bottles from the fridge.

"This is your place, right? Not Sherlock's?"

Irene didn't miss a beat. "Sherlock lives outside The City."

"Huh." I could see Wiggins mentally filing that tidbit away for later.

"Have a seat," Irene offered, indicating the stools lined up at the granite-topped center island.

I sat on the far right. Wiggins sat next to me. Uncomfortably close. I-could-almost-feel-the-heat-emanating-from-his-body close. I cleared my throat, scooting over a few inches. Instead of looking like he took it personally, Wiggins gave me that amused smile of his again.

Irene leaned her elbow on the counter opposite us, fixing her green eyes on Wiggins. "So spill it. What do you know about Rebecca Lowery and Vincent Gordon?"

"Well, I can tell you Vinny Gordon is not a nice guy."

"It doesn't take a crack detective to figure that one out," I said, laying the sarcasm on thick.

Wiggins shook his head at me before addressing Irene. "This one's feisty, isn't she?"

I narrowed my eyes at him. "Just try me."

"Start talking," Irene cut in. "We haven't got all day."

He sipped from the water bottle, drawing out the moment. "Okay, here's the deal." He pushed up his glasses and leaned forward on his crossed arms. "It's hard to find the details on Vincent Gordon, but I've run across him a few times in the course of my investigations. The stories about how the guy does business are not pretty."

"For example?" I asked.

"For example, one night a Lyft driver named Henry Harvey picked up this old guy someplace in The City. Harvey was never seen again. They found the burned-out car a week later in East San Jose." He paused for effect. "Harvey had been set to talk to the feds about Vincent Gordon in connection with money laundering."

"I didn't read anything about that when I looked into Vinny," Irene said, frowning.

"It's not public record. No charges were ever brought against him. Not enough evidence."

I shivered. Irene and I had our doubts about how legit the Gordon bothers were, but hearing Wiggins' story made me realize just how bad news these two could be.

"There are more stories like that," Wiggins said, "but they're pretty similar. Vinny's been the subject of numerous legal investigations, but nothing ever comes of it. And it's not because Vinny's the luckiest guy in San Francisco." Insert smirk. "It's because witnesses have a habit of retracting their statements or getting short memories. Or disappearing." He sipped his water. "You get on Vinny Gordon's radar, and you won't need to worry about getting gray hair, because you won't live that long."

A tiny frown of concentration knit Irene's forehead. "What about his brother?"

"Dominic?" He shook his head. "Dom's got his own problems. He's been hauled in a few times on minor league stuff. Flashing women in the park, creeping around peeking into windows, that kind of thing. Perv stuff."

"That fits," Irene said. "What'd he get in the way of punishment?"

"Not a thing," Wiggins said. "Dom *may* be the luckiest guy in San Francisco, because Vinny's his fixer. Vinny stepped in, and the problems disappeared, just like that." He snapped his fingers.

"A lot of things seem to disappear around Vincent Gordon," I noted.

"Including Rebecca Lowery," Irene added. She turned to Wiggins. "You said Vinny was involved in her death. How?"

He paused, looking from Irene to me. "I *am* going to get a story out of this, aren't I?"

I blinked innocently at him. "Of course." I had to admit, the reporter had good instincts.

He took a sip of water again, eyeing us. Finally he must have decided he had no choice but to trust us, as he set his bottle down and leaned his elbows on the counter again. "Okay, Rebecca Lowery's boyfriend is on the take from Vinny Gordon."

I gasped out loud.

There went Wiggins' self-satisfied smirk again.

I shut my mouth with a click. "Are you sure?"

Wiggins nodded. "I'd bet money on it."

"Whoa," Irene said. "That paints a different picture."

No kidding. So much for my theory about Vincent being Rebecca's secret lover. If what Wiggins was saying was true, Vincent would hardly be worried about Bryan finding out he was the one sleeping with his girlfriend. He'd just *fix* him.

"How do you know all this anyway?" I asked Wiggins.

"I looked into Bryan Steele as soon as I saw you visit his house."

I blinked at him, letting that implication sink in. "You followed me to Bryan Steele's house too?!"

Wiggins gave me a *well, duh* look.

"Great! Is there any place you haven't followed me?"

"I haven't seen you shower yet." Wiggins grinned, sliding his gaze up and down me in a way that told me he wouldn't look away if the chance arose.

"Back to Bryan Steele," Irene prodded.

Wiggins turned away from me (reluctantly) and toward Irene. "Right. When I figured he had something to do with the Disappearing Diva, I looked into him. He's on suspension for roughing up a suspect."

"That much we know," Irene told him.

He looked surprised for a moment, as if shocked we weren't totally deficient detectives.

"Well, I recognized the name of the suspect he beat up," he went on. "He's a member of Vinny's crew."

"Why would Vinny pay Steele to beat up his own crew member?" I asked.

"These guys do that all the time. Look, they don't have dental plans to ensure employee loyalty. When someone messes up, the enforcers come in and make an example of them."

"So, you think Steele is one of Vincent Gordon's enforcers."

Wiggins nodded. "He works the same areas of The City Vinny does. And according to public records, he's crossed paths quite a few times with other of Vinny's suspected associates."

"So, maybe Dominic 'losing' Rebecca had nothing to do with the Fluffy Bunny after all," I mumbled more to myself than the room at large.

Wiggins gave me a funny look. "Fluffy Bunny?"

I waved him off, lost in thought. "Maybe Bryan Steele really did lose his temper with his girlfriend, kill her, then in a panic, thinking the police would find some evidence of his crime, he called his buddy Vincent to dispose of it."

Irene nodded. "It's the classic you scratch my back, and I'll dispose of a corpse for you."

It all sounded frighteningly plausible to me. Of course, while it was a nice theory, there was still one little problem. "How do we prove any of this?"

Wiggins looked at me with a blank stare. "That's your job—you're the detectives. I just spin the stories."

"No, that's *Watson's* job," Irene insisted. "If Steele was afraid, something about Rebecca's body would give him away. That evidence has got to still be there."

"Which means we're banking on Lestrade convincing Watson to do a full autopsy." I paused, thinking back to our conversion with the detective. "You know, there's still one thing bothering me."

"*One* thing?" Wiggins asked.

I shot him a look.

"What is it, Marty?" Irene asked, playing referee again.

"Who is Jane Doe?"

"Right." Irene nodded. "You think she was killed too?"

I nodded. "Maybe if we knew more about her, it would lead us to some evidence of who killed both women."

"But we never even saw her," Irene said. "We don't even know what she looks like, expect that she was the same age and coloring as Rebecca."

"I wish we'd thought to look while we were at Gordon's," I mused.

I glanced up to see Wiggins grinning at us both like a Cheshire cat again.

"What?" I asked him.

"Well, good thing *I* did look. And I've got the photo to prove it." He held out his phone, displaying a picture of a blonde woman lying peacefully in a casket. Dominic Gordon had been right about the two women looking similar. At first glance, she certainly could have been Rebecca, though the more closely I looked, the more I could see subtle differences—the shape of the ears, the tilt of the nose, the shape of the eyebrows.

"Where did you get this?" I asked.

He shrugged. "Like you're the only person who can break into a mortuary."

I blinked. "You followed us there too?!"

"Honey, I've followed you everywhere."

"Except the shower," Irene added, on the verge of laughter.

I shook my head. "Okay, so we have Jane Doe's picture. Maybe if we show it around, someone might recognize her?"

"'Around'?" Wiggins did air quotes. "Exactly where would that be?"

"To our suspects," Irene said. "Maybe they'll let something slip. Or maybe someone saw one of our suspects with her?

I mentally ran through the list. Vinny, Dominic, Bryan Steele. A conversation with any one of them sounded dangerous. "Let's start with Tara," I suggested.

"I'll drive," Irene said.

\* \* \*

Parking was scarce today at the Bayside Theater, forcing us to park two blocks down and around the corner before hoofing it back toward the theater. Luckily, the wind had died down, though the sunshine was still struggling to burn off the fog rolling in from the bay. As soon as we stepped into the theater, I realized why the street was so parked up. Dozens of people filled the audience as well as the stage and the orchestra pit. It appeared a full-scale rehearsal was going on, complete with several costumed divas on the stage, including Tara Tarnowski. She stood front and center in the spotlight, though she wasn't singing today. Instead, she was simultaneously yelling at Diana, the wardrobe woman, about the tightness of her bodice; someone named Elli, about her wig being crooked; and her male costar dressed in tights, about standing too close to her spotlight.

"Is that the understudy?" Wiggins leaned in and asked.

I nodded.

"Delightful," came his sarcastic opinion.

I couldn't help a grin. That was about my assessment of Tara as well.

"You again." PS Rossi spotted the three of us standing in the aisle and charged toward us, his hands balled into fists at his side. Though whether he was truly that excited to see us or just frustrated at his star, it was hard to tell. Granted, every time we had come to his theater so far, we hadn't exactly been the bearers of good news.

"We're sorry to intrude again," Irene said, stepping forward.

"What do you want this time?" he asked. His tone was irritated and urgent, as his gaze pinged from Irene to me to Wiggins. "Who's this? Another investigator?"

"Something like that," Irene glossed over. "I know you're busy, so we won't take up too much of your time."

The frowns etched in Rossi's forehead smoothed a bit at that promise. "We've only got a week left until we open, and rehearsals are not exactly going smoothly." He gestured his head behind him and rolled his eyes.

"Tara isn't the easiest coloratura to work with?" I asked

"Let's just say she's no Rebecca." He glanced to Irene again. "What is it you said you needed?"

"We wanted to talk to Tara—" Irene started.

But Wiggins jumped in. "We were actually wondering if you had ever seen this woman around the theater." He held out his phone, displaying the photo of Jane Doe. "We think she might have been a friend of Tara's."

Rossi blinked at the photo, his frown deepening again. "Is she dead? It looks like she's in a casket?"

"Um, yes, unfortunately she is deceased." I looked from Wiggins to Irene. It would have been so much easier to gauge a natural reaction to the photo if it hadn't been taken in the Platinum Slumber.

"What does she have to do with Rebecca's death?" Rossi asked.

"That's what we're trying to find out," Irene said. "Have you ever seen her around? Maybe with Tara?"

Rossi shook his head. "No, I'm sorry. I don't recognize her. But it's not like I know all of my casts' friends. We're on a tight schedule here. There hasn't been a lot of time for socializing."

"Would you mind if we ask some of the other cast and crew if they might've seen her?" Irene pressed.

Rossi blew out a deep sigh and pulled a pack of cigarettes from his pocket, smacking them against his palm. "We really can't afford any more delays. My backer is concerned enough about the production as it is."

"We completely understand," I assured him. "We'll be very quick and very discreet."

Irene and I both flashed him our biggest smiles. Wiggins attempted one as well, but as usual came off a little too cocky.

Rossi shook his head and looked upward, as if trying to draw some help from above. "Fine. Ask around, but please don't interrupt the rehearsal. We don't have time for any more setbacks." He shoved an unlit cigarette into his mouth and walked away, waving his hands in the air and gesturing to the orchestra to begin again.

"That guy's tightly wound," Wiggins said as we made our way down the aisle and around the stage toward the dressing rooms.

"If I had to deal with Tara on a daily basis, I might be too," I admitted.

"Looks like Tara's going to be a while," Irene said, gesturing to the stage where Rossi was trying to soothe the savage diva into singing her song.

"Let's start with the crew," Wiggins suggested, gesturing to the buzz of activity behind the scenes. "Maybe someone has seen them together."

We did, showing the photo to one crew member after another and getting much the same response. Shock that we had a picture of the dead woman on our phone, questions about why she was in a casket, and absolutely no recognition from anyone. No one seemed to have seen her with Tara or Rebecca. One of the makeup artists said she *might* have been a delivery girl she'd seen bringing in sandwiches to the theater last month. Diana Rossi said she resembled one of her favorite soap opera actresses. And the bassoon player from the orchestra said she looked a lot like his second ex-wife, only he would've paid good money to see the ex-wife in a casket. I chose to believe that wasn't an actual threat, but no one seemed to have any real information about who Jane Doe was.

I was about to call this the wild goose chase that it was, when I spotted Tara stomping toward her dressing room. I gestured to Irene and Wiggins to follow. However, when we got to her door, I paused. Tara wasn't alone. A male voice came from the other side of the door. A male voice that was raised and not very happy.

I held up a finger to my lips to signal my companions to be quiet as I strained to hear the conversation.

"…that detective…what did you tell her…gonna make someone pay!"

The hair on the back of my neck stood up as I recognized the voice. Bryan Steele.

*He's in there*, I mouthed to Irene.

"Who?" Wiggins asked.

"Shhh!" I admonished.

*Who?* he mouthed.

"The boyfriend," I whispered.

"The cop?"

Irene and I nodded.

"What's he saying?" Wiggins asked in a hushed tone.

"He's saying—"

Only I didn't get to finish that thought, as the door suddenly flew open and said boyfriend filled the frame. His brows hunkered down over flashing eyes, and every vein in his neck stood at attention. His gaze shot from me to Wiggins to Irene, all hunched over and whispering.

"Uh, hi." I straightened up and did a little one-finger wave at the Hulk.

His eyes narrowed at me. "What are you doing out here?"

"Uh...us?" I squeaked out, my voice an octave higher than normal.

"We wanted to know if you've ever seen this woman," Wiggins said, stepping forward to show Steele his phone. If he had any trepidation about taking on the bodybuilder/violent cop/possible murderer, he didn't show it.

Steele's eyes narrowed even further as he looked at the photo. "She's dead."

I rolled my eyes. "Yes, we're aware. Do you know who she is?"

His shoulders bobbed up and down in a shrug. "Beats me."

I had to admit, I had no idea if he was telling the truth or not. Though I noticed he had barely looked at the picture, his eyes flickering to it just once. Either he had an aversion to the image of people in caskets, or he was purposely avoiding making an identification.

"Who's out there?" I heard Tara ask from the room beyond. "What's going on?" She shoved Bryan Steele away from the door, taking in our trio. I wasn't sure who she had been hoping to see, but her face registered disappointment at seeing us.

"Oh. You again."

If everyone seemed so happy to see me, I was going to get a complex soon.

"Here to apologize for threatening me the other day?" Tara asked me, crossing her arms over her ample chest. I was impressed she could even get them to touch.

"Threatening her?" Wiggins asked me, raising his eyebrows in a question as that smirk tugged at the corner of his lips.

I could see his story brewing behind his eyes, and I quickly nipped it in the bud.

"Hardly. Do you know this woman?" I asked Tara, grabbing Wiggins' phone and showing it to her.

Tara's nose scrunched up in disgust. "Ugh. She's dead."

"But do you recognize her?" Irene jumped in.

Tara rolled her eyes and shook her head. "Do I look like the kind of person who hangs out with dead people?"

"We think she might have been a friend of...Rebecca's," I prompted. I didn't add *or yours*. "Maybe she was at one of Rebecca's performances? Or a rehearsal?"

"Well, if she was a friend of Rebecca's, then I definitely don't know her."

Wiggins narrowed his eyes at her. "Are you sure?"

Tara's head snapped up to meet his gaze. "Yes, I'm sure. What, are you calling me a liar?"

Wiggins held both hands up in a surrender gesture. "No, I just noticed you didn't really look at the picture very long."

"Yeah, well, I'm not really into looking at dead people, okay?"

"Tara?" a voice called behind us.

I turned to see Diana Rossi standing in the hall. "PS is ready for you on stage again," she told the redhead.

Though I noticed her eyes were on Wiggins and the phone.

"Great. We were done here anyway," Tara said, sending a pointed look our way. She followed Diana in the direction of the stage.

Bryan Steele ducked back into Tara's dressing room and slammed the door shut so hard I felt a breeze ruffle my hair.

"Well, that was a bust," Irene said as we made our way back outside. "Apparently whoever Jane Doe is, she didn't hang out with the theater crowd."

"I don't know if it was a total bust," Wiggins said, shoving his phone back into his pocket. "Tara barely glanced at the picture. It's possible she was lying about not knowing the woman. She certainly didn't want to talk to us about it very much, did she?"

"Bryan didn't look at it very hard either." I turned to face him. "You think maybe they were both lying?"

"Or they're both telling the truth, and they just don't like us very much," Irene reasoned.

Which was just as plausible.

We stepped outside into the struggling sunshine, and Wiggins paused, his gaze going up and down the street. While it wasn't the heart of the theater district, the Bayside was popular enough that a smattering of restaurants and small businesses catering to tourists lined the sidewalks.

"Maybe I'll take the photo around to some of these places," Wiggins said, nodding toward the coffee shop across the street. "It's possible maybe one of them saw Tara with Jane Doe."

Irene nodded. "Good idea. Send me a copy of the photo, and we'll take the right side of the street. You can take the left."

"Actually…" I looked down at my phone, noting the time. "I have an appointment."

Irene shot me a sly look. "This wouldn't happen to be an *appointment* with a certain doctor, would it?"

Out of the corner of my eye I saw Wiggins' head snap up.

"No," I said honestly. "My electrician."

"Oh." Irene looked visibly disappointed. "Right. The estimate."

Wiggins, on the other hand, registered a different emotion. One that I couldn't quite put my finger on, before he quickly turned his head away.

"I could cancel," I offered.

But Irene shook her head. "I'll text you if we find anything. Good luck. I'll think low thoughts for you."

"Thanks. I'm going to need all the good thoughts I can get." If only good thoughts could pay for new electrical.

# CHAPTER SIXTEEN

———

"My guys can finish up the rewiring by the end of next week."

I was back at the house, standing in the foyer with the electrical contractor, Delvecchio, studying his final estimate. His multi-paged final estimate, full of big plans and bigger numbers. I knew full well the work had to be done, but the prospect of laying out thousands of dollars at once was more than daunting. It was terrifying. Especially now that my payday was precarious.

As if on cue, a knock sounded at my front door. A loud, insistent one. I excused myself from Delvecchio to answer, still holding the estimate, and opened the door.

Barbara Lowery Bristol barged in, jaw clenched with anger. She zeroed in on me, her eyes narrowing. "How dare you!"

Her fury left me taken aback.

"Excuse me?"

"You called that police detective!"

Oh. That. Well, I hadn't expected her to be exactly pleased about us interfering in her plans. Then again, I'd barely expected our interfering to work. Usually it didn't.

"I know you had something to do with this," she practically shouted. "You knew I wanted to bury my sister. You deliberately went against my wishes."

"I'll just...uh..." Delvecchio edged out of the room, leaving us alone.

"Please let me explain," I said, trying to keep my tone calm, hopefully even reassuring.

It didn't work.

"You had no right to push for an autopsy," she snapped. "That's not your decision to make. I told you I just wanted to lay Rebecca to rest and go home. Our business was done. Yet for some reason, you saw the need to keep nosing in!"

*Nosing in?* "You hired us to find her," I reminded her.

"Your job was done." Her lips compressed into a bloodless slash. "Thanks to you, we almost had to cancel the burial."

"Wait—almost?" I felt that sinking feeling in my stomach again.

She narrowed her eyes at me. "Rebecca was already embalmed at Gordon's. A full autopsy is useless now. Which, if you had asked me instead of running off to the police, you would have known."

The sinking turned into a full-on hollow pit. We were too late. Of course Dominic Gordon would have embalmed her. He wouldn't have just had her sitting in his freezer as a ticking time bomb to point the proverbial finger at her murderer—he would have done anything possible to eradicate evidence of a crime from her body. And with us running all over The City looking for her, he'd had plenty of time to do it too. Whatever secrets Rebecca's body might have held were gone now. And tomorrow her sister would be burying her…and the truth along with her.

"Don't you care how your sister died?" I asked, shaking my head in disbelief. "Don't you want to know why someone took her?"

"What I want to do is lay my sister to rest."

I opened my mouth to speak, but she ran right over me.

"And you can tell Mr. Holmes that I'm canceling the check!"

I stared at her, blinking, letting that unsettling implication set in as she turned on her sensible heels and marched out of the Victorian. I was still staring when I faintly heard a voice behind me.

"Uh, ma'am?"

I turned to see Delvecchio standing on the second-floor landing, clutching his clipboard. His pained expression and the nervous shifting of his feet suggested he'd overheard our conversation.

"Did you want me to come back later?"

Warmth suffused my cheeks. He was worried about being paid, and he was right to be. I had no way to pay anyone without Barbara's check. That meant no new electrical system, no roof, no hot water heater. Nothing.

"Uh, yeah. I mean, no. Maybe…another day…" I trailed off as despair coiled deep in my belly. This was all Sherlock Holmes's fault. If he hadn't come along, I'd be putting in extra shifts at work and saving for the repairs like a normal person. I wouldn't be breaking into funeral homes and hiding in caskets and buying drugs in questionable delis and holding up someone's burial. Normal law-abiding citizens didn't do things like that. But I was a criminal now, thanks to Sherlock Holmes.

I should have cut it off at the knees, just refused to go along with Irene when she'd conjured up the great detective. I'd only wanted to get information about my great-aunt; I'd never intended for it to go this far. It had been a bad idea from the start, and it hadn't gotten any better. Let Lestrade take over, do what needed to be done, arrest who needed to be arrested. That was *his* job. Wiggins could out Sherlock Holmes and stop following me. I was done. And Watson…well, Watson would probably never speak to me again. That stung the most, turning that sinking pit into a gnawing ache that made me yearn for chocolate and chick flicks starring Renée Zellweger. But, since I had neither, I headed for the kitchen to pour myself a glass of water, gulping it down while staring out into the tiny backyard that I'd never be able to afford to landscape. It belonged to the weeds now.

My cell phone buzzed, alerting me to a text. I pulled it out, glaring down at the screen. It was from Tara Tarnowski.

*I know who the girl in the picture is. Meet at Bayside 8p. Use stage door n come alone.*

Yeah, right. I let the phone clatter to the counter, annoyed that she'd assume I was gullible enough to accept her invitation. I still had the lump on my head from my foray into Lampley Park. No way was I falling for *that* again. I might be delusional, thinking I could solve this case, but I wasn't stupid.

I glanced down at the phone. But I *was* curious. I mean, did Tara really know who Jane Doe was? This didn't feel like a confession text. But maybe *Bryan* had recognized the woman and let something slip.

I glanced at my phone. As much as I wanted to pretend I didn't care, the truth was a little part of me felt guilty if I didn't at least check it out. I mean, what if Bryan *had* done something to Rebecca…and what if he did it again to Tara? While I didn't harbor any thoughts of becoming besties with the singer, I didn't want her to end up dead. Especially if it was because I didn't do something as simple as answer a text.

I picked up the phone, I closed my eyes, and I let my conscience war with my better judgment. But I shouldn't have bothered. When had my better judgment ever won?

*I'll be there*, I texted her back.

I stared at the words for a few second, wondering what I was getting myself into now.

Then I sent Irene a quick text. *Busy tonight?*

I pulled in a deep breath, staring out into my backyard. Done. I'd meet Tara, but I wouldn't meet her alone.

My phone chimed. *Free as a bird. What's up?*

*Meeting Tara at Bayside. 8pm. She knows Jane Doe.*

*Great. We'll be there.*

I paused. *We?* I texted back.

*Wiggins and me.*

Oh boy. Whatever I was getting myself into just got that much stickier.

\* \* \*

"How come Sherlock Holmes has you two doing the legwork all the time?" Wiggins asked. "Does the great and powerful Oz just sit behind the curtain doing data analysis or something?"

"He's out of the country," Irene said, easing her car to the curb in front of the Bayside. Because the stage was dark on Mondays and the rehearsals long over, the neighborhood was quiet. The theater loomed over the sidewalk, silent and dark. I noticed the marquee had removed Rebecca's name and now reflected Tara Tarnowski's promotion to prima donna.

I shivered, glad I'd trusted my instincts to bring along company. Even if Wiggins was part of the company. As irritating as having a reporter along was, something about the extra muscle was a little comforting. And it didn't hurt that his hoodie was tight enough on his biceps to show off said muscles. I'd even caught Irene giving him an appreciative stare or two in the car.

When Irene had shut off the engine, I turned to face them before we got out. "Here's the thing. Tara is expecting me to come alone. You two should hide somewhere close enough to hear everything, but let me meet with her alone, okay? At least until I know what she has to say."

"Sure thing." Wiggins winked at me. "You won't even know we're there."

It didn't matter what I knew. I just needed him to fool Tara.

"She said to use the stage door," I told them when we'd gotten out of the car. I pointed. "I think that's it there."

The door was unlocked, and we let ourselves into the theater, Irene and Wiggins slipping into the shadows out of sight while I went in the opposite direction, through the parted stage curtain, down the stage stairs, and into the seating bowl, which was empty. Safety lighting on the risers stretched fingers of faint light up the two aisles but left the stage itself draped in shadows. Twin *Exit* lights glowed an eerie red above the doors leading to the lobby. The oppressive silence was nearly noise unto itself, almost a sensory overload.

Until I heard a muffled thump and faint giggling. Wiggins or Irene must have walked into something in the dark and had promptly forgotten about the need for stealth. I rolled my eyes, thinking this whole thing was a bad idea.

I texted to Irene *shhhh*

Nothing back. But I didn't hear anything else either, which I took as a good sign. In fact the entire place was eerily quiet. And dark. As bumbling as my two hidden cohorts were, I was glad not to be alone. The creepy factor here put Lampley Park to shame.

Reaching into my bag, my fingers curled around the only conceivable weapon in there—a travel-size can of hairspray. Better than nothing, I supposed. Flicking off the top, I palmed it as I moved carefully toward the stage, purposely letting my footsteps be heavy in the hope of providing Irene and Wiggins a trail of aural bread crumbs. Hopefully, they'd stayed close enough to hear them.

I was infinitely glad I'd worn chunky wedge shoes and not heels, as I stumbled in the darkness. My toes butted up against the steps at stage left, and I paused there, straining to discern some kind of form from the amorphous darkness. Nothing but silence, ahead and behind. Still, the hairs on my neck prickled as I climbed the steps. My heart clattered chaotically against my ribs. Something felt off, something more than the solitude, the silence, and the darkness.

My eyes scanned the surroundings, adjusting to the dark.

And that was when I saw it.

A metallic glint coming from the shadows behind the parted stage curtain.

The glint of a gun barrel pointed directly at me.

Every part of my body froze except my heart. *That* ran at full speed, hammering so hard I could practically hear it pounding in my ears.

I was out in the open, with nothing to duck behind for cover, and no real weapon unless a stream of Extra Hold could stop a bullet. Somewhere in the theater sat Wiggins and Irene, but I had no idea where. I didn't even know if they could see me from their hiding place.

I cut my eyes left and right, hoping for some small indication of where my backup was.

"Don't bother." The voice was muffled, impossible to recognize but too deep to be Tara's. Whoever was behind the curtain was male. "Your friends have already been taken care of."

Taken care of? *Keep it together, Marty.* I couldn't think about what that might mean. Not now. I'd dragged Irene and Wiggins into this situation. If they didn't come out of it, I couldn't live with—

No. Bad choice of words. I could live with anything, and so could they. They had to. Power of positive thinking, right? I just had to concentrate. Use my head for something other than impending hysteria.

*Think.*

So the person in the shadows wasn't Tara. Who, then? Bryan Steele, who beat up people for Vinny Gordon? And maybe worse.

"Officer Steele?" I said, hoping I didn't sound as terrified as I felt.

The curtain was brushed aside with a rustle, and PS Rossi stepped out.

"Wrong again," he said.

# CHAPTER SEVENTEEN

His smile was pleasant, with a dark sort of emptiness behind it. The kind of smile you might see at a psychopath cocktail party. It chilled me to the core.

"What's going on?" I asked, the confusion in my voice genuine as I tried to comprehend the truth that was holding a gun on me. Suddenly it was clear to me that PS Rossi's biggest crime was not smoking in the theater lobby.

"What's going on is I'm tired of you stirring up trouble." His smile might be psycho-pleasant, but his tone was not. It was flat and cold. He held the gun in a rock-steady, nerveless hand. Clearly it wouldn't bother him at all to usher me into the afterlife.

If I couldn't focus, that was just where I'd find myself. I glanced to the left and right, trying to find anything I could use as a weapon. Wouldn't it have been handy if some Viking sword props just happened to be lying around? Why did their current production have to be a love story?

"I'm not here for trouble. I'm…I was just supposed to meet someone."

"I know. But, sadly, she doesn't."

I blinked, realization dawning. "You sent me that text. From Tara's phone."

He nodded slowly.

"You wanted me to meet you here tonight."

"Alone," he emphasized, chiding me with the one word.

I swallowed hard. "Yeah, well, that didn't turn out so well for me last time."

"I don't think it's going to turn out well for you this time either," he told me without a hint of sympathy.

I licked my lips, my heart rate going practically heavy-metal speed. "You killed Rebecca," I said. Which felt a bit like stating the obvious at this point, but I had to keep him talking. It was the only chance I had of coming up with a way out of this life-or-death drama currently playing out on the stage. I glanced to my right. A stray water bottle, a discarded jacket hanging over the back of a chair, a script on the floor. Unless I could defend myself by paper cutting him to death, I was out of luck. "She didn't die by accident. You killed her."

"Did you figure that all out on your own, detective?" Rossi taunted me.

Actually, the gun in his hand had been the dead giveaway, but I kept that to myself. Best not to upset the psycho. "But why?" I asked, hoping the explanation was a long one. "She was your star."

Rossi shook his head. "Does it matter now?"

"Humor me," I asked.

He grinned, though there was little humor involved on either side. "Yes, she was my star. She was also a conniving and thoroughly selfish diva."

Suddenly it dawned on me.

"You were sleeping with Rebecca," I said. "*You* were the other man."

"I guess it turns out you're not as dumb as you look."

Ouch. "The fight Bryan and Rebecca had at the theater. You must have overhead it and been jealous she still cared about Bryan."

Rossi threw his head back and laughed, the sound echoing off the walls like a creepy funhouse gag. "I take it back—you are as dumb as you look."

I narrowed my eyes at him. "Enlighten me then."

"I didn't care in the least who Rebecca cared about. Granted, she was a bit of fun when it all started. One does need distractions now and then, you know."

Yeah, like the one I was hoping this conversation provided him while I figured a way out of here. My eyes cut to the stage behind him. I could faintly make out the *Exit* sign glowing above the door, but there was no way I'd be able to get to it before he could fire off the gun in his hand.

"So what happened?" I prodded.

"What happened is she was an addict. And, like any addict, her next fix was all she really cared about." He paused, almost looking sad for a moment.

"The Fluffy Bunny."

"So you knew about that too. See, I knew you were getting too close."

Oops. Me and my big mouth again. "You killed her because she was doing drugs?" I had to admit, it wasn't adding up as a great motive.

Rossi shook his head very slowly. "No, I killed her because addicts are sloppy and dangerous. Rebecca was threatening to expose our entire operation, and my backer was getting nervous."

"Entire operation…" Facts, faces, and tidbits of information were swirling around in my brain so fast I was having hard time keeping up with all of them. "You're not just talking about the opera production, are you?"

Again with the head shake. "No. Don't get me wrong— we will put on a very nice production of *Ethereal Love*. But ticket sales will pale in comparison to how much we'll make with our real business."

"Selling Fluffy Bunny," I guessed.

He nodded. "A traveling tour is a wonderful way to move things around the country without questions. No one ever looks very closely at our props. And it's a marvel what my wife can sew into a hoop skirt."

"And Rebecca found out?" I still felt like I was missing a huge part of the puzzle. And running out of time to find it.

"Rebecca was no angel," he said. "Even before I met her. Oh, she'd gone to some meetings, tried to get clean, but at heart, she was still an addict. When she found some pills among my things one day, she knew just what they were. So, I gave them to her."

"You hooked her on drugs again," I said, honestly disgusted. Rebecca had been trying to get her life together, and he had known exactly what her Achilles' heel was. And exposed it.

"I gave her what she wanted to keep her mouth shut. But then she started demanding more and more. She started threatening to expose the show for what it was. My backer doesn't take kindly to threats."

It hit me like a mental ton of bricks. "Your backer is Vincent Gordon. He's the one you were worried about offending with bad publicity." Although I guessed it was less *offending* and more *drawing the attention of law enforcement* that he'd been worried about.

"You can see why," he said dryly.

"And she figured that out," I said, remembering her visit to Lucky's Deli.

"She was greedy, but she wasn't stupid. Yes, she figured it out. So, she had to go."

I shivered at just how coolly he said the words. Like it was a line in the opera he was cutting and not cutting a woman's life short.

"You killed her, and Vincent's brother, Dominic, was called in to dispose of the body."

Rossi nodded, and an awful thought struck me. Would he call Dominic Gordon to dispose of *my* body? The idea of it made my skin crawl. I didn't want Dominic Gordon stashing me in his basement refrigerator like some slab of beef. And I certainly didn't want to be propped up in his kitchen to keep him company.

"You had Dominic follow me to Lampley Park?" I said, connecting the dots. I knew that I knew that mud.

Again, Rossi nodded. "Tara told me you'd been leaving her harassing messages all day. It was my suggestion that she agree to meet you there."

"Where you had Dominic hit me."

Rossi shrugged. "It was meant to be a warning. One you didn't heed," he added, clearly none too happy about that.

"But what I don't understand is *why*?" I pressed, cutting my gaze to my left. Sadly no handy weapons had miraculously appeared. I could only keep him talking for so long, and I was running out of options. "Why hide the body? And if Rebecca was an addict, how did the tox screen come back negative?"

Rossi cocked his head at me, and a slow smile snaked across his face. "So you hadn't figured *that* part out yet."

Clearly. I puckered my brain trying to figure out exactly what "that" was.

"Rebecca Lowery didn't die from a blow to the head. She died from a drug overdose. Two weeks ago."

If I were a cartoon, my jaw would have been on the floor. Puzzles pieces swirled around me. None of Rebecca's neighbors had seen her in over a week. Neither had her coworkers—she'd been calling in sick. At least according to Rossi. In fact, it was also Rossi who had identified the body in Watson's morgue… "Oh my God, it was never Rebecca!"

His smile grew into a self-satisfied thing that said he thought it was all pretty clever. "No, it wasn't. When Rebecca threatened to expose Vincent if we didn't keep up with her demands, he supplied me with a special blend for her. One that was sure to put her out for good. Only an overdose would require a full autopsy and an inquiry, and that kind of scrutiny wasn't good for anyone. So we silently moved her to Gordon's mortuary, where Dominic kept her on ice for a few days." He paused. "No pun intended."

I cringed. "So who was the Jane Doe?"

Rossi waved that question off as if it were insignificant. "Some woman Vinny knew. A prostitute. She looked reasonably like Rebecca, so we had her meet us in Rebecca's apartment, where she had a nasty fall and hit her head. When the police came, she looked enough like the photos in Rebecca's ID that, along with my positive identification, everyone believed she was Rebecca Lowery. They had no reason not to."

"And no one looked into Rebecca's death."

"Exactly. Once we had Jane Doe at the mortuary, all we had to do was swap out the bodies and cremate the real Rebecca."

"Only no one counted on Rebecca's will stating she wanted an open casket viewing."

His smile faltered. "A diva to the end," he spat out. The gun wobbled in his hand as he grew agitated. "Dominic assured us that he could make Jane Doe look enough like Rebecca to pass her off, but then that sister came nosing around before

Dominic had an opportunity to make up the corpse, and he panicked."

"And everyone thought Rebecca was missing."

He nodded. "And she would have stayed that way if you hadn't come along." He paused, taking a step toward me. "And now you have to go."

"I can go now," I offered. "Give me thirty seconds, and it'll be like I was never here."

He shook his head with a sad little smile. "It's too late for that, Miss Hudson. You know far too much. Mr. Gordon won't stand for it. And trust me—my way is much better than his way."

He raised the gun to head level. My head.

A flash of pure terror left me in an instant cold sweat. If I died, who would take care of Toby? Who would taste Mr. Bitterman's toxic creations and run interference with Mrs. Frist? Who would move into the Victorian and finish the repairs? Who would rein in Irene's harebrained schemes and moon over Watson's pouty lips? A terrible thought occurred to me. Would someone else lay claim to those lips?

I couldn't let that happen. I took a deep breath. It was now or never. I might not have a whole lot in the weapons category, but I had one thing he didn't.

Accessories.

I kicked my right foot forward as hard as I could, sending my chunky wedge flying toward the corner of the stage.

Rossi's eyes followed its arc for just a second.

But that was all I needed.

Immediately I shot a stream of hairspray at his eyes, taking grim delight in his pained shriek when it hits its mark. He slapped both palms to his face.

I jumped to my left, grabbing the wooden chair in such a force that the jacket hanging off the back flew to the floor. I swung blindly toward Rossi's head. He went down in a heap, eyes squeezed shut, hopefully glued shut by the Extra Hold hairspray, as the gun clattered to the floor. I grabbed it, holding it in front of me more as a shield than a weapon.

"Don't move!" I yelled. If he had any idea I didn't know the first thing about guns, he might have moved. As it was, I must have been convincing enough, as he just lay there, moaning as the hairspray wore off. I fumbled for my phone and quickly punched in 9-1-1.

# CHAPTER EIGHTEEN

————

Detective Lestrade arrived in record time with reinforcements, and the dark theater was soon filled with light, uniformed officers, and dozens of crime scene techs. Which, at the moment, were the most welcome sight I'd ever seen. It was all I'd been able to do to keep from breaking down in tears as the first officers on the scene had taken the gun from my hands and slapped a pair of handcuffs on Rossi. I'd been in the midst of giving a semi-coherent statement to another one when two more uniformed officers had come from backstage, Irene and Wiggins in tow. Then I did break down, blubbering like a baby as Irene and I wrapped each other in a hug that might have lasted longer than most people's entire friendships. She told me they'd been hiding backstage in a dressing room, and someone had shut the door and propped a chair against it. I guessed that had been Rossi's way of "taking care" of them.

While Irene told me her side of the story and I told her mine, Wiggins made himself scarce, taking advantage of the situating to no doubt get his blog written before any other news outlets carried the story. I cringed to think what he'd print about Sherlock Holmes, but at least he had his exclusive story and hadn't dug any deeper into *our* story.

"Marty?"

I looked up to find Watson jogging up the theater aisle toward me. The look of concern on his face melted me faster than any sunshine ever could.

As soon as he reached us, he pulled me into a hug to rival Irene's, crushing me to his chest. Which was warm, solid, and felt so safe I never wanted to let go.

"Are you okay?" he finally asked when we pulled apart. "You're ice cold, Marty." He took my hand in his.

I was fairly sure that if I tried to speak, I'd break down in tears. Again. Instead, I nodded and covered our clasped hands with my free one. "Hairspray," I managed.

"You don't need it," he said. "You look fine, considering what you must have been through."

"No," I said, my voice shaking. "I hairsprayed *him.*"

"You hairsprayed a killer holding a gun on you?"

I tried to smile, but I couldn't manage it. "It's all I had."

Watson grinned at me. "You never cease to amaze me."

I wasn't entirely sure he meant that in a good way, but at the moment I wasn't into overanalyzing anything. All I wanted to focus on was the way his hands were so warm and tender over mine. The way his eyes were crinkling at the corners slightly as he smiled down at me. The way his soft lips were parting just so as they moved toward mine.

I blinked.

His lips were *moving* toward mine. Slowly, leisurely, almost as if he couldn't even control the pull between us. I knew how he felt as my body started automatically moving forward to meet his until I felt his lips lock over mine. Then he was kissing me. And oh boy, what a kiss. I felt heat pool in my belly then start to head south.

"Ahem." I heard Irene clear her throat. Was she still there? "Uh, maybe I should give you guys a little privacy…" She trailed off.

But the moment was over, and Watson had pulled away. "Uh, no, it's…fine. I need to go chat with Lestrade anyway. It sounds like I'll be transporting someone back to my morgue after all." He paused and must have seen the confused look I felt forming on my face. "Jane Doe."

I nodded, hoping we'd soon have a real name to go with the face.

"Why don't you go on home," Watson continued. He turned to Irene. "You can take her?"

Irene nodded. "Come on, Mar. Let's go fill Sherlock in on everything." She winked at me.

If *filling in* meant a long bubble bath and my nice warm, safe bed, I was all for it.

* * *

"You know, he's really a pretty good reporter," Irene said the next day.

The Victorian was quiet around us, with only the sound of Toby's soft panting as he slept at my side. An empty pizza box sat on the coffee table with paper plates and crumpled napkins piled on top. We were working our leisurely way through a bottle of wine while we waited for a *very* important phone call to come in. Irene had her laptop set up to accept the call via some program I suspected she'd coded herself. While we waited, she scrolled through Wiggins' *Irregulars* article.

I grinned. "You're just saying nice things about Wiggins because he mentioned Sherlock Holmes about thirty times."

"Hey, this story has gotten even more hits than the last one," she said. "It's free advertising. I bet we'll get tons of new business from this."

I wasn't so sure that was a good thing. I hadn't recovered yet from the old business. I had a feeling it was going to take some time before I didn't see that gun pointed at me whenever I closed my eyes. Absently, I stroked Toby's soft ears. He snuggled up against me with a contented sigh.

"I wonder who his sources are," Irene mused. "He tied up a lot of loose ends. Did you get to the part where he says Dominic Gordon has disappeared? He's probably wearing cement shoes fitted just for him by Vincent."

I shuddered. "He might just be in hiding from his brother. I know *I* would be."

"Yeah, you've got a point. If any more bodies go missing, we'll know for sure." She sipped her wine while she scanned the article. "The Jane Doe's name was Amy Balentine. She's from Bakersfield."

I shook my head, my heart going out to her family. While it sounded like she hadn't lived a strictly straight and narrow life, she hadn't deserved the end she'd gotten.

"And Bryan Steele's Internal Affairs investigation has expanded to look into his connections to Vincent Gordon," Irene added, finishing the article.

"That's a good thing. That man has no business being a cop."

"Agreed." She glanced up. "Did you ever find out what happened to Tara?"

I nodded. "She called me last night after the story broke. She claimed she lost her phone yesterday, and she thinks that Rossi stole it from her dressing room to send me that text. He must have deleted it off her phone, but I'm sure the police will be able to check her records with her cell provider."

"She can't be too happy to be out of work just when she was elevated to prima donna."

"Actually, I don't think she'll be out of work for too long. She's front and center in this story, and it sounds like she's loving the limelight. She said she's fielding offers to appear on a few daytime talk shows. Who knows, maybe she'll ditch opera for Hollywood."

"She can be a diva anywhere," Irene said, smiling.

I leaned forward, looking at Irene's screen and noticing a photo beside Wiggins' article, of an angular-looking man in a ridiculous looking deerstalker cap. "Who on earth is that?"

"That, my dear Hudson, is Sherlock Holmes."

I shot her a look. "You've got be joking."

Irene shrugged. "What? You don't like it?"

"That hat's a bit much."

Irene shrugged. "I like to think Sherlock has his own sense of style. Very retro rural England chic, no?"

I shook my head. "No." I paused. "Where did you even get this?"

"I pieced it together in Photoshop."

I opened my mouth to ask more, but didn't get the chance, as the doorbell rang.

Irene set her glass down. "Are you expecting someone?"

I shook my head. I went to answer it with Irene and Toby at my heels.

Barbara Lowery Bristol stood on the porch. "I'm sorry. I should have called." She looked away, clearly ill at ease. "I wasn't sure you'd want to see me after…"

"I understand you were upset," I said. "Please come in." I stepped aside.

"I won't take up much of your time." Her fingers worried the clasp of her handbag. "I really just came to apologize for being so unfair to both of you. I hired Mr. Holmes to do a job, and then I behaved miserably when you tried to do it."

"This wasn't an easy situation for you," I said gently.

"No." She started to speak, hesitated, and fell silent for a moment. "Losing Rebecca has just been so hard. I—" She paused, looking from Irene to me. "Well, I just feel so guilty. You were right. I did try to nudge Rebecca out of our parents' inheritance. She caused them nothing but grief when they were alive, and I was the one who stayed behind to pick up the pieces and take care of them in their later years." Tears formed behind Barbara's eyes. "But she was my sister. I should have loved her despite her faults. Now I have to deal with the fact we'll never have the chance to reconcile." Her voice broke.

Reflexively, I reached out to touch her hand. There was nothing either of us could say to lessen her pain.

After some time, she regained her composure. "I've said what I came to say. Now I have to attend Rebecca's funeral." Her smile was small and weak. "At Haley's Funeral Home. Oh. Here. I've cut another check for you." She handed it to me. "I hope you'll accept my apology." She offered her hand, and we shook it in turn.

We watched her return to her car and drive away.

"We should send some flowers to her back in Iowa," Irene said.

I glanced at her, surprised. "You're getting sentimental."

"And then we should get you a new roof," she said. "Can you feel that draft?"

I rolled my eyes. Although she had a point. With Barbara's check in hand, anything felt possible. Maybe even new electrical too. I knew it wouldn't cover everything the old place needed, but you had to start somewhere.

The sound of an old-fashioned phone ringing came from Irene's open laptop.

"That's him!" she shouted, diving for it.

I shut the front door and joined her, taking a spot next to her on the sofa as she put on a headphone set, adjusting the microphone to her mouth.

"Ready?" she asked.

I nodded, my heart in my throat.

Irene hit a button on the computer to answer the call and spoke into the microphone. Only the voice that came out was two octaves deeper and distinctly male. And if I listened carefully, even modulated with a hint of a British accent.

"Sherlock Holmes speaking," Irene's alter ego said.

"This is Detective Lestrade of the SFPD," came the reply from the other end. "Mr. Holmes, you're a hard man to get ahold of."

"My apologies, Detective. As you know, I do travel quite extensively."

"So I've heard."

I held my breath, almost not believing our ruse was working.

Irene and I had assumed that our "end of the day" timeline to have Mr. Holmes contact Lestrade would have vanished when we'd hand delivered a murderer to the detective. Not so much. He'd given us a small stay of execution to have Holmes contact him the following day instead. A day that Irene had spent the better part of loading her computer with this software, practicing her "Sherlock" voice, and trying to come up with answers to whatever hard questions Lestrade might throw her way. She was putting it to the test now, and I was mentally crossing all ten fingers and ten toes that we wouldn't need Barbara Lowery Bristol's check for bail money if she didn't succeed in pulling the wool over Lestrade's eyes.

"What can I do for you this evening, Detective?" Irene/Sherlock asked.

"I'd like to speak with you about two of your investigators, Irene Adler and Martha Hudson."

I bit my lip. What could Lestrade possibly have to say about us?

"Yes?" Irene prompted.

"Uh, before I go on, I'd like to let you know I also have the medical examiner, Dr. John Watson, on the line."

I froze. Irene shot me a questioning look. I shrugged and shook my head. This wasn't in the plan.

"Uh, yes, I'm familiar with Dr. Watson's work," Irene answered slowly.

"Nice to finally talk to you, Mr. Holmes," came Watson's voice from the laptop.

Oh boy. If this went sideways, we were all in now.

"Likewise, Dr. Watson," Irene answered.

"As I said, I have a few questions for you about Ms. Adler and Ms. Hudson," Lestrade went on.

"They are two of my best investigators. Outstanding individuals. Highly intelligent, hard working, and not bad to look at either," Holmes told them.

I rolled my eyes at Irene and thought I heard Watson chuckle in the background.

*What?* she mouthed.

"Uh, yes," Lestrade continued. "Anyway, as I was saying, I have a few questions. Specifically about their credentials."

Uh-oh. There it was. He knew we were hacks.

"Go on," Irene prompted.

"I don't seem to see a private investigator's license on file for either of your employees."

I closed my eyes and thought a dirty word.

But Irene wasn't fazed. "Of course not. They're still in training."

I heard rustling on the other end, like Lestrade was mumbling something privately to Watson. "In training?" he asked finally. "You mean, taking classes?"

"I mean, they're working as apprentices under me to accumulate their necessary hours to apply for the license in California. I believe it's six thousand hours, correct?"

"Oh, uh, er. I'm not sure…" Lestrade paused, whispering to Watson again.

I held my breath.

"Uh, yes, I believe that is the requirement."

"Well, that takes some time, Detective."

"But, you see, the problem is that I actually can't seem to find a license on file for you either, Mr. Holmes."

I shot Irene a helpless look. Last year when we'd first made up our phony baloney employer, Irene had forged a license for him, which she'd then sent to Watson to prove our credential. Of course, if anyone actually went digging into the real records at the Bureau of Security and Investigative Services, it wouldn't exist. And apparently Lestrade had dug.

"No, of course not," Irene said, sounding completely unruffled by the question. "I'm not licensed in California."

I blinked at her. She was just admitting it like that?

I heard more rustling. "Uh, Dr. Watson here," came Watson's voice. "I distinctly remember you sending me a license issued by the state of California when you were looking into the death of Miss Hudson's aunt."

"Yes, I did," Irene agreed. "But that's expired. So, at current, you would find no record of an *active* license for me in California."

"Then you can't practice in California," Lestrade jumped in. "And neither can your apprentices."

I hated how satisfied he sounded about that.

This was not going well. My gaze pinged to Irene again.

"Actually, I do believe I can," she went on, cool as a cucumber. "You see, I'm licensed in Georgia."

"Georgia?!" Lestrade said.

*Georgia?* I mouthed to her.

She winked at me.

"That's correct," she answered us both at the same time. "And, I believe the Bureau has a reciprocity agreement with Georgia, which allows me to conduct business in California."

"Well…I…I'm not sure about…" I heard Lestrade try to cover the mouthpiece of his phone and address Watson. "Is that true?" he mumbled. "Can they do that?"

I didn't hear Watson's reply, but it must have been affirmative, as Lestrade came back on the line a much surlier man. "Don't think I won't be checking Georgia's records!" he warned.

"Please do," Sherlock said smoothly. "Now, if there's nothing else, I do have a rather busy schedule today."

"I'm sure you do," Lestrade said, laying on the sarcasm.

"Oh, but before I go, my associate Miss Hudson wanted me to relay a message to Dr. Watson."

I did? I narrowed my eyes at her and shook my head in the negative.

"She did?" Watson's voice asked. If I didn't know better, he sounded hopeful.

"Yes," Sherlock went on, completely ignoring my ever-increasing head shaking. "In fact, she said she's quite sorry she had to run out on your—"

I gave Irene a look that could kill.

"—*business* dinner the other night and would like to make it up to you."

*I would not!* I mouthed vehemently.

*Liar*, Irene mouthed back.

Okay, so maybe it was a slight fib, but the last thing I needed was "Sherlock" to do any matchmaking for me. He'd already screwed up every other area of my life—he could leave my love life alone. Measly as it was.

"Well, you can tell Marty that I'd like that very much," Watson answered.

Irene shot me an *I told you so* look. "Splendid!" she answered him. "I'll have her text you the details."

"Uh, Mr. Holmes." Lestrade bustled back on the line, clearly out of patience with all of us. "When will you be in town so that we can meet face to face?"

"Oh, I'm so sorry, Detective, but I'm afraid my business will keep me here a bit longer."

"Exactly where is *here*?" Watson asked.

"Sorry. My connection isn't very good. I'm having a bit of a time hearing you. I'm afraid I must go now, but thank you for the very lively chat, Detective. I do so look forward to meeting with you when I'm in town again. Cheerio!"

Amid Lestrade's protests, Irene disconnected the call and removed her headset.

"You don't think the 'cheerio' was a bit over the top?" I asked.

Irene grinned, refilling our empty wineglasses. "Relax, Hudson. I got you a date, didn't I?"

I shook my head. "Yeah, I guess you missed my violent *no* to that."

"Watson sure seemed to like the idea."

He had kind of, hadn't he? "Fine. Thank you for the *business dinner*." I paused. "But what was all that about Sherlock being licensed in Georgia?"

She sipped her wine, looking supremely pleased with herself. "Turns out, Georgia has the most lenient licensing requirements of all the states with California reciprocity. So Shinwell went on a little vacation last week to Georgia to get licensed. You know, just in case we needed it."

I blinked at her. "You sent Shinwell to impersonate Sherlock Holmes to the Georgia state licensing board?"

She nodded. "He's a great actor, really."

She was missing the point. "We've now committed fraud in two states," I mumbled.

Irene handed my wineglass to me. "You worry too much, Marty. Besides, Sherlock has to keep doing business somehow."

"No! No, he does *not* have to keep doing business."

Irene shot me a look of mock hurt. "Marty. How much is that check worth that you're holding?"

I didn't realize I was still clutching Barbra Lowery Bristol's check. I glanced down at it. "Three thousand."

"And how much was your electrical estimate?"

"Ten thousand." I sighed.

A slow smile snaked across Irene's face. "So, want to check Sherlock's email and see if his newfound fame has caused any new cases to come in?"

I glanced up at my water-stained ceiling, my knob-and-tube wiring, my single-paned drafty windows, and my crumbling plaster walls. "Maybe just one more case."

Irene's smile stretched from ear to ear. "Sure, Marty. Just one more case…"

# ABOUT THE AUTHORS

Gemma Halliday is the #1 Amazon, *New York Times* & *USA Today* bestselling author of several mystery series. Gemma's books have received numerous awards, including a Golden Heart, two National Reader's Choice awards, three RITA nominations, a RONE award for best mystery, and two Killer Nashville Silver Falchion Awards for best cozy mystery and readers' choice. She currently lives in the San Francisco Bay Area with her large, loud, and loving family.

To learn more about Gemma, visit her online at
www.GemmaHalliday.com

From her first discovery of Nancy Drew, *USA Today* bestselling author Kelly Rey has had a lifelong love for mystery and tales of things that go bump in the night, especially those with a twist of humor. Through many years of working in the court reporting and closed captioning fields, writing has remained a constant. If she's not in front of a keyboard, she can be found reading, working out or avoiding housework. She's a member of Sisters in Crime and lives in the Northeast with her husband and a menagerie of very spoiled pets.

To learn more about Kelly, visit her online at:
www.kellyreyauthor.com

Other series in print now from Gemma Halliday...

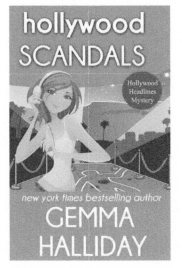

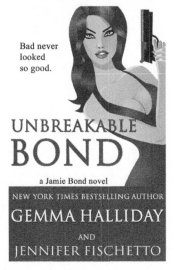

www.GemmaHalliday.com

76772174R00132